PROSE AND CONS

PROSE AND CONS

Wendy Corsi Staub

SEVERN
HOUSE

First world edition published in Great Britain and the USA in 2021
by Severn House, an imprint of Canongate Books Ltd,
14 High Street, Edinburgh EH1 1TE.

Trade paperback edition first published in Great Britain and the USA in 2022
by Severn House, an imprint of Canongate Books Ltd.

severnhouse.com

British Library Cataloguing-in-Publication Data
A CIP catalogue record for this title is available from the British Library.

ISBN-13: 978-0-7278-5016-4 (cased)
ISBN-13: 978-1-4483-0598-8 (trade paper)
ISBN-13: 978-1-4483-0597-1 (e-book)

All Severn House titles are printed on acid-free paper.

Typeset by Palimpsest Book Production Ltd.,
Falkirk, Stirlingshire, Scotland.
Printed and bound in Great Britain by
TJ Books, Padstow, Cornwall.

For all the Muldowneys,
my second family,
with lifelong memories and so much love.

And, as always, for my three guys: Mark, Morgan and Brody.

'It was one of those March days when the sun shines hot and the wind blows cold: when it is summer in the light, and winter in the shade.'

– Charles Dickens, *Great Expectations*

ONE

'Isabella? *Halloooo*, Isabella?' calls the only person in Lily Dale who addresses Bella Jordan by her full first name. 'Where are you?'

'Up here, in the tub! Give me a second and I'll be right—'

The bathroom door is thrown open.

'. . . down.'

Pandora Feeney is framed in the doorway. Sharp-featured and angular, she reminds Bella of the portrait of Sir Isaac Newton that hung in her classroom when she taught middle school science, not quite a year – and yet a lifetime – ago.

Last spring, the world had screeched to a terrifying halt amid a heartbreaking trifecta: her husband Sam died, her longtime landlord evicted her and their six-year-old, Max, and she lost her job.

But look at you now.

Well, not *now*, on her hands and knees in the cast-iron clawfoot tub with a scrub brush, wearing ragged clothes, her long brown hair in a bedraggled ponytail. But generally speaking, she's come a long way.

'Blimey! You are a sight, Isabella! I'd assumed you were soaking in the bath, not . . . What, pray tell, are you doing?'

'Trying to remove the rust stains so that I can reglaze the enamel. And if you thought I was *in* the bath, shouldn't you have knocked first?'

'I *did* knock, luv, on the front door, and I rang the bell. But you didn't hear me.'

'So you let yourself in.'

'Of course.'

It's hardly the first time. As the former mistress of this three-story Victorian manor, Pandora maintains a proprietary interest in the place, though she lost it years ago in a messy divorce. It's since been converted from private residence to guesthouse, now managed by Bella with plenty of input from Pandora.

Bella hoists herself to her feet with a groan and brushes flecks of scouring powder from her favorite soft-as-velvet faded jeans.

Pandora eyes the frayed holes in the knees. 'Oh, you poor thing! You seem to have torn your trousers.'

Oh, you poor thing. Your frock seems to have sprouted a small cabbage, Bella longs to reply, eyeing the floral-sprigged dress with an enormous rose corsage appliqué jutting beneath one of Pandora's long gray braids. But if she's learned anything in the nine months she's lived in Lily Dale, it's that Pandora Feeney – for all her haughtiness and maddening overstepping – means well.

'I'm loath to trouble you, luv,' she says, 'but might you have a few moments for a tête-à-tête over a cuppa?'

'Is this about book club again? Because I told you, if you don't agree with Misty's choice for the first month's read, you can just opt out.'

'Goodness, no, it isn't about that, although now that you've brought it up, in hindsight, I believe we should have elected officers at our inaugural gathering. We're in dire need of a governing body to keep unruly members in check.'

'There are only five of us, Pandora. I don't think we—'

'I'm going to throw my hat in the ring for president, and I've chosen you, Isabella, as my running mate.'

'So this little tête-à-tête *is* about book club?'

'No, an issue has arisen that's far more urgent. Please, Isabella. I shall only require a few minutes of your time.'

Bella glances at her watch. 'All right. I guess I can spare a few—'

'Splendid! I put the kettle on before I came up. Shall we?'

Bella sighs and climbs out of the tub. 'I guess we shall.'

Pandora leads the way down the grand polished staircase to the kitchen as though she's still the lady of the house, commenting on the 'clutter' along the way. Coats draped over the newel post, cat toys scattered across the parlor hardwoods, polished mahogany dining room table buried under overdue library books, clean laundry waiting to be folded, and a large – and largely unfinished – jigsaw puzzle.

'What were you thinking, Isabella, opening all these windows in the dead of winter?'

'I was thinking that it's the first day of spring. Because it is,' she reminds Pandora. The day had dawned with sunny blue skies, and the temperature had leapt well into the fifties by noon. 'You know what they say. In like a lion, out like a lamb.'

'I beg your pardon?'

'The old proverb. If March comes in like a lion, with terrible weather – and it did, with that roaring blizzard, remember? – then it goes out like a lamb.'

'A lamb? Did I ever mention that I dated an Uplands shepherd back in the UK? I was studying music at Leeds, and I met Duncan at the Christmas market. He had a stall, and I purchased a pair of woolen mittens. He was quite flirtatious – said he'd knitted them just for me. Do you know that they were precisely the color of my hair?'

She waits for a response.

'Uh . . . gray?'

'Not my hair *now*, my hair back then, when I was just a lass! Do keep up with the conversation, Isabella. Those mittens were dyed a rich shade of brown. I kept them and treasured them long after Duncan broke my heart. Oh, he was quite the strapping bloke. I often wonder about the path not taken, where he is now, whether he's forgotten me after all these years.'

'I doubt it. You're pretty . . . unforgettable, Pandora. Anyway . . . March is going out like a lamb. I'm feeling really optimistic about the weather.'

And other things, she thinks, glancing at the jigsaw puzzle and remembering Saturday night.

'One must never be optimistic about springtime, Isabella. She's a cruel tease here in the Dale. Some years, July is the only month of the year we've not seen snow. This cold draft is aggravating my chilblains. Please do close the windows.'

Pandora sails on toward the kitchen, pausing to adjust the vintage thermostat dial.

An icy breeze jangles the wind chimes on the porch and blows through the open screens as Bella tugs down the sticky window sashes. The skies have indeed faded once more to a familiar wintry monochrome.

She can hear the furnace creaking and groaning into action beneath the scarred floorboards. Like many things here at Valley View Manor, the ancient ductwork needs costly attention that will have to wait.

Bella checks the thermostat and finds that it's been raised to seventy-five, with the recklessness of someone who's no longer paying to heat this drafty old house. The money doesn't come out of Bella's pocket, either, but Valley View's owner, Grant Everard, expects her to stick to the budget.

She lowers the thermostat ten degrees, then stoops to pick up a jigsaw puzzle piece from the floor beneath the table. It's mostly blue, with a narrow triangle of pale green. She glances at the image on the puzzle box – a dazzling New York city-scape – and sees that the piece is mostly sky, pierced by the tip of Lady Liberty's crown. Leaning over the puzzle, she tries the piece in various locations, remembering how touched she'd been when Drew Bailey showed up with it last weekend, along with pizza, a bottle of pinot noir, and . . .

'Is that a puppy?' Max had asked, peeking into the blanket-covered crate. 'Yes! It's a puppy! Is he a present for me?'

Bella's 'No!' was decidedly more forceful than Drew's, hers accompanied by a *how-could-you?* glare, and his by a chuckle. He explained that the pup was the last of the litter born to an injured dog he'd rescued at his veterinary hospital around Christmas.

'This little guy is lonely because his mom and brothers and sisters have all gone to their new homes.'

'Yep, and one of those new homes is at my friend Jiffy's house down the street. His little guy is a boy dog and his name is called Jelly. So I want to keep this one. Then me and him can visit his brother Jelly, and Jiffy's kind of like *my* brother since I don't have one. So can I have the puppy, Mom?'

Drew responded for her. 'Actually, Max, he's already spoken for. But his new family can't take him until next week, so until then, he's hanging out with me. I thought maybe you could play with him tonight?'

'Yes!'

It had been a perfect Saturday night. Puppy, pizza, pinot, puzzle . . .

'I thought you'd like this view of the Statue of Liberty better than the one you had when you were a little girl,' Drew had said, showing her the box.

'What? I can't believe you remember that.'

A while back, she'd mentioned to him that she only ever saw the back of the statue's head when she was growing up in Bayonne. And after she and her widowed father moved into the city, she didn't even see that.

'Our first apartment in Queens faced the brick wall of the building next door,' she'd told Drew. 'The next one overlooked a bodega. One night, I was looking out of the window and saw the owner being held up at gunpoint.'

Drew cringed. 'That had to be terrifying.'

'Oh, he didn't get shot.'

'But still . . .'

'Yeah, Dad moved us out a few weeks later. We moved a lot.'

'I hope the views got better?'

She smiled and shook her head. 'Mostly alleys and dumpsters.'

'That makes me sad for little Bella.'

'Don't be. My dad did the best he could, and even though it was just the two of us, I always felt loved and protected.'

After her father passed away, she had her husband. And then Sam, too, was gone, and for the first time in her life, she was alone – homeless, jobless, terrified.

Some days she still feels that way. She's learned, however, that she doesn't have to rely on anyone else to take care of her and Max. She's found a new home, a new job, and provided her son with steadfast love and stability, with a strong support system among their friends here in Lily Dale. Now, she's never alone unless she wants to be – and often, not even then.

Loneliness, though . . . Loneliness is different. It's a pervasive ache that can't always be assuaged by kids and kittens, small town bustle, daily chores, an endless to-do list.

But lately, with Drew, she almost feels a sense of—

'Isabella? Where are you?' Pandora calls as the kettle starts to whistle.

With a sigh, Bella gives up on the puzzle piece and goes into the kitchen.

Pandora has taken a canister of imported leaf tea from one cupboard and a pair of bone china cups and saucers from another. Supermarket teabags and mismatched coffee mugs won't do for the Dale's self-proclaimed royalty.

Pandora may not be descended from Queen Victoria or King George, but she claims to chat with both on a regular basis, along with other illustrious departed souls. She's a psychic medium, as are the fellow residents of this tiny western New York village. Lily Dale was the birthplace of the nineteenth-century Spiritualist movement and remains populated by people who can speak to the dead . . . if one believes in that sort of thing.

Bella would like to think that her late husband can communicate with her and Max from beyond the grave, but she's found logical explanations for most so-called paranormal incidents that have occurred since their arrival last summer. As for the seemingly inexplicable ones . . .

'Not now,' Pandora tells a patch of empty air over her left shoulder, then pauses, head tilted as though listening. 'Yes, yes, darling, I'm quite aware . . . No, just you . . . Yes. Tomorrow, then. And *do* make yourself more presentable.'

Catching Bella's raised eyebrow, Pandora says, by way of explanation, 'Winston. Why on earth does he wear those awful jumpsuits? They don't do a thing for him, do they?'

Again, she pauses, and shakes her head at her invisible – imaginary? – visitor. 'No, I'm afraid not. I've nothing to say to *you*.' To Bella, she adds, as if it means anything at all, 'Wallis.'

'What?'

'Not *what*, *whom*. Wallis Simpson. She's the dreadful divorcee for whom King Edward VIII abdicated the throne in '36'

'No, I know who she is. Uh, *was*.'

'And always shall be. A leopard doesn't change her spots in the hereafter, Isabella. I saw you shiver just as she touched in. Clearly, you felt the chill of Spirit in the air.'

'What I *felt* was the chill because it's still cold in here from the open windows.'

Pandora regards her from behind steamy vapor rising from her cup like ectoplasm from a grave . . . if one believes in that sort of thing.

Bella does not. Yet through the mist, she sees – or imagines she sees – a pair of hands close around Pandora's spindly neck.

She blinks, and they're gone.

Yes, she finds Pandora irritating, and maybe there are times when she'd love to strangle her, but merely figuratively. This felt . . . malicious.

Could it have been a ghostly vision?

No, because you don't see ghosts, and anyway, ghosts aren't real.

She shivers again. Turning to make sure the window above the sink is closed, she sees Chance the Cat, tail twitching, green eyes fixed on the vacant spot behind Pandora's chair.

If Odelia were here, she'd probably claim it's Nadine, the mischievous household spirit. But she's away today at a vernal equinox seminar, and there's about as much mischief in the air as there is springtime.

'There now, do you see, Isabella? Chance sensed Wallis as well. When I was a girl, my darling little Scottish Fold, Dodger, reacted precisely the same way whenever that woman was in our midst. And to unsavory living souls, as well. Dodger always hissed before my piano teacher, Miss Brinkman, even rang the bell at Marley House.'

'Marley House?'

'My childhood home in London, of course. Years later, Mother discovered that the woman had been a Nazi spy in her youth. Felines are acutely aware of negative energy. Now then, where were we?' she asks, sounding impatient, as though Bella's the one keeping her off-topic.

'I don't know, but Max will be coming home soon, Pandora, and I really should—'

'Ah, yes. As you were saying, your guestrooms are vacant at this time of year, and—'

'I wasn't saying that. I had a nice Canadian couple check out yesterday, and a group is coming from Pittsburgh at Easter—'

'By that time, we'll be gone.'

'Who, exactly, is *we*?'

'My dear Auntie Eudora sent word that she's coming from London, accompanied by a gentleman friend. They're in Southampton as we speak.'

'The Hamptons?'

Bella flashes back to her old life in the New York City suburbs. A stolen newlywed weekend with Sam at a colleague's oceanfront house. Lazy beach days that began with watching the sun rise above a sparkling ocean in what her poetic husband deemed a sushi sky.

'All those streaks of red and pink and orange – it reminds me of the omakase platter at Oishii,' he'd told her. 'You wait and wait for it, and it's absolutely beautiful when it gets there. But it lasts only a few seconds before it disappears.'

Oh, Sam.

Pandora yanks her back to the present. 'My goodness, no, not the *Hamptons*, Isabella. Auntie Eudora is in Southampton, *England*, about to make the transatlantic crossing.'

'On a ship?'

'Of course. She doesn't *fly*,' she says, as though Bella should have known that. 'She's the old-fashioned sort. It's all rather spur of the moment – you've heard of Beacon Atlantic?'

'The new bargain cruise line? Oh, yes.'

Their pervasive commercials feature a cloying and annoying jingle.

If adventure you're a'seekin' . . .

You can't go wrong with Beacon . . .

'They were booking suites for a steal on the *Queen Jane*'s maiden voyage, and so Auntie Eudora and Nigel thought, why not?'

'Well that's . . . nice.'

Bella wonders what any of this has to do with her, a trend in most conversations with Pandora.

'*Carpe diem*, Isabella! Oh, you'll adore Auntie Eudora. I idolized her when I was growing up. My father passed away when I was a girl and she was his younger sister. People always said I bore far more resemblance to her than I did my own mother, and they couldn't have been more different. Mummy was rather frumpy and plain, you see, and Eudora quite glamorous, a *real* looker.'

Bella keeps a straight face. 'I see.'

'She attended one of the finest finishing schools in Switzerland for a while, but it wasn't her cup of tea. She was a feminist – never married, had no children, and devoted herself instead to building a career as a renowned chef. She had a splendid restaurant in Covent Garden, not far from where we lived. How I miss her beef Wellington. And oh, her steak and kidney pie. Tender, flaky pastry – she trained at Le Cordon Bleu, you know.'

'I . . . uh, didn't know.' She clears her throat. 'Pandora, this is all very . . . exciting for you, I know, but—'

'It's exciting for you as well, Isabella. A much-needed breath of fresh air in Valley View.'

'Oh! So you're saying your aunt and her friend want to stay here?'

'Where else would they stay? It isn't a problem, is it?'

'No, of course not. We can use the extra income, especially since the furnace is—'

'I'm afraid we can't have Auntie Eudora and her beau as *paying* guests, Isabella.'

'But—'

'Absolutely out of the question.'

'Well, I don't know how Grant would feel about that.'

In truth, Bella knows exactly how he'll feel. When the globe-trotting entrepreneur inherited Valley View from his Aunt Leona last year, he made it clear he had no use for it unless it was fully renovated and began turning a profit. He gives Bella a commission on new reservations, as well as bonus pay for household repairs she does herself.

'Isn't Grant in Patagonia?' Pandora asks.

'That was last month. He's in Myanmar now.'

'Precisely. And Auntie Eudora *is* family.'

Not Grant's, though. And not mine.

Then again, haven't the people of her new hometown, Pandora included, embraced Bella and Max as just that?

She sighs. 'I suppose it wouldn't hurt for a couple of days. I can let them have two rooms on the third floor if—'

'Auntie Eudora prefers the Teacup Suite on the second floor. She adores the turret alcove, and there's plenty of room there for two.'

'Oh – when you said she was old-fashioned, I assumed she wouldn't be sharing with her . . .' She can't bring herself to say *beau*.

'His name is Nigel, and Auntie Eudora is old-fashioned in some ways, but not in others. They'll have the Teacup Suite, and as long as you don't mind being uprooted for a couple of nights, luv, I'll take the Rose Room.'

'What? Of course I mind. That's *my* room, Pandora.'

'Yes, but the window seat does have a lovely view across Melrose Park to Cotswold Corner for Lady Pippa.'

Bella rewinds the sentence in an attempt to make sense of it. Lady Pippa, of course, is Pandora's Scottish Fold, easily the most pampered pet in town. And Melrose Park is the small clearing out front of Valley View, more mud than grass at this time of year.

'What's Cotswold Corner, Pandora?'

'My home, of course.'

'Your home . . . here? In the Dale? It has a name?'

'Doesn't everything?'

At a loss, as is often the case when she's dealing with Pandora, Bella shrugs. 'I don't follow.'

'When I was a girl, Mummy and I spent the most brilliant holiday in the Cotswolds, a picturesque region west of London – charming cottages along winding lanes, very much as there are here in the Dale, and cobblestone—'

'No, I know where the Cotswolds are, and what they are. I just didn't know that you'd named your house after them. Or . . . at all.'

'Yes, a rather recent turn of events, but it's tradition back in the UK, you see.'

'I don't. What does it have to do with Lady Pippa and the window seat?'

'Isn't it obvious? You can't tell *me* cats don't suffer from homesickness, Isabella!'

'I wouldn't dream of it, Pandora. But I still don't get it.'

With an exaggerated sigh of patience, she says, 'If dear Lady Pippa becomes homesick during our Valley View sojourn, she can gaze from the window upon our home across the way.'

'Your . . . sojourn?'

'It means "temporary stay."'

'No, I know what it means, but—'

The front door bangs open. 'Mom? Hey, Mom! Me and Jiffy have a *great* idea!'

'Ah, the lads have returned from school,' Pandora says, pushing back her chair as Max bursts into the kitchen.

As always, Bella is struck by how much he looks like his father – same cowlick in the same sandy brown hair, same earnest, bespectacled brown eyes. And as always, she notes with gratitude his transformation from a shy, grieving kindergartener who'd struggled to make friends, to a happy-go-lucky first-grader, accompanied by his inseparable sidekick, Jiffy Arden, who lives two doors down.

'Mom, since it's so nice and sunny out—' Max notices Pandora. 'Hi, Miss Feeney. Mom, since it's so nice out, we want to run through the sprinkler, right, Jiffy?'

'Right, since it's so nice out,' Jiffy agrees. 'Like summer. Only not hot.'

'But not cold, either.' Max shoots him a warning look. 'Not like winter or March or anything.'

'Nope. By the way, today is the vernal equinox. That means the first day of spring, Bella.'

She smiles. 'I'm aware, Jiffy.'

'Are you studying astrology, too?'

'Too? Are *you* studying it?'

'No, my mom is. She's taking a Zodiac class online. That's why I'm going to stay at your house a lot more. Because my mom's homework is working on signs and charts and when I'm there I disturb her and you're not busy like my mom is. So anyway, since it's spring today—'

'Sorry, Jiffy, but we're not going to be running through sprinklers.'

'Well, we didn't mean *you*. Just me and Max. And Sanchez. And maybe Jelly.'

'Ah, Sanchez.' Pandora nods. 'Albie's cat.'

Albie, according to Jiffy, is a man who lived in Lily Dale almost a century ago. Died here, too. He wears a fedora and likes to whistle. His cat, Sanchez, is black with green eyes. Albie and Sanchez hang around the Ardens' home.

Bella knows that although Pandora can't see them, she's sure they're real because Jiffy says so.

That's Lily Dale. Anywhere else, adults would regard a child's visible-only-to-him friends as imaginary.

'By the way' – Max borrows Jiffy's catchphrase – 'Jelly is Jiffy's puppy. I wish I could have a puppy. I want to get one for my birthday. It's in April.'

Bella sighs. 'I know, Max, but—'

'I was saying all of that stuff for Miss Feeney, Mom, in case she doesn't know about my birthday and in case she wants to get me a great present. And I would want it to be a puppy.'

'Duly noted, young man,' Pandora says. 'But I shall leave it up to your mum.'

Max turns back to Bella. 'Can I—'

'Not now, Max. We're not talking about puppies now.'

'I was going to say, can I have my after-school snack?'

'Oh – sure. That, you can have.'

'Good. We want chocolate ice cream cones.'

'With chocolate sprinkles,' Jiffy adds. 'Because *sprinkles* are a good treat for after the *sprinkler*. Get it?'

Max and Jiffy's uproarious laughter is contagious. Even Pandora chuckles, ruffling Jiffy's gingery hair on her way to the door.

'Don't touch anything, boys. I'll be right back.' Bella hurries after her. 'Wait, Pandora, I don't understand why you'd stay here when you live right across the way.'

'Because Auntie Eudora hasn't been to the Dale since the wedding.'

'Which wedding?'

'My own, of course. Oh, Isabella, if you could have seen me then . . . I was such a dainty, dewy bride.'

'Your . . . wedding? To, um, Orville?' Pandora's been divorced from him for decades.

'Of course, Orville! I've only been married once, Isabella. What do you take me for? Do you think I've taken a string of husbands like that strumpet Jillian Jessup?'

'Jillian . . .'

'The movie star! Orville's second wife! He was her third husband, and she's had at least two more since. What would you expect from a woman so perpetually and precisely papaya?'

'I . . . I'm not sure what you mean by that.'

'Her *aura*,' Pandora says, as if Bella had failed to compute that two plus two equals four. 'It's that ripe shade of reddish orange.'

Pandora, like many of the locals, believes that living beings are surrounded by bioenergy fields that change color depending on a person's circumstances, health and emotions. She considers herself the Dale's foremost expert in aura interpretation, and has been known to deliver passionate monologues on the subject.

Sometimes she's so convincing that Bella would buy into her theories if she hadn't taken enough college psych classes to know that a neuropsychological phenomenon called synesthia can trigger the brain to perceive color where there is none.

'You know, Pandora, that ripe shade of reddish orange is my favorite color,' Bella says. 'But it doesn't make me think of papaya.'

'Ah, yes, you and your sushi sky.'

Bella's heart slams into her ribcage and she stares at Pandora. 'How did you . . .'

'But we're talking about auras, Isabella. And very much like the sky – anywhere but Lily Dale, that is – *your* aura is blue.'

It isn't the first time Pandora has made that claim. According to her, a blue aura means Bella is 'bloody logical. Stubborn. Intuitive and serene. You feel deeply, but you refuse to allow your emotions to impact your decisions. You guard them quite fiercely. You don't wear your heart on your sleeve. It takes you yonks to let someone in.'

'Yonks?'

'That's a long, long time. But when they're in, they're in for yonks. You're true blue, darling.'

All Bella knows is that 'Bella Blue' had been Sam's nickname for her, in reference not to her aura, but her cobalt eyes.

And that Sam had talked about a sushi sky.

But Pandora couldn't have known that . . . unless Bella had mentioned it. Maybe she had, and has forgotten, though it doesn't seem likely that she'd confide such an intimate detail in Pandora, of all people.

On the other hand, how likely is it that Pandora – of all people – is channeling Sam's spirit?

Soon after Bella's arrival, retired police detective Luther Ragland had given her a folded slip of paper. He said he'd carried it in his wallet throughout the years on the job, where he'd often collaborated with Bella's next-door neighbor, psychic medium Odelia Lauder.

The handwritten quote is attributed to Albert Einstein: *Everyone who is seriously involved in the pursuit of science becomes convinced that a spirit is manifest in the laws of the Universe.*

If a Nobel Laureate in Physics believed that, who is Bella to rule it out entirely?

'As I was saying,' Pandora goes on, 'Jillian Jessup's papaya aura indicates a voracious sexual appetite.'

'I see.' Bella clears her throat. 'Getting back to your aunt . . .'

'Ah, yes. She's a yellow. Jolly, optimistic, creative. She—'

'I don't mean her aura, Pandora. Tell me about her visit.'

'Well, you see, I haven't quite conveyed to her the entire truth about my . . . current situation.'

'You mean she thinks you're still married?'

'Are you daft? Orville is a household name! His subsequent divorces have been highly publicized.'

Rather than remind Pandora that that depends on the household, Bella asks, 'So what *does* she think about your situation?'

'She believes I still reside here at Valley View Manor.'

'Why didn't you just tell her you moved after the divorce?'

'There was no need. And now, I'm afraid the shock might

be too strenuous for her. She hasn't been well, and she's getting up there in years.'

'But we can't just—' Hearing a chair scrape in the kitchen, she calls, 'Max, what are you doing in there?'

'Nothing.'

'I said don't touch anything. Where are your listening ears?'

'We're not touching things, Mom, we're checking things.'

'I'll let you be, luv, now that we're all sorted, and you have your hands full with the lads. We'll reconvene to plan our strategy,' Pandora says.

'Our strategy? For what?'

'For the book club election! My goodness, Isabella, where are your listening ears? Now, I'm assuming we'll be unopposed on the ticket, but we'll need a clever slogan. Something like "Tippecanoe and Tyler Too", but not quite as—'

'Pandora, I'm sorry, but I really don't think the club needs—'

'You're right. Perhaps a vice president is unnecessary. You can be my campaign manager. We'll need posters and hand-bills, and I'll consult Susie B for advice on getting out the vote.'

'Susie B . . .?'

'. . . Anthony. The suffrage and Spiritualist movements coincided here in the Dale. She was a regular, and still pops in from time to time. Toodle-oo!' Pandora disappears out the door.

Bella shakes her head and hurries back to the kitchen, just in time to pluck Max from a wobbly chair pulled up in front of the refrigerator.

'Max! What are you doing?'

'Finding the chocolate ice cream.'

'With sprinkles,' Jiffy says.

Bella sets Max on his feet, returns the chair to the table, and opens the freezer. She'd bought three pints of Triple Fudge Fusion on sale last weekend. They've gone through two and part of a third, but she can't find it.

'That's odd,' she says, rummaging among frost-coated packages of chicken, bagged vegetables and ice cube trays. 'Where's the ice cream?'

'I bet Nadine ate it,' Jiffy says. 'Right, Max?'

'Right! I bet she did!' he agrees too quickly. 'Like, maybe she ate it yesterday after school when you were upstairs working on the bathtub, Mom, and me and Jiffy were down here in the, uh . . .'

'Not in the kitchen. Except for, like, two seconds. Just to find a healthy snack,' Jiffy adds. 'Right, Max?'

'Right. But not ice cream.'

Choose your battles, Bella Blue, Sam's voice whispers in her head, and in her memory, but not, of course, here in the room. Because regardless of what Pandora and Jiffy and . . . and Einstein say about it, Bella isn't convinced that dead people can communicate with the living any more than they can . . . eat ice cream.

Bella closes the freezer, looks at the pressed tin ceiling, and counts to three before smiling at the boys.

'OK, guys. I'll cut up some apple slices.'

'With cinnamon sugar?' Max asks.

'Sure.'

'And chocolate sprinkles?' Jiffy asks.

'Sure, why not.'

'And then maybe we can do the sprinkler, Bella? Please?'

'Please, Mom?' Max chimes in. 'We're sick of winter. We want to have fun.'

'Yeah, and adventure. If adventure you're a'seekin',' Jiffy sings, 'you can't go wrong with Beacon! Or the sprinkler!'

He and Max find that hilarious.

Bella, not so much.

Ten minutes later, the boys are settled in front of the TV with their snack, and Bella is back in the bathtub, this time with that damned jingle on an endless loop in her head.

If adventure you're a'seekin' . . .

You can't go wrong with Beacon . . .

March 27th
Somewhere in the North Atlantic

When the *Queen Jane* hits rough seas on the sixth night of the transatlantic journey, Nigel can delay no longer. Pity it has to be this way, but time is running out. They'll be in New York tomorrow.

That she doesn't expect a thing renders the ghastly task much easier from a physical standpoint. From an emotional one, however . . .

Well, he isn't made of stone, is he? They have enjoyed some jolly laughs and splendid meals together.

Ah, well. As the great Geoffrey Chaucer said, all good things must come to an end.

After completing the first, and most unpleasant, part of the deed, Nigel is catching his breath and contemplating the next when someone knocks on the cabin door.

'Bloody hell,' he whispers, and glances into the mirror. Bloody clothing, as well. And gloves.

'Who is it?' he calls.

'Room service.'

'I'm afraid you must have the wrong cabin. I haven't ordered anything.'

A pause. 'Miss Feeney called about twenty minutes ago for her chamomile tea.'

Twenty minutes ago? Nigel had been out in the torrential night, pacing the rain-slicked sundeck in the dark, working up his nerve to accomplish the task that now lies behind him. Unfortunately, the evidence remains.

He clears his throat and calls loudly, 'Eudora? Did you order tea?' He pauses while removing the gloves and yanking a dressing gown over his stained shirt and trousers.

Tying the sash tightly at his waist, he strides to the door and opens it a crack.

A young man stands in the corridor beside a small tea cart. 'Good evening, sir.'

'Good evening. Miss Feeney is in the bath, if you wouldn't mind leaving that until she's finished.'

'Why don't I just roll it inside for you?'

Nigel offers him a smile and a wink. 'Sorry, mate, I'm afraid I'm not quite . . . presentable. If you must know, I was about to join her.'

The man reddens. 'I do apologize, sir. I'll just leave this here.'

Nigel thanks him, closes the door, and slides the bolt. 'Coming, Eudora,' he calls, stripping off the dressing gown.

He crosses the cabin and opens the door, not to the bathroom, but the balcony.

A wet wind pelts him as he leans over the rail to make sure the adjacent and overhead balconies are vacant.

Every other night of the cruise, despite the frigid North Atlantic sea air, he's glimpsed fellow passengers out here, or he's heard their voices, or smelled their cigarette smoke. Tonight, even the hardiest and most nicotine addicted are safely inside as the ship barrels through towering waves toward New York.

Stepping back inside, Nigel finds the duct tape he'd brought on board in his luggage, along with the large plastic shower curtain now spread on the floor beneath the corpse. In a matter of moments, he's dragging a tidy, if unwieldy, sealed bundle onto the balcony.

Hoisting it onto the rail with a grunt, he whispers, 'I'd say you've had one too many trips to the buffet, darling. Another day at sea, and this might have been quite impossible.'

He pushes it over the railing. In this weather, at this speed, from this height, he hears no satisfying splash below.

Back in the cabin, he closes and locks the balcony door and then opens the one to the corridor. After peering out to make sure the coast is clear, he reaches for the tea cart and pulls it inside.

'Thank you, darling Eudora,' he murmurs, heading for the bathroom. 'Hot tea will be just the thing after a nice long bath.'

TWO

March 29th
Lily Dale

'W here does this go?' Drew asks Bella, standing at the sink with a dish towel over his shoulder, holding up a skillet.

'Oh . . . I was going to wash it, and the breakfast dishes.'

'I just did.'

'You scrubbed dried eggs and bacon grease off a sink full of dishes that have been sitting there for hours, from a breakfast you didn't even get to eat?' She sets down a laundry basket filled with linens she'd stripped off the beds upstairs. 'Drew, that's . . . Wow. Thank you.'

'It's the least I can do.'

'The least *you* can do? After you drove all the way over here to drop off the Revolution?'

That's Chance and Spidey's prescription medication. Bella forgot to get the refill at their checkup, and it's hardly urgent, but when she called Drew about it this morning, he insisted on bringing it right over.

'I'm happy to help. I know you've got your hands full getting ready for your guests.'

'You mean *Pandora's* guests.' She takes the pan from him and opens a cabinet. 'It took forever to make up the beds. I'd already put away the flannel sheets and extra comforters in the storage closet because I didn't think we'd be using them again till the fall.'

'It's a little warm for flannel, don't you think?'

'Well, they're elderly, and if they're anything like my mother-in-law, they'll be bundled up in cardigans even in July.'

'True. My father is the same way.'

She wedges the pan into its spot in the stack with a clatter and closes the cabinet. 'Pandora keeps reminding me that if

she were running Valley View, everything would be "spot on
for their stay – It's the small touches that make things *brilliant*, Isabella!"'

Drew laughs. 'You sound just like her. And how are those
small touches coming along?'

'So far, not so good. Would you believe Walmart was fresh
out of crumpets?'

'You don't say.'

'Clotted cream, too. And I have to go pick up the ingredients
for a full English breakfast.'

'Which are . . .'

'Eggs, toast, back bacon, bangers, baked beans, mushrooms,
black pudding.' Bella rattles them off in Pandora's accent,
adding an exaggerated, 'Oh, and *toe-mah-toes*, lightly seared,
Isabella, in a cast iron skillet.'

'I don't know if I want to know what bangers and black
pudding are.'

'Bangers are sausages, and black pudding . . . don't ask.
Oh, and she wants me to order English bluebells from a florist
for vases in the guestrooms because hers aren't in bloom yet.
I told her it's not in the budget but I'll pick up some lilies at
the supermarket this afternoon, to which she said, ". . . lilies
smell like funeral parlors, and it's *most* unwelcoming to remind
people of a certain age that death is just round the corner,
Isabella."'

'Would that be her age, or her aunt's age?'

'Both, I guess. Pandora is no spring chicken herself.'

'Well, if you want guestroom touches for people who are
"of a certain age", I can give you some drugstore reading
glasses for their nightstands. My dad is always losing his, so
I have a supply from all the pairs he's left behind at my house.'

'Pandora might not approve of the poor dears staying up
reading past their bedtime – and that's going to be extra early
with jet lag, according to her. She basically wants me to tuck
Max into bed after school so that he won't raise a ruckus and
rouse the guests.'

'Wait, jet lag? Didn't they sail here from England on the
Queen Mary?'

'The *Queen Jane*.'

'Wasn't she beheaded?'

'Yes, after only nine days on the throne, according to Pandora, but her ship's maiden voyage fared better. It arrived in New York harbor yesterday.'

'When does her family get here?'

'Not until later tonight. They're stopping off for lunch at the Culinary Institute of America on the way. Eudora's a chef, and I made the mistake of suggesting it to Pandora. My old home in Bedford was only an hour's drive from there, and we, uh, ate there a few times for special occasions.'

We – Bella and Sam, celebrating wedding anniversaries. Toasting their love and the future with champagne and never the slightest hunch that their lives together wouldn't extend into old age.

'A mistake?' Drew asks, and it takes her a moment to realize he's not referring to her lack of foresight, but merely echoing her own words.

'Right, a mistake, because Pandora assumed I had some kind of pull and insisted that I make a lunch reservation for them. Which took a lot more time and energy than I had to spare.'

'Well, at least you've stalled their arrival, so why don't we go take a walk around the lake? I've got some time before I have to get back to Miraculous Maisie.'

That's what he's dubbed his ailing poodle patient whose previous vet wanted to put her down. The distraught owner came to Drew for a second opinion. It was a long shot, but his immunotherapy treatments have Maisie on the road to recovery.

'I'd love to, but I was planning on going to the supermarket with Pandora's list before Max gets home.'

'Do it later, with him, and spend time with me now.'

'You say that like someone who's never gone grocery shopping with a six-year-old.'

'I say it like someone who's going to miss you while you're tied up with Pandora and her high-maintenance guests.'

Bella smiles and picks up the laundry basket. 'A walk would be perfect. I'll just start this load and grab my sneakers and jacket.'

In the windowed mudroom that doubles as a laundry room off the kitchen, she doesn't find her jacket hanging on the hook where it should be. She does find wet clothing in the washer, dry clothing in the dryer, and a full basket of whites waiting to be washed.

She shouldn't have said yes to a walk when she has so much to do. But how could she refuse on a beautiful day like today?

Beyond the open screened window, a balmy breeze sways the vast Ginkgo tree's bare branches beneath a bleached blue sky. Chance the Cat is perched on the deep sill, gazing at a sparsely visited birdfeeder, awaiting the return of the flocks that had fled south for the winter.

Bella sets the laundry basket on the floor. It can wait. Drew and Miraculous Maisie cannot.

'*Carpe Diem*, Isabella,' she murmurs.

As she slips her feet into her sneakers, she notices the tabby's striped tail twitching, the way it does when Chance is wary of a threat.

'What's going on out there?' She leans closer to the window. Maybe a deer has wandered onto the property, or one of the neighbors' dogs has gotten off the leash again.

Looking from the woodpile to the tarped patio furniture to the gray water lapping at the grassy shore of Cassadaga Lake, she sees nothing amiss – not that she can perceive, anyway.

But Chance has turned away from the yard, and is looking in the opposite direction now. As Bella reaches to give her a reassuring pat, the cat arches her back, fur standing straight up, and hisses.

'Whoa. Sorry. I won't touch you. But what's wrong?'

The cat leaps from the sill and darts from the room.

Bella shakes her head, stepping back into the kitchen.

Drew's wearing a khaki barn coat over his red plaid shirt, and he holds out her fleece jacket. 'Looking for this?'

'Yes, and Chance.'

He jerks a thumb toward the front of the house. 'She went that way. Did you step on her tail again?'

'No! She was fine one second, and then she bolted, almost as if . . .'

As if she saw a ghost.

'Cats are quirky.' Drew shrugs, as always uninclined to attribute bizarre behavior – animal or human – to ghostly activity.

Still, even pragmatic Bella sometimes wonders whether Chance has . . . mystical qualities.

Last June, she and Max were en route from the New York suburbs to Chicago to make a reluctant fresh start with Sam's mother when the cat turned up in the middle of the road, enormously pregnant and refusing to budge. She bore an uncanny resemblance to an also enormously pregnant doorstep stray they'd left behind nearly five hundred miles and twenty-four hours earlier.

Max remains convinced the cats were one and the same, with magical powers. Odelia fuels that theory with her claims that all felines are spiritual, intuitive and highly evolved. Bella only knows that if it hadn't been for Chance, she wouldn't have found her way to Lily Dale, Valley View, or Drew.

She'd detoured to the animal hospital in search of the stray's owner. Drew had traced her embedded electronic chip to the guesthouse, where Bella discovered that Leona Gatto, mistress of the house and cat, had 'crossed over', as the locals say, in a tragic accident that turned out not to have been an accident.

While the resident mediums attempted to channel the victim's spirit to find out who'd killed her, Bella solved the case using good old-fashioned common sense. She agreed to stay on and run the guesthouse through the Dale's busy summer season, and when autumn came, this strange little town already felt like home, and its quirky residents like family. Drew, too, though he lives and works fifteen miles away, a fellow outsider.

'OK, I'm good to go. Thanks for being the most patient man in the world,' she tells him. 'Oh, wait, I just need—'

'Right here.' He plucks her cell phone from behind a thick library book on the table. 'You're reading *A Tale of Two Cities*?'

'For book club. Pandora's selection. Retaliation for Misty choosing that reality TV star's memoir last month, which I have to admit was—'

The doorbell blasts.

'Expecting someone?' Drew asks.

'No, it must be a package delivery. I ordered a new shower curtain for the third-floor bathroom, though it's not supposed to be here just yet. Guess it's my lucky day.'

Or not. Bella opens the front door to an older couple surrounded by luggage.

'You must be Isabella, Pandora's new girl,' the woman says in an English accent.

'I'm . . . I . . . you can call me Bella. Everyone does.'

Everyone except Pandora.

New girl? Seriously?

At least Eudora didn't say it with a condescending tone, as her niece might have.

'Pleasure to make your acquaintance, Bella,' the man says, shaking her hand. He's dapper in tweeds, with silver hair, mustache and beard. 'I'm Nigel Spencer-Watson, and this, of course, is Miss Eudora Feeney.'

Of course. The woman bears an unmistakable resemblance to Pandora, similarly long-limbed with angular features. But she's far more attractive, especially for a woman of her age, which is . . .

Well, Bella doesn't recall how old Pandora had said she was, but she'd anticipated a little old lady. This one is remarkably spry and lively, insisting on pulling her own bag over the threshold until Drew joins them and takes it from her.

'Drew Bailey,' he says, setting the bag at the foot of the stairs and shaking their hands. 'It's nice to meet you.'

Recognizing the brisk efficiency and taciturn set to his face that she'd found so daunting when they first met in his office last June, Bella is reminded anew that Drew isn't Sam.

And he isn't me, or Max, or Odelia, or even Pandora.

No, Drew keeps strangers at arm's length. Sometimes she wishes he were quicker to warm up, but other times, usually in retrospect, she thinks she might benefit from his brand of restraint.

'Good man, there are several more bags in the boot,' Eudora tells Drew.

'The boot?'

'Of the hire car,' Nigel explains, gesturing at a dark sedan
parked at the curb and handing Drew the keys. 'This button
pops the boot, see? Do be careful not to leave anything behind.'

Bella opens her mouth, not even sure what she's going to
say in response to his presumption, but Drew grins at her and
gives a little shake of his head.

'Got it. Happy to help,' he says, and is out the door.

Eudora turns to Bella. 'Where is Pandora? I've been trying
to ring her for the last hour, but she doesn't answer.'

'She's . . . she was here, but she's not, at the moment.' It
isn't a lie.

This morning, having failed to convince Bella to vacate the
Rose Room, Pandora had moved her belongings – including
Lady Pippa and every feline accessory imaginable – into the
third-floor jungle-themed room. It's located directly above
the Rose Room, affording a similar view of the little pink
cottage across the park, to stave off feline homesickness.

In parting, Pandora gave Bella strict instructions not to
disturb Lady Pippa between one and six o'clock, when she
naps.

'But, uh, don't all cats pretty much nap all day?'

'Lady Pippa is very particular, Isabella. She requires a quiet
house and a dim room.'

'Does she wear a little sleep mask, too?'

'I'm most serious, Isabella.'

'Sorry. But if she's so sensitive, maybe you should keep
her at home.'

'Out of the question. I've scheduled an aura and chakra
cleansing session this afternoon,' she said, as if that – whatever
it was – explained everything.

Now, presumably, she's in the midst of her cleansing
session, but Bella isn't sure whether Eudora is aware of
her niece's spiritualism and mystical activities, or if she's
similarly gifted.

Pandora often mentions that she inherited her paranormal
abilities from her mother's side of the family. Eudora is on
the paternal side and more likely . . .

Well, *normal* is the word that comes to mind. Certainly at
a glance, in contrast to Pandora. Eudora's gray hair is a frosty

salon shade as opposed to Pandora's drab salt and pepper. Nor is it long and braided, but short and stylish beneath the blue cloche that matches her long wool dress coat.

'How was the drive from New York?' Bella asks.

Nigel says, 'Splendid! Quite scenic. I highly recommend it, if you ever have the opportunity.'

'Oh, I've had the opportunity.'

She'd made the trip with Max last June, covering nearly five hundred mountainous miles from one end of the state to the other. She'd been too preoccupied to notice the scenery, mourning what they'd left behind and worrying about what lay ahead.

They had been planning to move into her mother-in-law Millicent's pristine Chicago penthouse. Back then, Bella secretly referred to the woman as 'Maleficent'. Turns out she and Sam's mother have more in common than she'd ever believed. They'd both loved Sam, they both love Max, and nowadays, they've even come to love each other. From a healthy distance.

Drew is back with the rest of the luggage. 'Is the room ready, Bella? I can take this right up.'

'Yes, I just . . . never mind. Thanks.' She flashes him a grateful smile, and turns back to her guests as he heads upstairs. 'Sorry. I was planning to add a few finishing touches to your room before you arrived. I assumed that would be later tonight because you were stopping off in Hyde Park for lunch.'

'We decided to forego that little detour. No reason to make a long trip even longer, is there?'

'But . . . Pandora said Eudora was anxious to visit the Culinary Institute.'

'Yes, well, she was even more anxious to get to Lily Dale, weren't you, darling?'

'Aye, and it's truly as lovely as I imagined.'

Bella frowns. 'I thought you'd been here before, Eudora? I could have sworn Pandora mentioned that you—'

'Of course, and it's as lovely as I remember. Might you direct me to the nearest loo, luv?'

She shows Eudora into the half-bath tucked under the stairs. It would be just like Pandora to finagle the stay at Valley

View by claiming her aunt adores it and has a 'favourite' room, even if the woman has never set foot in the place in her life.

Nigel helps himself to a handful of M&M's from a crystal bowl on the registration desk and turns to watch Drew lug the second load of bags up the flight. 'The staircase and moldings are smashing. Honeyed oak?'

'Yes.'

'Original, are they?' He crunches his candy and reaches for more.

'Pretty much everything here is original.'

'Splendid. All precisely as Eudora described it. Quite remarkable, isn't it, to find ancient lights in perfect working order?' He indicates the creamy ochre gaslight globe atop the newel post, the pendant suspended from an ornate plaster medallion high overhead, and matching sconces along the stair wall.

'Well, I wouldn't say *perfect*. Sometimes when you press a switch, nothing happens.'

'Ah, but it happens to the best of us as we age,' he tells her with a sly grin, and gestures at the brown and amber brocade walls. 'That wallpaper is in pristine condition.'

'Up close, you can see the wear and tear, believe me.'

'Remember, my dear, "Every wrinkle is but a notch in the quiet calendar of a well-spent life."'

'That's lovely.'

'I'm afraid I can't take credit. The quote belongs to Charles Dickens. He's been on my mind this journey. Did you know that he visited Western New York at this time of year, during his first American tour back in 1842?'

'No, I didn't know. That's fascinating.'

'Yes. That was the era of the Second Great Awakening, a revivalist movement unfolding right here in the Burned-over District, as this region was known at that time, when it was deep in the throes of fiery spiritual fervor.'

'And Dickens was . . . *here*?'

'He traveled through the area, from Cleveland to Buffalo and Niagara Falls. He later became one of Victorian England's most outspoken critics of spiritualism as it pertains to communicating with the dead, though he quite famously engaged in mesmerism, a form of psychic healing.'

'So basically, he was a hypocrite?'

'One might say so. In any event, one year after his visit to the Burned-over District, in 1843, Dickens published what is arguably the world's most enduring and well-loved ghost story.'

'*A Christmas Carol*!'

'Precisely.' Nigel smiles at her.

'You're all set in the Teacup Suite,' Drew says, coming down the stairs. 'I'm going to head out if you don't need anything else, Bella?'

I do – more time with you.

She keeps that to herself. By the time she gets her guests settled, Max will be getting off the bus, and anyway, Miraculous Maisie needs Drew more than she does.

'It was nice meeting you,' he tells Nigel, extending a hand.

Instead of shaking it, the man presses something into it. 'Here you are, then.'

Seeing Drew gape at the five-dollar bill, Nigel rifles through a wad of cash and lays a twenty on top of it. 'Apologies. I'm still learning your currency.'

'But why . . .?'

'Begging your pardon? I was under the impression that it's customary in the US to provide the bellhop with a gratuity?'

Bella jumps in. 'It is, Nigel, but—'

She breaks off as the bathroom door creaks open and Eudora sails out. She's applied fresh lipstick, removed her hat and has her coat draped over her arm, revealing a trim figure in a well-cut charcoal herringbone suit.

Suddenly self-conscious of her own pilling fleece, well-worn jeans and dingy sneakers, Bella silently completes the sentence, and then some.

Drew's not the bellhop, and I'm not Pandora's new girl, and I can wear whatever I want, and Eudora's ridiculously over-dressed. Who wears a blazer, skirt, hose and heeled pumps for an eight-hour road trip?

Pandora's family, that's who.

'It's so lovely to be back at Valley View again,' Eudora

comments, with a contented gaze around the hall. 'How I've missed—'

Her jaw drops and she gapes at the parlor beyond the archway.

Bella swivels, sees nothing out of the ordinary, and heaves an inner sigh. *Spirit* again?

'Is that . . . an *animal*?' Eudora points, and Bella sees a twitching tail poking from beneath a skirted table.

'It's just Chance.' She strides over and lifts the hem, revealing the fat tabby. 'She's our – hey, what are you doing?'

The cat sits up, back humped and fur standing on end, and emits a loud hiss before darting toward the back of the house.

Bella stares after her, then turns back to her visitors. 'Sorry. She's very sweet, I promise. She never behaves this way. I don't know what's gotten into her today.'

'Perhaps she has an aversion to strangers,' Eudora says. 'Most cats are rather standoffish, aren't they?'

'Not Chance. She's a people person – er, cat. She lives in a guesthouse, so she's used to strangers coming and going.' She looks at Drew. 'Maybe she's not feeling well?'

'Could be, but more likely she's reacting to something that's imperceptible to us. Some cats get skittish when they sense a predator in the vicinity, or when there's an electrical storm looming . . .'

He glances at the sunny window. Bella follows his gaze, as do the others.

'Guess it's not the weather,' she says. 'Maybe there's a stray dog in the neighborhood or . . . something.'

'A ghost?' Eudora suggests.

Bella shrugs. 'That depends on who you ask. Drew?'

'I can't confirm that I've ever seen a cat react this way to a supernatural threat. Only to natural predators, weather . . . *humans*,' he adds pointedly.

Eudora is equally pointed 'And if you ask someone other than the bellhop?'

'Drew – *Dr Bailey* – is a veterinarian and an expert animal behaviorist,' Bella informs her, and relishes her obvious dismay.

'Yes, well . . .' Eudora falters, looking at Nigel.

'I'm afraid this won't do. Eudora suffers from acute ailurophobia.'

After a brief pause, she agrees. 'That's, ah . . . that's right. Ailurophobia. Most acute.'

Uncertain she even knows what the word means, Bella clarifies, 'So you're afraid of cats?'

Nigel answers for her. 'Quite. You'll have to put her out, Isabella.'

'Well, if you insist. Come along, Eudora.'

Drew muffles a laugh.

Unamused, Nigel snaps, 'Not Eudora! The feline!'

'I know. It was a joke. But Chance is an indoor cat, and part of our family. So is Spidey – he's my son's kitten.'

'Your *son*?' Nigel raises his white brows as if the place is infested with vermin and rodents. 'There are *children* here?'

Remembering that things hadn't ended well for the last visitor who'd asked that question in that tone, Bella says, 'Just Max.'

'I hope you don't suffer from pedophobia,' Drew says.

It's Eudora's turn to answer for Nigel, with an indignant, 'Certainly not! Mr Spencer-Watson is a most respectable, decent gentleman, I assure you.'

'Not—' Bella begins, but Drew catches her eye and winks. She shifts gear, swapping *pedophilia* for '. . . to be rude, but if you'll excuse me for a moment, I'm just going to check on Chance.'

She hurries away, calling for the cat. Passing through the dining room, she casts a wistful glance at the unfinished New York City puzzle on the table. She and Drew haven't had a chance to get back to it, and it's probably going to have to wait a while longer now that she has guests to tend to.

In the kitchen, she finds Chance perched on a chair grooming Spidey, the runt of her litter last summer. He's since grown into a robust kitten, thanks to Drew's veterinary expertise and Bella's willingness to bottle-feed the ailing newborn round the clock.

'Hey, guys,' she says softly, going to the cabinet for a box of dry food. The moment she shakes it, the cats leap from the chair and follow her to the feeding station in the mudroom. She fills their bowls with food and fresh water from the laundry sink. There's a litterbox in the corner, and a couple of toys scattered on the floor.

'You two will be fine in here for a while, OK?'

She closes the mudroom door – not to protect her skittish guests from the cats, but the other way around.

Returning to the front of the house, she hears Drew talking about Jiffy. 'He lives a few doors down the street, but he spends more time here than there. His dad is serving overseas and his mom, Misty, has her hands full, so Bella's taken him under her wing.'

'Lovely,' Eudora says tautly. 'I'm sure the children are delightful.'

'That's one word for them. Boisterous is a better one. So, as I was saying, if you were counting on getting some R&R while you're here, you might want to consider staying someplace else.'

'R&R?'

'Rest and relaxation,' Bella explains, re-entering the room, 'and he's just teasing. The boys will be perfectly well behaved.'

'I'm certain they will be,' Nigel says. 'I'm looking forward to meeting them.'

'In the most proper way, of course,' Eudora clarifies, still stuck on her own pedophobia misinterpretation.

'Of course,' he agrees. 'In the meantime, Eudora and I would fancy a nip of gin, wouldn't we, darling?'

'Gin?' Bella sighs. 'Pandora had mentioned that you like wine, so I got a nice cabernet, and a sauvignon blanc if you prefer white.'

'I do enjoy both, with dinner,' Eudora tells her. 'But a gimlet would be lovely this afternoon. The famous Feeney family recipe, of course.'

'Oh . . . I don't know what that is.'

'I'm sure Pandora has it. And a light snack, please. We'll take it in our suite.'

Drew intervenes. 'Don't you have to go meet the bus, Bella?'

'I . . .' Catching the pointed glint in his eye, she glances at her watch. 'Yes. Yes, the school bus . . . it's coming. I have to go meet it.'

It's not entirely a lie. The bus is coming . . . eventually. But she hasn't met it at the bus stop ever since Max – with Jiffy pleading his case – convinced her that her daily presence there was humiliating for a big first-grader.

She strides to the tall registration table as if she's pressed for time, digs through a drawer, and thrusts several items into Eudora's hands.

'Here are instructions on using the keypad on your room door, if you want to lock it.'

'Isn't that standard procedure?'

'I mean . . . it depends on what you're comfortable with. When I first moved here from New York, I kept my room locked, but now I hardly ever do. The Dale is safe, and you're the only guests we have right now, so you might not want to bother. Oh, and here's an information packet for Valley View, and a brochure about Lily Dale.' Following Drew out onto the porch, she calls over her shoulder, 'End of the hall on the left. I'll be back shortly if you have any questions.'

Drew pulls the door closed after them and they exhale in unison.

'You OK?'

She nods, descending the front steps with her hands thrust deep into her jacket pockets. 'I'm fine. Just irritated. I was trying to figure out how to explain that I don't do room service, or cocktail service, and . . . anyway, thanks for rescuing me.'

'If ever there was a woman who didn't need rescuing, it's you. Who else can juggle endless chores and renovations with kids, cats and guests, and make it look so easy?'

'You forgot ghosts.'

'Ghosts, ghouls, goblins . . . guys like me.'

'Guys like you are the best part, pulling pedophobia out of a hat. Did you see the look on their faces?'

He grins. 'I was hoping they never took college psych.'

'Did you?'

'Of course. I was planning to become an MD before I switched over to veterinary science.'

'Really? So was I, before I switched to teaching. What made you change?'

'I realized I prefer animals to most humans. How about you?'

'I realized I prefer kids to most adults.'

'You could have become a pediatrician.'

'That's what my father wanted me to do, but . . . well, we couldn't afford med school.'

Frank Angelo couldn't afford undergrad tuition, either, but he scraped up what he could. Bella worked her way through college, supplemented by loans she is still paying.

'Maybe someday you can go to med school, if that's what you want,' Drew suggests. 'When Max is older, and—'

'What? No, it isn't what I want. Not at all. I don't even miss teaching, most of the time. I'm happy doing exactly what I'm doing right now.'

Funny – she hadn't even realized it until the words came out of her mouth. In the whirlwind since she lost her job, she hasn't had time to adjust career goals or analyze whether she should strive for something more in line with her original life plan. And if the past year or two have taught her anything, it's that plans are meaningless. The best you can do is just try to maintain some semblance of control over your immediate future, and adapt to the inevitable complications.

Like guests who want gimlets – from specific recipes, no less.

She checks her watch and sighs. 'I guess I'd better get more gin. I'm pretty sure there's a bottle in the liquor cabinet, but I'm not sure there's much in it.'

'Send them out to fetch it themselves.' Drew gestures at the rental car parked alongside his pickup truck.

'No, it's all right. It's in the budget, and whenever my regulars mention things they like, I make a note to stock up for their next visit. And to be fair, these two were basically fine until Eudora made that comment about Chance.'

'Personally, I think you should have put Eudora out. Nigel, too. Here, take the money he gave me and treat yourself and Max to dinner tonight.'

She looks down at the cash in his hand and shakes her head. 'I can't do that. You should give it back to him.'

'Come on, Bella, it's not like I picked his pocket. He *gave* it to me.'

'Because he thought you were the bellhop.'

'Listen, that luggage weighed a ton, and they were designer bags. He obviously doesn't need the money as much as you do.'

'Maybe, but the animal hospital needs it more. Let's donate it to the rescue fund in Chance's name. Use it to save a kitten.'

'That's perfect.' Drew smiles, pockets the cash, puts his arms around her and presses a light kiss to her forehead. 'You're good people, Bella.'

'So are you. Maybe Nigel and Eudora are, too. I shouldn't make assumptions about them just because they're connected to—'

'Isabella? Isabella!'

'*Pandora* . . .' She completes her sentence on a sigh, and turns toward the shrill voice.

A gawky figure has emerged from the little pink cottage across the park.

'Have you heard she's named her house?' Bella murmurs to Drew. 'She calls it Cotswold Corner.'

'I hadn't heard. But that's . . . a very Pandora thing to do.'

'I've a message from Auntie Eudora saying they've arrived!' Pandora calls, barreling toward them in a flapping red parka and matching wellies. 'Why didn't you summon me immediately?'

'I'm summoning you right now,' Bella says. 'In person.'

'I do hope you didn't slip up and reveal that I'm no longer in residence at Valley View Manor?'

'No, but I really think you need to explain that you don't own it anymore.'

'I shall, in due time. But first, we must allow dear old Auntie Eudora to recover from the strenuous journey.'

'I don't know . . . she seems pretty sturdy to me,' Drew comments.

Bella nods. 'Yes, she's not as old and frail as you made her seem, Pandora.'

'That's because we Feeney women are genetically gifted with a remarkable youthful countenance. Why, to look at me, one would never suspect that I'm a day over twenty-nine.'

Drew emits a cough that masks a laugh, and Pandora turns a sharp gaze on him.

'Sorry. Tickle in my throat.'

'*Do* distance yourself if you've caught the lurgy, Dr Bailey.'

'I'm feeling . . . actually, that's a great idea. I'm going to distance my lurgy self right now.' He pulls his keys from his pocket and leans toward Bella. 'I'll talk to you la—'

'You mustn't spread germs to Isabella!' Pandora steps between them. 'We need her in perfect health while she's tending to her guests.'

'But, Pandora, if they think you own Valley View, wouldn't *you* be tending to the guests?' Drew asks. 'I'm sure Bella would welcome a few days off.'

'Don't be silly.' Pandora chuckles. 'Now then, Dr Bailey. You'll want to get home before the storm.'

He looks at the milky sky. 'What storm? The forecast says—'

'Why on earth would I have donned my rain gear if we weren't in for a lashing?'

'But—'

'I assure you, I'm *never* wrong,' Pandora informs him.

As if to punctuate her comment, the wind kicks up to jangle the wind chimes suspended from the porch eaves.

'I guess we know what's wrong with Chance now,' Bella says.

'Maybe,' Drew says. 'Or maybe she just senses that Eudora is terrified of her.'

'Terrified! My aunt? Of a cat? Pish posh.'

'That's what she said.'

'Ah, it's the fever talking.' Pandora takes a step back from him and gestures at the truck. 'Pip-pip, Dr Bailey.'

'Well . . . Pip-pip, I guess.' Drew gets behind the wheel with a last sympathetic glance at Bella.

'Oh, thanks for bringing the Revolution!' she calls after him.

'He brought a revolution?' Pandora asks. 'Are you feverish as well, Isabella?'

'Revolution is medicine for the cats.'

'Are they ill?'

'No one is ill, Pandora, including me. Don't worry. I'm in perfect health to tend to your guests.'

She sighs, watching Drew drive away as quickly as one can safely navigate the pothole-pocked Cottage Row.

Turning back to Pandora, Bella sees her narrowed eyes fixated on the house.

Pandora frequently reminds her that despite its gables, cupolas and turrets, Valley View Manor isn't much of a manor compared to the grand estates back in England. Painted a lavender-gray that compliments the backdrop of March sky and lake, it towers over the other Victorian residences that line this narrow and rutted lane, aptly named Cottage Row. Most were built in the nineteenth century, when Lily Dale was established as a summer colony for members of the burgeoning Spiritualist movement. Some homes have been updated and winterized, with cars parked out front, lamplit windows, shovels and bins of rock salt by the door. Others are shuttered, boarded up and abandoned until the vigorous Western New York weather turns balmy again. Nearly all are fronted by painted wooden shingles that dangle from signposts and doorstep brackets, advertising the residents' metaphysical specialties.

REVEREND DORIS HENDERSON, SHAMANIC HEALER
MISTY STARR, PSYCHIC CONSULTANT

And of course, right next door to Valley View: ODELIA LAUDER, REGISTERED MEDIUM.

Pandora clears her throat. 'Isabella . . .'

Noting the peeling paint on the scalloped trim and the slight tilt to the copper finial above the turret where the Teacup Suite is located, Bella braces herself for a scolding.

'Far be it from me to interfere with your parenting . . .'

Uh-oh.

'. . . but spoiling the lad won't do him any favors. My own dear father crossed over when I was the same age as your Max – he'll be six in April, you said?'

Did she? Thoughts whirling, she tells Pandora, 'Actually, he'll be seven, but—'

'Ah, I was only five, but to her credit, my own mum was not overly indulgent – not indulgent in the least, really, where I was concerned. On the contrary, she—'

'Pandora, I don't know what you're talking about.'

'The puppy, of course.'

'What puppy?'

'The one your young Max requested.' She waves a hand at the house. 'I can hear the poor thing yipping from here. It just won't do. Auntie Eudora is quite fearful of the creatures.'

'*All* creatures, apparently.'

'Pardon?'

'I know she has a cat phobia, but she didn't mention dogs.'

'Wherever did you get that idea?'

'She told me. Well, Nigel did, when they saw Chance.'

'I'm afraid you must have misheard, because she told *me* that she was looking forward to meeting Lady Pippa.'

Rather than suggest she was probably just being polite, Bella focuses on the nonexistent puppy.

'Pandora, getting back to the barking—'

'Yipping. Rather a yowling now.'

'Oh, Doris Henderson must be holding a drumming circle by the lake,' Bella says.

She'd run into the shaman in the supermarket a few days ago, and Doris had invited her to join the healing ritual sessions. 'People who have been through a loss like yours often harbor repressed grief,' she'd told Bella. 'Drumming and howling can be a tremendous release.'

'Howling?'

'Yes, like this.' Doris, a petite gray-haired woman, tilted her head back and emitted an unearthly sound right there in the produce aisle. Most people stopped and stared, a few shrunk away, one howled back, and a manager came rushing over to see what was going on.

'Just letting it all out,' Doris said cheerfully. 'Try it, Bella. It works wonders! Go on. Howl!'

Bella had politely turned down the invitation, assuring Doris that she was healing just fine on her own.

'According to the flier Doris gave me, they meet twice a week over at the gazebo, rain or shine,' she tells Pandora. 'Although considering that it's March in the Dale, it should probably say rain or snow instead, right?'

Pandora, who like most locals never misses an opportunity to elaborate on the extreme Western New York weather, shakes

her head firmly. 'What I heard isn't coming from a drumming
circle at the gazebo. It is inside Valley View.'

'Well, you know how sound carries across the water and
makes it seem as though it's—'

'Isabella, I *assure* you it's coming from the second floor.'

'And I assure *you*, Pandora, that there's no dog in that
house.'

Although Chance *was* behaving as though a predator was
lurking . . .

But, no. There is absolutely no way Max smuggled a puppy
into the house.

'Right, then,' Pandora says. 'It must be Spirit.'

'Spirit is howling?'

'*Yowling*. My guides are attempting to convey a message.'

'What do you think it—'

'Shhh.' She tilts her head, eyes closed, as if listening intently.

Nine months into Lily Dale life, Bella is aware that her
local friends believe they have an assemblage of guides from
a higher realm to see them through their earthly mission. Some
are animals, like Odelia Lauder's oft-consulted great white
hawk; some humans, like the Native American maiden to
whom Odelia was married in a previous lifetime when she
was a male tribal chief – or so she claims.

As much as Bella would like to think that she and Sam are
destined to find each other over and over again for all eternity,
reincarnation is, like drumming circles and countless other
aspects of Lily Dale life, a concept Bella finds difficult to
embrace.

Pandora opens her eyes and shakes her head. 'All will
become clear in due time, but I'm afraid it does seem rather
ominous.'

'The message? Ominous . . . how?'

'That remains to be seen. Let's go in, shall we, before we're
drenched?'

'It's not—' Bella looks up and sees a storm cloud that wasn't
there a moment ago.

Back inside, Eudora is just descending the stairs.

'Auntie!'

'Pandora, luv!'

Watching them embrace, Bella wonders how it feels to connect with someone who carries your own DNA as obviously as Eudora does Pandora's.

As an only child, like her parents, Bella had no siblings, no aunts and uncles. Her mother's best friend, Sophie, did her best to see Bella through a motherless childhood. But of course she looked nothing like Bella or her mom. The resemblance between Pandora and her aunt is striking.

Eudora turns to Bella. 'Have you dispatched the lads to another location, then?'

'Pardon?'

'Your son Maxwell and his chum . . . Geoffrey, is it?'

'Jiffy. And Max is just Max. And no, I just . . . I just came back to grab an umbrella and raincoat to take to the bus stop.' She plucks both from the coat tree beside the door and hurries back out to the porch, pulling the door closed after her.

'It's OK,' she murmurs to herself as she heads down the steps. 'You'll get through this. Just like everything else.'

Hearing a tinkling sound overhead, she glances up at the twirling, melodious cascade of pretty stained-glass angels hanging from the gingerbread trim.

The wind chimes had been Sam's last birthday gift to her. She hears them far more often here in Lily Dale than she ever did back home. She's well aware that's due to meteorological conditions on this blustery eastern edge of the Great Lakes. But at times like this, she'd like to think that her husband is letting her know he's still with her. She'd like to think she might even be able to see him, or hear him.

Odelia compares communication with the dead to a radio that tunes in to vibrations that operate on an atypical frequency. In order to connect with lost loved ones, a medium receives and interprets energy that's different from what most people can readily perceive.

'And just as an electrical storm can wreak havoc with an electromagnetic receiver, strong human emotions can create interference between the earthly plane and the Other Side,' she told Bella. 'It takes a long time to heal grief as profound as yours, my dear. It's a burden that at first seems impossible to bear.'

'It doesn't seem impossible. It *is* impossible.'

'Nothing is impossible. In time, you grow accustomed to carrying it, and it does grow lighter over time, bits and pieces falling away.'

It's true. Bella experiences far more good days than bad now. She's even starting to wonder if there's something to this spiritualist belief that dead isn't dead after all. If it's true that nothing is impossible.

She looks toward the heavens.

The sky, rapidly darkening, spits a fat wet droplet onto her cheek.

'Seriously?' Bella sighs and pulls on her slicker. 'Unbelievable.'

I'm never wrong.

Pandora's words follow her into the rain, along with a faint bark overhead.

Bella stops and looks sharply up at the windows tucked amid the clapboards, fish scale shingles and ornately carved cornices. There's no dog, of course. She imagined it.

But the turret's copper spire seems to point like an arrow at the lowest, blackest storm cloud perched directly overhead.

THREE

A s luck would have it – good luck, for a change – Bella finds her car keys and wallet in the pocket of the raincoat she'd grabbed when she left the house. She drives over to the bus stop and parks beside the gatehouse. Of course there's no actual gate, or even a fence. Just a couple of red-brick pillars and a painted blue sign declaring Lily Dale: THE WORLD'S LARGEST CENTER FOR THE RELIGION OF SPIRITUALISM.

During the summer season, an attendant occupies the low-roofed windowed hut, collecting a modest visitors' fee from a line of cars that sometimes snakes along the two-lane shore-line road.

The daily calendar is packed with guest lectures, celebrity psychic appearances, and workshops on everything from numerology to past life regression. People come from all over seeking psychic guidance, healing, or contact with the dearly departed. Veteran visitors book their individual readings well in advance, while first-timers and day-trippers wander the streets knocking on doors in search of mediums who have walk-in availability.

Like any other small town, the Dale has shops, a library, post office and fire department. It also has distinctly local landmarks like the Fairy Trail, Pet Cemetery and Inspiration Stump, the remains of a tree that once stood in the mystical Leolyn Wood, hallowed ground teeming with energy vortexes. The grove is now used for group readings, with a row of benches for those who flock to the Dale hoping the mediums will deliver personal messages from their lost loved ones.

When Bella was growing up in New York City, her widowed father warned her to stay away from the neighborhood fortune teller who could supposedly talk to the dead, predict the future and remove evil curses, all for a hefty fee.

'Shame on her, convincing gullible people that she's got

supernatural powers,' Frank Angelo said. 'She's nothing but a shameless opportunist. Steer clear, you hear me?'

She heard him, so well that when she got to Lily Dale years later, she initially pegged the local spiritualists as similar charlatans.

But nothing could be farther from the truth. Her friends here aren't doing what they do for financial gain, and many barely earn enough to get by. Their vocation is faith-based and meant to be used for the greater good – even Pandora's.

She turns off the engine and settles back, wishing she'd grabbed *A Tale of Two Cities* to read while she waits.

The book's opening lines run through her mind as she takes in the shuttered gatehouse and a family of ducks bobbing amid hoary ice slabs in the lake.

. . . *it was the season of Light, it was the season of Darkness, it was the springtime of hope, it was the winter of despair . . .*

Nigel might speculate that the words had been inspired by Charles Dickens' early spring travels through Western New York – the so-called Burned-over District.

Bella's cell phone vibrates, and she sees a text from 'Dr Drew Bailey'. That's how she'd entered his contact information in her phone back before he became so much more than her veterinarian. Every time it pops up, she thinks that she really needs to change it to just 'Drew', but never seems to get around to it.

All OK?

She sends him a thumbs up emoji and, *How's Maisie?*

He responds with a selfie. He's changed into scrubs and has the ailing poodle cradled in the crook of his arm.

So sweet, Bella writes back. It applies to both patient and doctor, as does her follow-up heart emoji, which he promptly returns.

She leans back, listening to Pandora's rain pattering on the roof and thinking of all the things the little red heart conveys that neither of them would dare to say. At least *she* wouldn't, navigating this budding romance as if she was wading toward a drop-off in the icy lake across the road.

Her caution is for Max's sake as well as her own – not because her son doesn't approve of her new relationship, but because he so wholeheartedly does.

In December, a year after Sam's death, she'd removed her wedding and engagement rings to do some painting. After the job was finished, it felt right to leave them safely tucked away in her jewelry box along with a tourmaline necklace that may – or may not – have been a gift from Sam.

At first, she was constantly running her left thumb along the base of her bare ring finger, acutely aware that something was missing. But eventually, she grew accustomed to it.

Yes. You get used to things – people, too – not being where they once were. You grow conditioned to absence. You even allow other things – other people – to take up some of the space in a void you know will never be filled again.

Drew isn't Sam. He doesn't clatter around singing off-key, toss Max playfully into the air, or lead him on lively, whimsical romps. He's much more reserved than Sam ever was. Intimidating, even – until you see him bottle-feeding an orphaned kitten, tenderly cradling a fallen bird . . . or reading a bedtime story to a fatherless little boy. He plays as important a role in Max's life as he does in Bella's own.

She and Drew would have been better off remaining platonic friends, though it's too late to go back to that. But if they break each other's hearts, her son's will be shattered. And Max can't lose anything – anyone – else. He just can't.

She hears a rumble down the road and turns to spot the big yellow bus rounding the bend. It pulls up at the gate with a hiss and squeak to dispatch a gaggle of Dale kids.

Max and Jiffy are the smallest of the group, dwarfed by their backpacks. Bella is gratified to see that her son has on his parka, even if it's not zipped, and she isn't the least bit surprised that Jiffy is wearing only a short-sleeved Buffalo Sabres T-shirt.

But wait – he's pausing on the bottom step of the bus to dig his jacket out of his backpack. Pleased that her maternal nagging has rubbed off on him at last, she rolls down her window to shout her approval.

Then he shouts 'Geronimo' and jumps into the streaming gutter, clutching the cuffs in his upstretched hands, coat flapping above his head like a parachute.

'Like that,' she hears him tell Max. 'See?'

'Yep. Great landing.'

'Climb back up and try it.'

'Sorry, fellas, but I've got to move on. See you tomorrow.' The driver closes the doors and the bus rattles away.

'Boys!' Bella calls.

They turn, dismayed.

'Mom! Why are *you* here?'

'Because it's raining! Hop in. You, too, Jiffy!'

'Nah. I mean, no thank you,' he adds politely. 'Me and Max like the rain, Bella. We're going to climb on stuff and splash down in all the puddles and pretend that we're brave army guys jumping out of helicopters into the sea.'

'Yeah, like Jiffy's dad,' Max says.

Mike Arden is serving a tour of duty in the Middle East. Bella met him when he was on leave in December, and witnessed his son's hero worship.

'I have a better idea,' Bella tells the boys. 'How about if we go shopping for treats instead?'

'Treats? Can Jiffy come?' Max asks.

'And Jelly, too?'

'Not Jelly – puppies really can't have treats.'

'Mine can. He loves treats!'

'But not the kind of treats I have in mind. I'll call your mom and get permission for you to come, Jiffy,' she says, pressing Misty's autodial number on her phone as the boys climb into the back seat.

'You don't have to call her, Bella. She likes it when people take me places and give her some peace and quiet. Plus, she also likes treats. Only not the kind that get stuck on teeth, because this one time when she was eating taffy her tooth fell right out and she swallowed it. Only it wasn't a real tooth, by the way. It was a fake tooth that I didn't know was fake. And it wasn't an April Fool's trick. But did you know April Fool's Day is only—'

She holds up a finger to quiet him as his mother answers the phone.

Misty sounds groggy, as though she's been napping. 'Hey, Bells. What's up?'

The quirky nickname always makes her smile. She'd been

Izzy in childhood, Bella Angel to her dad, Bella Blue to Sam . . . but only Misty Arden has ever called her *Bells*.

'I'm down at the bus stop with the boys. Is it OK if I take Jiffy on a couple of errands with me? I'm just going to Fredonia and Dunkirk to—'

'Sure, go for it.'

'Great. I'll have him home by—'

But Misty's already hung up with a yawn and a click.

'Hey, I thought we were shopping for treats!'

'We are, Jiffy.'

'But you told my mom *errands*. *Errands* is not fun.'

Errands is especially not fun on a rainy March day with a couple of first-graders in tow, but Bella promises them treats, and off they go.

The boys spend the duration of the fifteen-minute drive to Fredonia discussing their postponed splashdown plans and brave army guy alter egos.

'We need to have hero names,' Jiffy tells Max. 'And they can't be Mike Arden, by the way.'

'OK. Mine will be Sam.'

'Sam Wilson? He's the Falcon. He's a pararescue jumper and this one time he—'

'No, not the Falcon guy. Just *Sam*.'

'Sam doesn't sound like a hero name.'

'Well it is!' Max insists with such conviction that Bella feels tears needling her eyes, and quickly presses a fingertip to the inner corner of each.

She doesn't cry in front of Max. Well over a year into widowhood, she doesn't cry much at all anymore. But sometimes, emotion sneaks up when she least expects it.

Jiffy is agreeable. 'OK, your hero guy can be Sam. What's his last name?'

'Jordan.'

'That's your last name in real life, by the way.'

'I know.'

'Just making sure. Do you want to know my hero name?'

'Yep.'

'It's Baba O'Riley.'

'Bobby doesn't sound like a hero name.'

'It's not Bobby. It's *Baba*.'

'Baba doesn't sound like any name.'

'It is. It's a real guy.'

'A hero?'

'Yep, in a song.'

'What's the song?'

'I told you! Baba O'Riley! Everyone knows that song and it's by—'

'Mom?' Max cuts in. 'Do you know—'

'I do. It's a great song. An old one, by The Who.'

'By the moon, my mom said,' Jiffy tells her. 'That's who.'

'No, the band who sang it – *The Who*.'

'The *moon*. I just told you, Bella. You need to use your listening ears better.'

She smiles. Maybe she does. It can be challenging following Jiffy Arden's line of reasoning on a good day, and today she has way too much on her mind.

Their first stop is Tuscany, a gourmet market that unfortunately doesn't stock crumpets or clotted cream. They do, however, have most of the ingredients for Pandora's full English breakfast. They also have a wide array of candy by the register.

'You can each pick out one thing,' she tells the boys as she takes out her wallet.

'But you said *treats* with an *s*, Mom. That means more than *one* thing.'

'Smart kid,' the clerk comments with a grin, and Max beams.

'I'm smart, too,' Jiffy speaks up. 'More than one thing is called *plural*. And today, when Mrs Schmidt – she's our teacher – asked if anyone knows three plural ways to be a good global citizen, I said, "Always recycle, always share, and always put the toilet seat up so you don't get pee on it," and Mrs Schmidt said, "Please remember to raise your hand, Michael" – that's my real name and she calls me it – and then I said, "And remember to raise your hand, but that's four ways, not three." I'm great at math, too. And then Mrs Schmidt—'

'Jiffy?' Bella cuts in, conscious of the line behind them. 'We have to let the next customer have her turn.'

'OK. Global citizens take turns. By the way, that's *five*

things. And they don't interrupt other citizens, Bella. That's bad manners.'

'I'm sorry, Jiffy. Come on, let's get moving.'

'Where are we going next, Mom?' Max asks as she hustles bags, boys and umbrella toward the door.

'Liquor store to pick up some gin.'

'I don't blame her one bit,' the clerk tells her next customer.

'It's not for me,' Bella calls back, shoving the door open with her shoulder and wrestling to raise the umbrella before they step out into the downpour.

'Sure it isn't, sweetie.'

Standing at the foot of the stairs watching her aunt and Nigel ascend, Pandora smiles contentedly. Finally – at least for the moment – all is well in her world.

'We'll be back down just as soon as we've freshened up, luv,' her aunt calls. 'I'm so looking forward to catching up on all you've been doing since my last visit.'

'Oh, I'd much rather hear about *your* adventures. And get to know Nigel.'

It isn't that Pandora doesn't enjoy talking about herself, under the proper circumstances, with the proper people. And of course her aunt is well aware that she and her ex-husband long ago parted ways. But having spent her girlhood looking up to Eudora as a successful, self-sufficient modern woman, she's loath to admit that she's barely scraping by, still saddled with the remnants of marital debt all these years later. She's two months behind on the leasehold rent for her tiny cottage, and it's due again in a couple of days.

Cotswold Corner. She'd been hoping the posh new name might elevate the place a bit, the way her gardens and red geranium window boxes perk it up in summer, and her holiday light extravaganza gives it a December glow.

At this time of year, though, it's all so dreary, really. Her home, the Dale, her life, the growing stack of unpaid bills, the phone ringing with collectors . . .

Opening a cupboard door, she hears a familiar, distinct creak.

'Quite like a vixen's scream, isn't it?' Orville had said the first time she'd heard it, back when this kitchen, and the house itself, belonged to them.

Rather, to *him*.

Not solely, of course. The land in the Dale is owned by the Spiritualist Assembly, whose members obtain property lease-holds. Orville bought Valley View when they were engaged. They – rather, *she* – restored the former rundown boarding house to its period grandeur and transformed it into a smashing private residence.

Ah, their life together had been brilliant, back when he was her husband and had eyes only for her. It truly was the best of times.

They'd met here in the Dale. At the time, Orville was a British banker who frequently traveled to New York City on business. He'd always been fascinated by the paranormal, and one weekend traveled across the state to attend a psychic seminar in Lily Dale.

Pandora, then a fledgling medium, had flown from London to attend. She and Orville discovered that they had far more in common than being the only two Britons among the attendees. He, too, was in his mid-thirties and never married. He, too, was an only child who'd lost both parents, and had no close family ties in London. By the end of that weekend, Pandora and Orville were smitten with each other, and with Lily Dale, and were seriously considering living there – not together, of course, at that early stage, but things fell into place and they seemed destined to live happily ever after at Valley View.

Then Jillian Jessup came to town, and thus began the worst of times.

If only Pandora had been the one to open the door when that trollop came knocking. But it was her evening to preside at the Stump service. Orville was home, and his last appoint-ment of the day had just been cancelled.

The funny thing – hardly amusing at all – is that while Orville was back at Valley View with the glamorous starlet, Pandora's spirit guides were attempting to warn her.

'I have a message for a woman in a troubled relationship,' she announced to the crowd assembled at the Stump. 'I believe

the man's name is . . . is it George? No, no, it's two syllables
. . . Boris?'

She kept hearing the 'or' sound, yet she never thought of
Orville. Why would she? She'd never suspected him of philan-
dering. Indeed, in that moment, he had yet to philander. That
night, he'd merely channeled Jillian's beloved father on the
Other Side. But Spirit knew what was coming and persisted,
though no one in the audience claimed the message.

'I do apologize,' Pandora said, 'but my guides are most
insistent that I touch in with the lovely lady who's involved
with . . . Norton, perhaps? Forrest? Something similar, but not
quite . . . ah, Warren?'

A woman raised her hand. 'My husband is Harrison.'

Pandora shook her head. She wasn't hearing *ar*, she was
hearing *or*.

Her guides showed her the famous hillside Hollywood sign.
'Right. California – this has something to do with California.'

A misstep. In her own shorthand, the Golden Gate Bridge
was the symbol that signified any message involving the state.
Yes, the Hollywood sign is also in California, but she should
have realized the meaning went deeper; that Spirit was indicating not geography but industry.

A woman raised her hand. 'My boyfriend's name is Cory,
and his mother is from California.'

'Los Angeles?'

'Palo Alto.'

Pandora had no idea where Palo Alto was located. Still
doesn't, for that matter.

But when the woman asked, 'Is the message for me?' she
went with it. It seemed to fit.

'It seems this man has a connection to a woman called
. . . Julia, I believe. Or . . . Juliana? No . . . that's not quite
it . . .'

The woman gasped. 'Cory's ex-girlfriend's name is Jolene!'

Pandora has long since forgiven herself for a misdelivered
message that may have planted dodgy concerns in an otherwise
healthy relationship. She wasn't nearly as seasoned a medium
back then, as yet unaware of the extent to which one's emotions
or personal involvement can blur a vision, muffle a voice.

What would she have done, had she grasped the meaning? Raced back to Valley View, barged into Orville's study and ordered Jillian Jessup from the premises? That might have kept the affair at bay. That particular affair, at that particular juncture.

'But it was bound to happen sooner or later,' she informs Nadine, the resident spirit, who drifts in a corner of the kitchen. 'If not with that woman, then with another.' Seeing Nadine's forlorn expression, she adds, 'Yes, I'm quite aware that any other woman would have been preferable to Jillian Jessup. We needn't rehash that angle again.'

Pandora herself had been utterly starstruck when Orville told her about his celebrity encounter upon her return from the Stump reading that night. Yes, and she'd asked him for every bloody detail. 'What was she wearing? What did she say? Did she mention Andrew Lane?'

Who'd have dreamed that Jillian would dump her dashing co-star of suitable celebrity caliber for doughy, middle-aged Orville Holmes?

Orville's wife wouldn't have dreamed it. No, she'd been happy, *thrilled*, when Jillian had summoned him to LA to do a group reading for her friends at her Bel Air mansion. She'd been thrilled, *over the moon*, when that trip in turn led to Orville's involvement as a consultant in a film project about the Dale.

By the time it stalled in development, he'd left the Assembly, the Dale, and Pandora, married Jillian, and become a celebrity in his own right, branding himself 'Psychic Guru to the Stars'. His popularity waned a bit after Jillian moved on – served him right, the two-timer – but he's been on the rise again since January, when a major network picked up his syndicated television program to air in prime time, accompanied by a massive advertising campaign. Every time Pandora goes online, opens a magazine, or even drives out on Route 60, she's forced to confront her ex-husband in pop-up videos, print ads, a giant roadside billboard . . .

She plucks a canister from a shelf, plunks it onto the counter, and closes the cupboard with the same distinct creak.

'A vixen's scream, Orville?' she'd asked so long ago, when

they were newlyweds, newly ensconced in this, their dream house. 'That sounds rather terrifying.'

'The term refers to a female fox's mating call, my dear. Nothing terrifying about a shag, now, is there?'

Closing her eyes briefly, she can still see that randy grin of his, revealing crooked teeth she'd found as endearing as his paunch and receding hairline.

The kettle begins to rattle on the gas burner.

She quickly fills a strainer with loose Earl Grey leaves and resumes her hunt through the cabinets and refrigerator for the items she'd asked Isabella to purchase. Coming up short, she sets strawberry jam and butter on a silver tray alongside the cups and saucers, and grudgingly toasts a pair of so-called English muffins – not English at all, but they'll have to do, given the absence of proper crumpets.

'Orville adored crumpets,' she reminds Nadine. 'He liked them drenched in butter and topped with strawberry jam or, better yet, honey.'

If Pandora neglected to set out the honey pot at teatime, he'd wink and ask, 'Won't you *bee* a love and bring some honey for your honey?'

He'd fancied himself quite the comedian and Pandora always rewarded him with a hearty laugh, a loyal audience of one, long before he found his way to the masses.

The first time she'd stumbled across him on the telly, she barely recognized the lean, suntanned, stylishly dressed man. His mousy brown hair had miraculously reversed its retreat, now a lush blond swoop above a surgically chiseled face and massive cosmetic dental work.

She later found some satisfaction in his well-publicized, messy divorce from Jillian, and from the wife who came after her. But now, *here*, in a house that had once been her own, she's steeped in fresh frustration and sorrow. Not to mention residual debt that may very well leave her homeless.

'Do you know, Nadine, that I've yet to pay off that ridiculous diamond necklace I had to pawn years ago – the one he bought me for our last anniversary together? That was after he'd met *her*, and he was trying to assuage his guilty conscience, of course, but I—'

She breaks off, realizing Nadine is no longer present. No surprise. The spirit never did care much for Orville, even when the marriage was stable. She has quite a mischievous streak, but where he was concerned, it bordered on spiteful, or so he claimed.

'I no longer feel safe here because of her,' he'd told Pandora the spring before he moved out. 'Sometimes she comes up behind me on the stairs and gives me a little nudge. I'm fortunate I haven't taken a tumble and broken my neck.'

'Goodness! I'll have a word with Nadine.'

'Do. In any case, I'll be busy during these next few months with the film, so I've been thinking the West Coast makes more sense. Jillian has a guest flat on her property and she's generously offered it.'

'But Orville . . . summer is the *season* in the Dale. If we're not here, we'll miss—'

'I'm aware, Pandora. I wasn't talking about *us*. I was referring to *me*.'

Even then, she hadn't quite grasped the situation. Even then, he hadn't confessed that the actress was far more than a benefactor and colleague.

'No, of course he didn't, the wanker,' she mutters, as the kettle boils into a high-pitched whistle. She lifts it and tips the spout over the tea leaves.

'Wanker?' a voice echoes directly behind her, and she jolts, splashing boiling water across the countertop.

Turning, she sees Nigel, looking casual in denim trousers and a cable knit jumper.

'Careful there. Don't burn yourself.' He steps forward, takes the kettle from her hands and sets it back on the burner. 'So sorry. I didn't mean to startle you. And I do hope you weren't referring to me?'

'I beg your pardon?'

'The wanker.' He winks, and she blinks, seeing her ex-husband's face transposed over Nigel's.

In reality, this man, with his distinguished gray hair and scholarly spectacles, bears little physical resemblance to old, ordinary Orville, nor to shiny plastic Orville. Yet there he is, such a clear vision that she takes a step back, wide-eyed.

'Pandora?'

'I apologize. I was merely thinking of a loathsome person I used to know. The, er, wanker in question.'

'Your former husband.'

'How did you—'

'Eudora mentioned him a time or two. The description seems to fit.'

'Oh, well . . . yes. But I prefer not to talk about him, really.'

'To anyone but yourself?'

'Precisely.' She picks up the pot again. 'I'll just steep the tea and we'll all have a lovely visit in the front parlor.'

'Right. Eudora and I had something a tad more . . . relaxing in mind.'

'The back parlor? It's less formal and more comfortable. The furniture, while true to period, offers deep seating and is generously upholstered with plenty of throw pillows.'

He chuckles. 'Either parlor will do. What I meant was that we thought perhaps we'd have gimlets instead. It's not quite teatime, is it?'

'It's not quite cocktail hour, is it?'

'Well past, in London.'

'Following that logic, it's also well past teatime, isn't it?' Pandora sets down the pot.

'I do like a quick-witted woman. Now then . . . where is this famous Feeney family gimlet recipe I've been hearing so much about?'

'I beg your pardon?'

'Eudora told me it's been handed down for generations and contains a top-secret ingredient.'

'Oh? What is it?'

'There's the rub. She can't remember. I'm sure you have it in the old family recipe collection?'

She's sure she does. But of course the handwritten booklet, compiled by her nineteenth-century ancestors and presented to Pandora as a wedding gift from Auntie Eudora, is over at Cotswold Corner with the rest of her belongings.

'I'm sure it's around here somewhere, but for now, I'm afraid a regular gimlet will have to do.' She opens the refrigerator to look for limes.

'Right then. I'll fetch the Tanqueray. I spied some in the dining room cabinet.'

Rather bold of him, Pandora thinks, and decides she doesn't particularly care for the man. His aura is gray – not a negative quality in and of itself, as it can indicate wisdom and maturity, but she senses emotional isolation within.

She rummages through the refrigerator, wrinkling her nose in distaste at the array of individually wrapped cheese cylinders, small foil-topped cups of custard and jello, little purple boxes of juice with tiny straws . . . and, ah yes, citrus fruit.

Nigel returns with the gin, a silver shaker and three crystal coupe glasses as she sets a couple of limes and a knife on a cutting board.

'I must commend your taste in literature.' He gestures at the thick copy of *A Tale of Two Cities* on the table.

'Yes, well, I've always loved Dickens. Our family home, Marley House, is on Doughty Street in London, just a few doors down from the Dickens Museum.'

He nods. 'A museum now, but of course Dickens lived there in the nineteenth century. It's where he wrote *The Pickwick Papers*, *Nicholas Nickleby*, *Oliver Twist* . . .'

'Oh, I'm aware. Marley House has been in the Feeney family for many generations. Our ancestors Cornelius and Theodora Feeney got along famously with Charles and his wife Catherine. In fact, Theodora herself had literary aspirations.'

'So Eudora has mentioned.'

She doubts her aunt mentioned that Pandora's own mother was also well acquainted with Charles, whose presence lingered on Doughty Street a century after he passed. He often touched in with Mum.

Ironic, since Dickens had taken a famously dim view of spiritualism in life. So had her Feeney ancestors, staunch Anglicans who handed down that sentiment through generations. Like his parents and grandparents, Pandora's father was skeptical of anything to do with channeling energy from the Other Side – although Dad, like Dickens, changed his tune after he crossed over.

'I'm pleased to see that Valley View offers plenty of reading material. I'm looking forward to browsing the bookshelves,' Nigel says. 'I wonder if the recipe collection is there?'

'I believe that it is, likely tucked away on a top shelf. Now then . . . gimlets?'

'I'll do the honors.' He reaches for the knife and a lime.

'You, Nigel, are the guest. You don't have to—'

'And you, darling girl, have already done so much for us. I can't tell you how pleased I am to meet you at last. You're just as kind-hearted – and as pretty, I might add – as I imagined.'

'Oh, I . . . thank you.' Pandora feels herself flush. It's been ages since anyone paid her such a lovely compliment, and even longer since anyone called her a *girl*.

'The wanker didn't deserve you, did he?'

'He most certainly did not.'

'"She deserves the best and purest love the heart of man can offer . . . the devotion and affection of her nature require no ordinary return, but one that shall be deep and lasting,"' he announces with a flourish and a bow.

'Why, er . . . that's quite the apt observation.'

'Dickens, *Oliver Twist*, of course. And it certainly applies to you.'

Clearly, she'd judged Nigel too quickly. He's a lovely man, and he is, after all, very nearly family.

He begins slicing the limes. 'Pandora, if I might have a word with you before your aunt joins us . . .'

'Yes?'

'I'm quite aware that you haven't seen each other in years . . .'

'Decades. Auntie Eudora was last here for my wedding. After she opened the restaurant, she couldn't afford to take time off for such a long journey, and I . . .'

Pandora couldn't afford it, period, after the divorce. Even when she was married, she didn't make the trip back home to London. It wasn't worth the time and expense, with her aunt working round the clock, her parents long gone, her old chums scattered. And as much as Orville adored travel, he preferred exotic holidays and island resorts.

'I do wish I'd been able to spend more time with Auntie

Eudora after I left the UK,' she tells Nigel. 'Life has a way of flying by, doesn't it?'

'Yes, it certainly does. And you're the only family Eudora has left, and she is getting up there in years, though one wouldn't suspect her age to look at her.'

She recycles the comment she'd made earlier to Isabella and Drew. 'Well, we Feeney women are genetically gifted with a remarkable youthful countenance.'

'And great beauty.'

Pandora blushes – prettily, she affirms, catching her reflection in the window above the sink. 'Why thank you, Nigel. I'm so glad you were able to make the trip with my aunt. She's spoken so highly of you, and I'm looking forward to—' She breaks off, hearing footsteps descending the stairs.

'Ah, there she is.' As Nigel sets aside the knife and wipes his hands on a dish towel, one of the limes rolls off the cutting board and hits the floor. 'Clumsy of me, sorry.'

Pandora doubts that he's responsible. Nadine is back, standing beside him and wearing a familiar, mischievous smile.

Pandora gives her a scathing look and turns toward the doorway to greet her aunt as Nigel stoops to retrieve the lime. Hearing him cry out, she whirls back to see the knife's tip embedded in the floor, handle straight up, scarcely an inch from his canvas trainer.

'Darling! Are you all right?' Auntie Eudora asks. 'You might have lost a toe.'

'I'm quite all right, I just . . . I've no idea how that occurred.'

Pandora does. She glimpses Nadine's smile – now a touch more malevolent than mischievous – before the apparition fades.

FOUR

Pulling up in front of the Arden home, Bella heaves a sigh of relief. Mission accomplished – and with a pair of sugar-fueled boys in tow. She deserves . . . a pat on the back? A hot bath?

'Thanks for the errands, Bella. They were great.'

She smiles. Heartfelt gratitude from a six-year-old? She'll take it.

'You're welcome, Jiffy. Make sure you grab your backpack.'

'And your chocolate cupcake for dessert after dinner,' Max tells him.

'And your jacket,' Bella adds.

'I've got it right here.' He pats his bag.

'You need to put it on, Jiffy. It's still raining and you don't want to get soaked.'

'I do want to get soaked, so I can pretend I'm a brave army guy who fell out of a helicopter into the sea. By the way, I think the cupcake fell out of the car.'

Glancing into the rearview mirror, Bella spots a telltale smear of fudge frosting on his freckled face. Little stinker must have gobbled it down without her noticing.

He elbows Max, who says, on cue, 'Uh-oh. Now Jiffy doesn't have any dessert, Mom! We should go back and get him another cupcake. Plus also an extra one for me in case mine falls out of the car.'

'Did you eat yours, too?' she asks, spying fudgy traces around his mouth.

'Nope. Got it right here.' He holds up the white paper bag. 'I just tasted it a little bit. By the way, how did you know Jiffy ate his?'

'Because I know everything.'

'She does, Max. She knows way more things than my mom

and she's not even a medium! She's going to be really hard to fool on April Fool's Day.'

Jiffy opens the car door and hops out. Bella spies a crumpled white bakery bag stuffed into his pocket. Evidence.

'Don't forget to ask your mom about your brainstorm,' Max calls after him.

'I won't! See you tomorrow!'

'What brainstorm?' Bella asks, watching Jiffy head toward the little Victorian cottage, going out of his way to splash through every puddle between the car and the porch.

'For school. We're writing books. Mrs Schmidt said to tell our moms and dads to help us think of an idea tonight. She said it's OK that Jiffy and me only have moms to help us.'

'Please tell me the story isn't due tomorrow, Max?'

'Nope. Not until April first. That's April Fool's Day, by the way. So someone might be playing a trick on you.'

'Guess I'll have to be careful.' Seeing Jiffy backtrack to revisit one of the larger puddles by the curb, Bella rolls down her window and calls, 'Go on inside! You're getting all wet and muddy!'

'Yep!' is the cheerful response.

'His mom won't care,' Max says, and he's probably right.

Misty is a few years younger and a lot more laid back than Bella. Sometimes, that's probably a good thing, but other times . . .

She shudders. Last December, Jiffy had been abducted. Luckily, that ordeal had had a happy ending, and had forced Misty to take a closer look at her parenting skills and priorities.

'I need to be more like you, Bells,' she'd said.

'Me? What? Why?'

'Because you're pretty much perfect.'

'I'm far from perfect, believe me.'

'I don't.'

'Misty, for one thing, I'm a total klutz. I'm always dropping things and tripping over my own feet. Just the other day, I—'

'That's different. I'm talking about the big things. Like, you never make mistakes.'

'I make mistakes all the time.'

'Not big, bad mistakes. Not the kind that can do serious damage.'

'Misty, I—'

'Name one. Name one mistake you've made.'

Bella could think of many.

She shouldn't have taken for granted that she and Sam were going to raise Max together and that their marriage would endure into old age. She shouldn't have convinced Sam to hold off on having more children because they were only in their twenties and there was plenty of time. No, she shouldn't have believed there was plenty of time for babies, and all the other things they wanted to do, and all the things they needed to say.

She should have paid more attention to their finances, too. Should have convinced her young and healthy husband to keep their life insurance policies current instead of funneling money into their dream house savings. Should have anticipated that a serious illness could swallow that nest egg in a matter of weeks. She shouldn't have assumed that the astronomically expensive treatments that plunged them into crippling debt would save Sam.

And then . . .

Even then, after the worst had happened, she'd made mistakes. She'd allowed grief and loss to consume her. She'd ignored the landlord's For Sale sign on the rental property, and the district budget cuts that jeopardized her teaching job, so that she was blindsided by the eviction notice and layoff.

'See?' Misty said. 'You can't think of anything!'

'Believe me, nobody's perfect.'

'Well, nobody's more *imperfect* than me. Just tell me what to do, and how to do it.'

'Misty, I don't know if I can . . . I mean, it's not like I can hand you a list.'

'You don't have to write things down. Just show me. Like, Jiffy tells me you're great at saying no. He says you say no all the time, to everything.'

'Not *everything*.'

'A lot of things. Especially dangerous things. And I . . . half the time I can't tell what's dangerous, and half the time even if I can tell, I can't figure out how to say no. And it's all on me, because his father is on the other side of the world and half the time I can't reach him to ask for advice.'

Bella didn't point out that Max's father is on the Other Side, period. Even here, in the town that communicates with the dead, she hasn't been able to reach Sam.

She just hugged Misty and said she understood, and would try to help.

After that, they'd started spending time together – not just with the boys, and not just working on helping Misty become a more responsible mother, with varying degrees of success.

Lily Dale has taught Bella to expect the unexpected, and her friendship with Jiffy's mom falls into that category.

Misty opens the front door as her son clomps up the steps. Yes, she's still wearing pajamas, and yes, they're mismatched – a slinky zebra-striped print top that's too snug on her ample figure paired with purple plaid flannel bottoms that are much too big. And no, she doesn't make him take off his muddy shoes before he goes into the house. But today, she's here waiting for him, and that's what counts.

'Thanks, Bells!' she calls. 'See you at book club!'

'Oh, right. Thanks for the reminder! I need to finish the book.'

'*Finish?* I barely got through, like, the first five pages. I mean, seriously, who reads *A Tale of Two Cities* for pleasure?'

'It's actually not so bad, once you get into it. I read it years ago.'

'Oh, yay! Can you just tell me what happens?'

'A lot, and I don't really remember it very well. That's why I'm rereading it.'

'Well, you know what I think? I think Pandora only chose this awful book to get back at me for my pick last month.'

She's right, of course. Pandora had raged about Misty's celebrity memoir selection.

'She's well aware, Isabella, that Hollywood is responsible for the demise of my marriage, and yet she—'

'I wouldn't say that *Hollywood* is responsible,' Bella had pointed out.

But there was no reasoning with Pandora about Orville's

betrayal, or about book club. Hardly the most reasonable person under ordinary circumstances, she's been downright insufferable for the past week. Having insisted that the club elect a president, she assumed she'd run unopposed and was flummoxed when her nemesis Odelia Lauder joined the ballot and won.

Driving on up Cottage Row, Bella reminds Max to be on his best behavior while Pandora and her family are visiting.

'I'm always on my best behavior.'

'I know you are, sweetie. I just need you to be extra good, because these guests are extra . . . um . . .'

'Bad?'

'*Special*. They're extra special.'

He weighs that, looking up at Valley View as she parks in front. 'I think they're kind of bad, Mom.'

'Why would you say that?'

'I don't know.'

'Something made you say it.' Just as something made Chance uncharacteristically aggressive. The cat's behavior might have nothing to do with a stray dog or the weather, and everything to do with Eudora and Nigel.

'My brain made me say it,' Max tells her. 'Plus also my mouth.'

'And what made your brain and your mouth say it?'

'Sometimes I know things, just like you do. Even though I'm not a medium. But I might be when I grow up so I can live on Cottage Row and have a sign on my house like Misty and Odelia.'

Bella turns off the engine and looks at her son. His brown eyes, behind his glasses, are earnest.

'When you say you *know* things . . . how do you know?'

He shrugs.

'Max?'

'I don't feel so good.'

'About these guests?'

'About my stomach.'

She sighs. 'Too many treats. I'll make you some ginger tea. Come on.'

Back out into the rain they go. She tells Max to go ahead

as she opens the trunk to retrieve the shopping bags, but he
wants to help her carry them.

'It's OK, sweetie, your tummy hurts and you already have
your backpack.'

'I know but I'm super strong. Plus you look super tired.'

She *is* super tired, and so touched by his empathy that she'd
hug him if she weren't weighed down with bags. He grabs
the last two from the trunk and they splish-splash into the
house, where Bella doesn't even have to remind him to wipe
his feet for a change.

'You're a good kid, Max. Daddy would be so proud.'

Setting the bags on the floor, he replies with a nonchalant,
'He is.'

Bella looks sharply at him. 'How do you know? Is he . . .'

Of course he isn't. Yet she glances around, half-expecting to
see Sam's ghost lounging on a step or leaning on the newel post.

'Isabella? Is that you?' Pandora calls from the front parlor.

She sighs. 'Yep! It's me.'

'And me,' Max adds. 'Hi, Miss Feeney.'

'Hallo, hallo, delightful lad!'

Max whispers to Bella, 'Wow. How come Miss Feeney
sounds so happy? She's usually kind of a grouch.'

'She usually is, isn't she.' Bella can't help but smile. 'Max,
I need you to go straight upstairs and start your homework.'

'But I need you to help me with it because it's a brainstorm,
remember? Plus, I also need ginger tea.'

'I'll bring it to you, and I'll help you. Go on.'

He plods up the stairs. Bella wishes she could follow him,
or that there was a route to the kitchen that doesn't entail
going through the parlor.

In truth, there very well might be. With ties to both the
Underground Railroad and Prohibition-era bootleggers, Valley
View has its share of hidden passageways. Every time Bella
concludes she's discovered all its secrets, the old house reveals
something new.

In the parlor, she finds Pandora holding court in a velvet
chair, like a queen on a throne.

Eudora and Nigel have changed into casual clothing and
seem to have managed to make themselves comfortable on an

antique sofa Bella knows is anything but. All three are holding cocktail glasses.

'Did you get to the off-license, then?' Nigel asks, gesturing at the bags she's carrying but not offering to help her.

'The . . . off-license?'

'They call it a liquor store here in the States, darling,' Pandora tells him. 'I do hope you bought more gin, Isabella?'

'Yes. But I went to three different stores looking for clotted cream and—'

'Never mind that. Do join us for a bevvy!' Pandora says, flushed and tipsy. If she were a queen, her crown would be askew.

'Thanks, but no day drinks for me. I've got to put everything away and help Max with his story and figure out dinner.'

'No need, Isabella. Auntie Eudora will whip up something for all of us, won't you, dear?'

Clearly taken aback, her aunt says, 'Oh . . . I . . . well, I was under the impression that guests' kitchen privileges are limited to the microwave and toaster?'

She looks at Nigel, who nods. 'Yes, that's precisely what it says in the welcome packet.'

Pandora snorts. 'Tosh. You are our special guests. Of course you can use the kitchen, Auntie Eudora.'

Bella clears her throat. 'I don't know if she *wants* to use the kitchen.'

'Of course she does. Why, the last time she was here, she made a positively scrummy fish pie using bass she caught herself, right out back in the lake. And of course, she made our wedding cake. She spent two days crawling about in the wood gathering English walnuts. Oh, it was a divine three-tier confection, soaked in French brandy.'

Gin-soaked Pandora is oblivious to the look that passes between Nigel and her aunt, who obviously and unsurprisingly isn't keen on the idea of fishing or foraging at this time of year.

'Ah, yes, well, we *are* on holiday,' he says. 'We can't have your aunt slaving away in the kitchen the very first night, can we? Perhaps tomorrow we'll break out the Feeney family cookbook and give it a go, eh, Eudora?'

'Smashing idea! I gave it to you as a wedding gift, luv, remember?'

Pandora nods. 'Of course. You gave me something old, something new, something borrowed and something blue. The recipe book was old – ancient, really. And the blue, of course, was my bouquet of *Hyacinthoides non-scripta*.' She turns to Bella. 'That's—'

'The botanical name for English bluebells,' she says. 'The national flower. You planted them in the beds out front when you lived here, and at—'

Seeing Pandora's look of alarm, she catches herself.

She'd been about to say, *and at your cottage*. Oops.

'I mean, in the beds when you lived in England, and now you've planted them here at Valley View,' she amends.

'You certainly know a lot about English bluebells,' Eudora comments.

'Yes, well, they're Pandora's favorite and she's told me a lot about them.'

Understatement of the year.

Nigel says, 'Getting back to the recipe book, Eudora tells me that your ancestor Theodora Feeney may have inspired Catherine Dickens to publish her own cookbook years later, under the pseudonym Lady Maria Clutterbuck. It's quite a collector's item, you know.'

'I'm sure it is,' Bella tells him. 'You know quite a bit about Dickens.'

'Yes, Nigel is a renowned Dickens scholar,' Eudora informs her. 'He can tell you anything you'd like to know.'

'I'll look forward to hearing more about that,' Bella says. 'For now, I've got to get back to Max, but if you need dinner ideas, I have a list of local restaurants and a binder filled with menus. And the Solstice Bistro is only a two-minute walk from here.'

'The Solstice Bistro, my arse!' Pandora shakes her head. 'That's out of the question, Isabella! It's little more than a canteen!'

'I thought you loved that place. Anyway, none of you can get behind a wheel after however many "bevvies" you've had.'

'That's true,' Nigel agrees.

'If you don't want to go to the Solstice, plenty of restaurants outside the Dale will deliver, so you can order in and eat right here.'

'That sounds lovely,' Eudora says. 'I believe we'll take your advice and order takeaway.'

'Yes, and being a chef, darling, you're quite anxious to try the local delicacies,' Nigel agrees. 'What do you recommend, Bella?'

'Beef on weck is a roast beef sandwich served with au jus and horseradish on kummelweck – that's a roll that has kosher salt and caraway seeds. Or wings. They're—'

'Have you gone mad, Isabella? You can't serve *chicken wings* to a world-class chef and literary scholar and . . . *me*.'

'No worries, Pandora. I wasn't planning on serving anything. I'll just put these groceries away and grab the list and binder for you and you can—'

'Mom?'

She turns to see Max in the doorway, clutching his stomach.

'Ah, the lad. Rather green, isn't he?' Nigel observes.

'Why, Nigel! You can see auras?' Pandora exclaims, and then peers at Max. 'I'd say he's yellow, though, with blackish streaks in the midsection, which might indicate—'

Max makes a terrible retching sound.

'—abdominal illness.'

'Max!' Bella dumps a bag of groceries on the floor and rushes to hold it open beneath his chin as he bends over and vomits into it.

Following the revolting incident with young Max, dining at Valley View was out of the question. Bella's quick thinking may have saved the carpet from being soiled, but nothing could scour the lingering stench from the air.

Pandora had no choice but to escort her visitors out into the rain to the Solstice Bistro, the last place she wanted to be this evening. Not because the restaurant isn't up to par. On the contrary, it's a delightful little café tucked into the basement of a new-age bookshop. The food is decent and reasonably priced, and they even brew a proper pot of tea.

The owners, longtime year-round residents Walter Darwin and Peter Clifford, are friends of hers. That's the case with just about everyone in the Dale, but this particular couple had been part of Pandora's close-knit marital social circle.

After her divorce, most of the others had made her feel like a fifth wheel, or were openly enamored of Orville's newfound celebrity status, but Walter and Peter were solidly Team Pandora. She's made them privy to the worst of her problems over the years, and fears they might allude to her sorry state of affairs.

She hasn't yet found an opportunity to tell Auntie Eudora that she no longer owns Valley View – that in fact, she never did. Orville had purchased the house solely in his name before the marriage, and never added hers. By the same token, he'd never put his own name on the credit cards they'd used to run up debt during the marriage.

Pandora had had every intention of confessing the truth as soon as they were settled in with their gimlets, but then Eudora and Nigel started going on about Valley View's many charms, and she found herself accepting full credit, and then some.

'I've been up to my eyeballs restoring and renovating the place of late,' she'd heard her voice say.

It isn't like her to lie. Embellish, perhaps, on occasion, should the situation warrant. But *lie*?

There's just something unnerving about being reunited with the only living person she's known all her earthly life; someone who is, effectively, a bridge to the happier past and the woman Pandora once was – or at least, strived to be.

'I'm so proud of you, Pandora,' Eudora had said when they'd last seen each other. 'I promised your dear father I'd look after you, but that's no longer necessary, is it? You're married to a good man, mistress of a grand mansion, building a wonderful life here in the States.'

Her aunt had been disappointed when Orville left her, though unaware he'd left her destitute.

'I won't say I told you so, but I've been single all my life with good reason,' she said when Pandora called her to break the news. 'I don't believe in contractual romance. Relationships should be allowed to bloom, grow, and fade away without fuss

and fanfare and restrictions. And your Orville never did strike
me as the true blue sort.'

'I do wish you'd mentioned this before I walked down the
aisle.'

'Would you have heeded my warnings? You were immersed
in bridal frivolities and giddily in love.'

'I was, wasn't I?' She'd done her best not to sniffle into
the phone. 'What am I to do now?'

'Chin up and carry on, I say, just as always. Feeney women
are perfectly self-sufficient.'

Ah, but a self-sufficient woman would have seen Orville's
prenuptial agreement as a red flag, instead of accepting his
claim that all couples have them and signing without a close
look or second thought. She wouldn't have allowed him to
access the profits she'd made selling Marley House after her
mother's death and lose it all to bad investments. She'd have
hired a reputable divorce lawyer instead of naively believing
that her husband would come to his senses and return to her,
or at least treat her fairly.

A self-sufficient woman wouldn't have spent the last few
years triaging the bills she could scrimp enough to pay and
ignoring the ones she couldn't, as interest and penalties
mounted. Now, she can no longer even afford the utilities.

At best, Auntie Eudora will know what a fool she's been.
At worst, she'll pity her – and Pandora loathes pity.

Is it any wonder she's feeling out of sorts this evening?
She'd hoped a cocktail or two might help her relax and ease
the pervasive disquiet within her, but it hasn't done the trick.

She's relieved to find that they're the only patrons in the
candlelit restaurant on this blustery March evening, seated at
a cozy rectangular table for four. Eudora and Nigel are across
from each other, with Pandora to her aunt's left. As always,
she finds facing an empty chair a most explicit reminder of
what might have been. She resolves to have a word with Walter
and Peter about installing round tables for three – and for one,
as she typically dines alone.

Ordinarily, one or both of the owners would peek out from
the kitchen to greet them, but tonight she sees only Calla
Delaney. She's Odelia's granddaughter, a fresh-faced brunette

in her late twenties, and recently moved back to the Dale from Buffalo.

'Working here now, luv, are you?' Pandora asks when she comes over with menus and a water pitcher.

'Not officially. Walt and Pete asked me to help out tonight because they had to help Jacy move.'

Jacy Bly is their adopted son, and Calla's longtime live-in boyfriend. Their recent break-up has been remarkably civilized, especially given the fact that Calla is once again involved with Blue Slayton, Jacy's rival in the love triangle that dates back to their teenaged years.

'Is he coming home to the Dale, then?' Pandora asks.

'No, but the lease on the place we had together is up on April first, so he's subletting a studio near the hospital until he finishes his residency.' She turns to Eudora. 'You look so much like Pandora that you must be her aunt. Gammy told me you were coming for a visit.'

'Gammy?' Eudora asks.

'My grandmother.'

'The nickname – rather cruel, isn't it?'

At Calla's blank expression, Pandora explains, 'In some parts of the UK, "gammy" means that she's got a bad leg or some such injury.'

'Oh! Well, she can be clumsy, and she *did* break her foot last year,' Calla says with a laugh. 'Anyway, it's so nice to meet you both. Eudora, if I didn't know better, I'd guess you and Pandora were sisters.'

'We Feeney women are genetically gifted with a remarkable youthful countenance,' Pandora informs her, with perhaps a tad less enthusiasm for the comment this time round.

Not that Auntie Eudora doesn't look wonderful for her age. But she's nearly two decades older than Pandora, who is suddenly feeling much the worse for wear.

Perhaps it's the . . . *day drinks*, to use Isabella's terminology. She's out of practice. It's been a while since Walter and Peter invited her to join them for late-day cordials – 'unhappy hour', as they drolly called it after her divorce.

All things considered, is it any wonder that her youthful countenance, now in juxtaposition to her aunt's, leaves a bit to be desired? Pandora's life, since Orville left, has been so bloody difficult, while Eudora's life . . .

It strikes her that she knows very little about her aunt's day-to-day existence over the past few years. Their regular telephone calls have long since given way to texting. Those brief missives, while perhaps more frequent, just aren't the same as chatty conversation. No wonder their reunion has been a trifle stilted.

Ah, well, they'll soon make up for lost time, and she'll get to know her aunt again. Nigel, too. She wonders about his intentions, remembering that he'd requested a private word with her in the kitchen before Auntie Eudora joined them. Perhaps he was going to request Pandora's blessing to advance their relationship. He may be quite unaware of Auntie Eudora's practical-minded approach to romance and planning a proposal.

Auntie Eudora is beaming at Calla. 'I am indeed Pandora's aunt, Eudora Feeney. And this is my good friend, Professor Nigel Spencer-Watson. You must be . . .' She pauses as though trying to place her.

'Calla Delaney.'

'Ah, right you are. Calla Delaney.' Auntie Eudora seems poised to add that she's heard so much about her, but of course, she has not. Pandora has never mentioned her.

Then again, Calla recently published a novel. Might she have achieved more fame than Pandora realized?

'Calla is an author. Her first book was well received and she's working on her second.'

'Indeed?' Nigel perks up. 'Congratulations, Miss Delaney. Have I read it?'

'I doubt it. My agent sold the UK rights, but it won't be out there until summer.'

'Well, I shall give it a read the moment it hits the stalls.'

'Oh, you don't have to wait that long. There are at least a dozen copies in Valley View's library. Grab one, and I'll autograph it for you.'

'That would be lovely.'

'Nigel is a writer, too,' Eudora speaks up.

'Yes, but *not* a novelist. Articles, research, that sort of thing. As they say in academia, publish or perish.'

'It's very kind of a woman of your stature to volunteer in a restaurant,' Eudora comments, and Calla laughs.

'Oh, I'm not volunteering. Helping out a friend, yes, but not merely out of the goodness of my heart. I need to make my rent. A few months ago, I moved into a little cottage over on East Street, not far from Pandora's—'

'I do beg your pardon, Calla, but let's not prattle on and bore our guests,' she cuts in. 'I'm certain they're quite famished and wondering about the evening specials.'

'Right. Sorry about that. Let's see . . . in addition to the menu, tonight we've got spaghetti and meatballs, chicken cordon bleu, and moussaka.'

'Rather unusual bistro fare,' Nigel observes.

'Yes, and I do love a wide array of choices, don't you?' Pandora doesn't wait for a reply. 'How fortuitous that chicken cordon bleu is on the menu this evening. Call, Auntie Eudora received her culinary training at Le Cordon Bleu.'

Calla raises an eyebrow. 'Then you'll probably want to avoid ordering that dish here. They make it with boloney instead of ham. Some people like it, but it's not for everyone. Oh, and the soup of the day is minestrone . . .' She leans in and lowers her voice to a whisper. 'But don't get that, either.'

'Whyever not?' Eudora whispers back, with a glance at Pandora, who nods.

The minestrone at Solstice is a notoriously unappetizing amalgamation of the weekly leftovers, from French fries to tuna melt, but no one has the heart to mention it to Walter and Peter.

'I'd prefer not to elaborate,' Pandora says, 'but do take Calla's word for it – particularly on the heels of the rather unfortunate episode back at the house.'

'Uh-oh. What happened back at the house?' Calla asks.

'I'm afraid the lad chundered in the parlor,' Nigel says.

'Wow. I'm, um, not sure exactly what that means, but I'm guessing I'd rather not know. Can I bring you some sparkling water for the table?'

'Do,' Eudora says, 'and a wine list, if you please.'

'Oh, sorry. Peter and Walt are still waiting for their liquor license. It's BYOB.'

'That means bring your own,' Pandora explains to her guests. 'But I didn't think of it, what with . . .'

'The chundering?' Calla supplies.

'Precisely. We'll just have our supper and a nightcap back at Valley View.'

'Great. I'll get the sparkling water while you decide what to order.' Calla walks away.

Nigel pushes back his chair. 'And I shall go back to Valley View for the wine.'

'In this weather?' Pandora protests.

'It really is siling down, darling,' Eudora tells him, looking toward the streaming rain beyond the plate glass window.

'Not a problem. Red or white?'

'Both. After all, we're on holiday!'

'Back in a flash.' He kisses her cheek, retrieves his raincoat and umbrella from the hook by the door, and disappears out into the storm.

'*Siling* down,' Pandora muses, staring after him.

'Aye, it is, isn't it.'

She turns toward her aunt. 'I haven't heard anyone say that in years. Not since I was in uni.'

'Up in Leeds, wasn't it? Your dear father's alma mater.'

'Of course. For a moment, when you said it was "siling down" in just that way . . . and "aye" too . . . well, you reminded me of someone I once knew.'

'Oh?'

Pandora nods, thinking of her strapping Uplands shepherd. 'He's the one who got away.'

'Rather, the sod who let *you* get away.'

'You remember!'

'Of course. His name was . . .'

'Duncan.'

'*Duncan!*' Auntie Eudora says, a split second behind her. 'Of course! I remember.'

'I was positively gutted when we broke up, but your pep talk helped me through. Chin up and carry on . . . It was brilliant, really. Just what I needed. You said the same thing years later, with Orville.'

'Always glad to help.'

They smile at each other awkwardly.

In her younger days, a heart to heart with her favorite aunt could cure just about anything that ailed her. Now, it's as though they're polite strangers, facing each other across a chasm. Maybe time and distance really do take an irreparable toll on relationships. Something is obstructing the flow between them.

Of course something is! It's your bloody lie!

'Auntie Eudora, there's something you should know about—'

'Sorry to interrupt, ladies.' Calla is back with a loaded tray containing a bottle of sparkling water, lemons and limes, and a basket full of hot rolls. 'Oops, I forgot the butter, sorry.'

'No butter necessary,' Eudora says, 'and you may remove the breadcakes as well.'

'It isn't that dreadful, tasteless bread you loathe, Auntie Eudora,' Pandora assures her, helping herself. 'These are hot out of the oven.'

'I'm certain it isn't, but I'll only be tempted.'

'Well then, we'll just keep them beyond your reach.' Pandora pushes the basket across the table as her aunt reaches for a lime. Their arms collide.

'So sorry, luv.'

'It's quite all right. Calla, I'd like some butter, please?'

'Sure, be right back.'

Auntie Eudora squeezes lime into her glass and sips. 'Refreshing. All that's missing is the gin.'

Pandora lifts the piece of bread. 'All that's missing is the butter. You know what they say about that.'

'What who says about what?'

'About a roll without butter? And it isn't what they say – it's what *you* say.'

'Perhaps you can jog my memory.'

'Perhaps it's my own memory that needs a good jog,' Pandora says, and bites into the roll as though nothing is amiss.

But something nags at her consciousness. It isn't simply that her aunt seems to have developed quite a taste for spirits – the liquid sort, anyway. Nor that Eudora always did love to start a meal with freshly baked bread, and in fact once remarked

that a roll without butter is like Christmas morning without
Santa.

A *roll*. Not a *breadcake*. She's never called them that.

Duncan had, however. And so had Pandora's friends at uni.

'Now then, Pandora. You were saying?'

'I was saying . . .'

Ah, yes. She was about to confess the whole sordid mess.

'I was saying . . .'

But before she can go on, Calla reappears with the butter.
And Nigel will be back any minute.

The moment has passed.

FIVE

'He's much better, thanks,' Bella tells Odelia, phone propped between her shoulder and ear as she rummages through the fridge and freezer for healthy ingredients to cobble into a meal for Max. 'It's totally my fault. I was so stressed, I let him have too many treats. I just hope Jiffy doesn't get sick, too.'

'Don't give it another thought. That child has the constitution of an okapi.'

'A . . . what?'

'It's a cross between a zebra, deer and giraffe. I got to know them a few years back when I was on African safari. They have four stomachs.'

'Well, Jiffy only has one, as far as I know. But I never knew you went to Africa, Odelia?'

'I did, with Leona Gatto. She'd been there several times. She was a wonderful travel companion. How I miss having exotic adventures.'

If adventure you're a'seekin' . . .

You can't go wrong with Beacon . . .

The jingle is back, playing in Bella's head as she grabs vegetables and a package of frozen chicken, then closes the fridge with her foot and the freezer with her elbow. She steps around Chance, Spidey and Lady Pippa, intertwined and napping on the floor in the worst possible spot. They don't stir when she dumps everything on the counter with a clatter.

Pandora had hand-delivered Lady Pippa to Bella's care before leaving for the restaurant. 'She'll need to be fed. She likes her food gently warmed, but not hot. She prefers a plastic spoon but if you must use metal, see that it's a teaspoon. And you'll want to keep her away from your two.'

'Right. I don't want them getting any ideas about being spoon-fed.'

'No, I just mean because Lady Pippa is unaccustomed to other cats and she's rather shy.'

As soon as Pandora and the others left the house, Bella let her own cats out of the laundry room. Lady Pippa made a beeline for them, tackling Spidey, wrestling with Chance, and leading a merry chase throughout the house. When Bella set three bowls of room temperature food on the floor, she dove hungrily into her own bowl, then polished off the others'.

Bella steps over the cats again and opens a cabinet. 'Odelia, did you make a decision about that trip with Luther next month?'

'No, and I just don't know what to do. Business has been slow and I'm broke.'

'I thought the cruise was Luther's treat.'

'Yes, but I wouldn't feel right about not paying my own way. He says he wouldn't feel right about that, and I told him he's being archaic.'

'What? He's just being generous, and a gentleman. If he wants to spoil you, let him. You should go.'

'He did say he got such a great deal that it's practically free.'

'Well in that case, how can you say no?'

'Because, Bella, in my experience, if something seems too good to be true, it probably is.'

'Are we talking about your relationship with Luther, or the deal he got on Beacon Atlantic?'

'Both. I'm just not sure I can commit.'

'Odelia, it's a cruise, not a marriage proposal.'

'A marriage proposal! Do you know something I don't?'

'I doubt it. You're the clairvoyant. But ever since I met you, Odelia, you've been infatuated with this man, and now that he's finally—'

'Infatuated! I'm a senior citizen, not a schoolgirl. And we have absolutely nothing in common! Luther has expensive taste, and I'm no-frills. I've been married with children, he's a lifelong bachelor. He's a dog person, I'm a cat person. He's into sports and physical fitness, I'm into relaxation and meditation. He's a drop-dead gorgeous black man, I'm a not-so-gorgeous white woman.'

'*You* are one of the most beautiful women I've ever known,' Bella assures her. 'Inside and out.'

She may not be a conventional beauty, with wayward pumpkin-colored curls and an eclectic fashion sense, but she's utterly captivating, and Bella isn't the only one who thinks so.

Odelia and Luther met years ago, when he was a police detective and she approached him about a case he was working on. It wasn't the first time she'd gone to law enforcement with information she'd received courtesy of her spirit guides, but it was the first time law enforcement was receptive. Thanks to Odelia's tip, Luther solved the case. They collaborated on many others before his retirement, and remained good friends.

A bit more than friends these past few months. But now that ladies' man Luther seems willing to put aside his freewheeling ways, Odelia has become uncharacteristically reticent, stalling on his invitation to accompany him on a spring getaway.

'Luther is crazy about you, Odelia,' Bella says. 'Don't hurt his feelings.'

'It isn't about *feelings*. It's about scheduling. I've got a business to run here. I need to make money. I can't go gallivanting all over the globe.'

'It's just to Bermuda.'

'Exactly. Bermuda.'

'Bermuda . . . what?'

'Strange phenomena occur in the surrounding waters.'

'Strange phenomena occur right here in the Dale, too. And there are no palm trees or pink sand beaches on Cassadaga Lake, and you said you miss travel, so you might as well go to Bermuda.'

'That's easy for you to say.'

'It isn't, really. You know how I feel about, um . . . strange phenomena. But while we're on the subject, I might as well ask . . . what are your guides telling you to do?'

'I sense that they're uneasy with the idea.'

'Why?'

'Hard to say. I've been meditating, but it's all unclear.'

'You must be too emotionally invested.'

'Listen to you, Bella. You sound like a seasoned medium.'

'I'm just telling you what you've told me many times about how things work around here. Now can I ask you something?'

'Anything.'

A question pops into her head. Not the one she was planning on posing, about the rock-solid hunk of poultry on the counter, but one she hadn't even known was on her mind.

But why would she ask Odelia about Drew Bailey? *What would she even ask about him?*

You wouldn't. You shouldn't. So don't.

Back to Question A: 'How long do you think I should microwave three pounds of chicken to thaw it?'

'It takes much longer than you think. You have to be patient. It's a delicate process.'

For a moment, Bella wonders if she's inadvertently asked the Drew question after all.

But then Odelia goes on, 'Set the microwave to fifty percent power and check it and turn it every minute or two.'

'Right. Too complicated. Forget it.' Bella opens the freezer and puts the chicken back. 'I guess it's buttered pasta for dinner again.'

Before she can shut the door, a bag of frozen organic pomegranate seeds slides out and plunks onto the floor. She sighs, retrieves it, and puts it back. The freezer is overpacked, thanks to Pandora's grocery requirements.

'Bella, why don't you come here for dinner? I'm making celery loaf and shrimp-stuffed apples.'

Odelia's culinary skills tend toward the experimental, sometimes with surprisingly delicious results, and other times . . . not so much. With business lagging she's been working on a cookbook, inspired by her granddaughter Calla's success in the publishing industry, and is always looking to recruit tasters.

Wedging the frozen fruit between a carton of ice cream and a bag of French fries, Bella says, 'Oh . . . thanks, but we'd better not tonight. Just in case Max is coming down with something.'

'Well, I'll run it over to you, then. I've cooked enough for an army.'

'Don't do that,' she says quickly, and a bit too forcefully. 'I mean, I appreciate the offer, and that sounds yummy, but I'd better keep Max on a bland diet for tonight.'

'Well, I'll bring you some fresh ginger root. You just grate it and steep it in hot water, then have him sip it.'

'I'm one step ahead of you, Odelia. I made him some ginger tea earlier and it helped. The last thing we need is a repeat performance of him throwing up all over Pandora and her family,' she adds, just as the pomegranate seeds fall from the freezer again.

'He threw up *on* them?'

Bella stoops to retrieve the bag, this time wedging it in more firmly. 'No, but every time I replay it in my head it gets worse. It wasn't *on* them. Just into a grocery bag.'

'I see.'

'You sound disappointed, Odelia.'

She chuckles. 'I'll admit I kind of enjoyed the image.'

'I'll bet you did.' There's certainly no love lost between the two women, especially now that the book club election is in the mix.

'Although, I don't suppose her aunt deserved it. What's she like?'

'Eudora? She's nice enough. And Nigel is too. But—' Bella shoves the freezer door shut with a grunt. As she holds it there to make sure it sticks, she hears movement in the next room. She looks down, counting cats. All still here.

'Max?' she calls.

No answer.

'Bella? Is everything all right?' Odelia asks.

'Sorry, I thought I heard footsteps down here, and he's supposed to be resting.'

'It's probably just the wind, or Nadine. She's always restless when it rains, poor thing. Just like Miriam.'

Miriam is the resident ghost next door. According to Odelia, Miriam's husband built the house back in the 1880s, and she's hung around to keep an eye on things.

'Now then, Bella, you were saying . . .?'

'I was saying . . .'

'Pandora's guests.'

'Right, Eudora and Nigel. They're fine. Lovely, really. It's just . . . you know what? It's probably nothing.'

'It's never nothing.'

She sighs. 'Chance just seems kind of . . . uneasy around them. She's usually fine with other guests, so it's out of character. I wouldn't think anything of it if it were just that, but just a few days ago, Pandora mentioned that felines are sensitive to negative energy.'

'As much as I hate to agree with anything Pandora says, she's right. So that's what has you troubled?'

'Not just that. After they got here, Max said something about . . . wait, I just heard it again. Hang on.'

She steps over the cats and peeks into the dining room. 'Max? Are you down here?'

No sign of him. No wind, either, at the moment. She hears only the rain, and the antique mantel clock ticking loudly in the next room.

Then Odelia's voice, calling through the phone, 'Nadine? Leave Bella alone, please! She's had a rough day.'

Bella smiles and returns to the kitchen. 'Thanks. I hope she listens to you.'

'She'd listen to *you*, if you'd just address her directly.'

'OK, well – oh no! How did that happen?' She stares in dismay at the pomegranate seed avalanche littering the floor in front of the open freezer.

'What happened?'

'A mess, that's what. It's like this bag of frozen fruit has a life of its own. It keeps jumping out of the freezer and now it's torn open and made a huge mess.' She plucks the bag from the freezer, closes the door, and steps over the three still-somehow-sleeping cats on her way to the sink.

'Is it something you bought for Pandora?'

Recognizing the thoughtful muse in Odelia's question, Bella assures her that it isn't. 'I must have bought it a while back. It was probably on sale. Or maybe one of the guests bought it and stuck it in here. I really need to clean out the freezer.'

She could have sworn the bag was sealed the first time it fell out, but she must have been wrong about that, or maybe it was damaged in her rough handling. There's a jagged tear below one seam. No wonder it made such a mess. She sighs and shakes her head.

'Bella? What kind of fruit is it?'

She sighs again, this time not about the red-pocked floor. She can picture Odelia on the other end of the line, wearing the familiar expression she gets when she's deciphering some symbolic other-worldly message.

'It's organic pomegranate seeds.'

'I see.' The words are loaded.

'Odelia? I didn't mean that this fruit actually had a life of its own. It didn't *literally* jump out of the fridge.'

Three times.

No, it absolutely did *not*.

'I'd better hang up now because I've got to clean up this—'

'Wait, Bella, what did Max say about the visitors?'

'He said they're bad people – something like that. And I wouldn't have thought anything of it if Chance hadn't hissed at them. She was on edge before they even got here . . . almost as if she was dreading something. Which makes absolutely no sense,' she adds quickly.

'It makes perfect sense. Cats are intuitive. Especially Lily Dale cats. And so are children. They're open to spiritual experiences because, unlike adults, they haven't yet fully learned what they're supposed to see and feel, and what they aren't.'

It isn't the first time she's told Bella as much. And there have certainly been occasions, since their arrival in Lily Dale, when Max has shown a level of perception that seems to defy logical explanation. She's learned to pay attention, in case there's something to it. But still . . .

'Odelia, Max isn't . . . you know . . . I mean, you told me that psychic gifts run in families, but there are none in mine or Sam's.'

'I did tell you that certain families have a genetic tendency toward mediumship, and it comes more easily to some, the same way some families produce musical virtuosos and sports heroes. But anyone can learn to play a piano or catch a baseball, Bella. And anyone can learn to communicate with Spirit. The key lies in willingness and practice.'

'I'm not so sure about that, Odelia.' She grabs a roll of paper towels, spray cleaner and the trash can from under the sink. 'I mean, I'd like nothing more than to communicate with Sam, and I've been open to that ever since I got here, but . . .'

'Have you, though, really?'

'What do you mean by that?'

'Just that you've approached these things with a healthy dose of skepticism, my dear.'

'Well, you can't fault me for that.' Bella drops to her hands and knees and starts picking up pomegranate seeds. 'It's not like I came to Lily Dale because I was trying to get in touch with Sam, you know, the way other people do. I'd never even heard of it before I wound up here, and for that matter, I never believed in this stuff before I got here, either.'

'But now you do.'

'Exactly. Wait, no! Not exactly! Not at all!'

'Not at all?'

'Not most of the time, anyway.' She spritzes spray cleaner on the floor and unsheathes paper towels. 'If I were going to believe in it, am I supposed to believe that I'm just not good at this thing that *anyone* can do? Or that my husband . . . what? Just . . . isn't speaking to me?'

'I think he's spoken to you many times, in many ways. Maybe you just don't always recognize him, but that doesn't mean he isn't there. Do you understand?'

'I guess so.'

Two summers ago, she and Sam had spotted a tourmaline pendant in a gift shop. He'd told her it was meant to be hers, and he was going to surprise her with it one day when she least expected it.

Last summer, she'd found an identical necklace in a hidden compartment under a stair tread here at Valley View.

The moment she saw it, she was certain Sam had sent it to her from the Other Side.

In the months since, she's scoured her brain for a logical explanation.

Had Sam told someone – Max, a friend, his mother – about the necklace before he died, and asked that it be planted for Bella to find . . .

In a guesthouse in a town they'd never heard of?

Coincidence is the only explanation that makes sense. Here in the Dale, however, coincidence is not accepted as coincidence, any more than dead is dead. And of course, nothing is impossible, or so they say.

She sighs. 'Odelia, I really have to . . .'

She freezes, her hand poised mid-scour on the wad of paper towels.

'Bella?'

'Hang on a second, Odelia.'

She just heard something creak in the dining room. She gets to her feet and peers around the doorway. The room appears empty. She flips on the light to be sure there's no one – well, Max – hiding behind the drapes, under the table, or in the adjacent alcove lined with floor-to-ceiling bookshelves.

No Max. No anyone.

She checks the back parlor, the breakfast room, the front parlor, and the small study beyond the curtained French doors. Other than the Rose Room, this is Bella's favorite in the house. It had been set up as Leona Gatto's reading room – not as in library, but rather the dedicated space where she practiced mediumship. Now it serves as an office, with a desk, file cabinet and computer for guests' use as well as her own. The walls are a vibrant yellow, and bright blue floral cushions line the window seat, with one of Valley View's many secret cubbies tucked beneath – too small for even a small boy, but she still lifts the lid and calls, 'Max? Nadine? Anyone?'

Only Odelia, on the other end of the phone. 'Bella, is everything all right? Do you need me to come over?'

'No, I'm fine, but thank you.' She closes the study door and goes into the front hall. 'Just exhausted, and it really has been a rough day. I'll talk to you tomorrow, OK? Enjoy your dinner.'

'Are you sure you wouldn't like some?'

'Positive.' She smiles. 'You're a good friend, Odelia. And don't mind my rantings about Lily Dale. You know I love it. And you.'

'I know. Sleep well, my dear.'

Bella hangs up and sighs. Then she notices the faint trace of water on the floor. She presses a wall switch to illuminate the hall. Bending closer to examine the spot, she sees what appears to be the faint partial outline of a shoe.

'Hey, Nadine . . . does Spirit leave footprints?' she asks softly, and finds herself listening for a reply.

She hears the ticking clock, and her own pulse pounding in her ears, and, somewhere in the distance, a faint . . .

Not a bark, exactly. It's that same strange *yip* she heard earlier.

Power of suggestion, that's all it is.

Realizing she's holding her breath, she exhales shakily. This is crazy. It's—

Out of the corner of her eye, she sees movement, gasps, and swivels.

'Oh! Chance! You scared me, kitty.'

The yip must have come from the cat.

Bella has never heard her make that particular sound before, though. Chance occasionally meows and sometimes chirps. And the yip seemed to come from outside, or upstairs, not right here in the room . . . if it had been real at all.

Come on, Bella. Pandora mentioned a yip, and now you're hearing yips? What does that tell you?

But it isn't just her. Maybe Chance heard it, too. Something roused her from a sound sleep. And now her tail is twitching, her fur is spiky, and her eyes are fixed on the door.

'Is something out there, Chance? Was someone in here?'

Bella looks again at the footprint, or rather, *for* the footprint. It seems to have dried and disappeared. Was it ever there at all, or is she seeing things? Hearing things?

It wouldn't be the first time that's happened since she moved to town. And some of the strangest things she's heard have had perfectly logical – well, using Lily Dale's unique brand of logic – explanations.

She goes over to the coat tree and grabs the down parka she wore throughout the snowy winter, pretty sure she'd had it on the day she ran into Doris Henderson at the store. Yes. The green flier is still in the pocket, transformed into scrap paper with various notes to herself jotted on the back.

Put wiper fluid in car

Pay electric bill

Buy 4 white posterboards

If Max needs supplies for a school project, she's learned to get extra for Jiffy, who invariably neglects to tell his mom. Or if he remembers, Misty forgets, then asks Bella if she can borrow whatever it is.

'It's so amazing the way you always have exactly what I need on hand, Bells!'

'Yep. Amazing.'

She checks the drum circle schedule on the flier.

Twice weekly . . . Rain or shine . . .

It's certainly raining tonight, but drum circle doesn't meet until the weekend. So who's yipping and yowling?

She turns off the overhead light so that she can see outside. Pressing her forehead against the glass, she finds the porch vacant, as it should be. The stained-glass angels are twirling slowly, lacking sufficient wind to make them chime. Beyond the porch lamp's glow, there's nothing but falling rain and darkness.

Bella turns away.

'See that, Chance? You don't have to worry, because everything's OK out there. In here, too.'

The cat's green eyes glitter at her across the dim hall.

'Yeah, I know. I don't believe me, either.' With a sigh, Bella slowly returns to the kitchen to clean up the pomegranate confetti. The seeds are starting to thaw, pooling and glistening like droplets of blood.

SIX

Yawning, Bella stands watching the coffee *drip, drip, drip* into the glass carafe, wishing she'd remembered to set the machine's automatic timer last night. There's nothing better than waking up to a full pot of hot, fragrant brew. Well, nothing better now that she doesn't have a husband to wake up to.

Last night, she'd gone to bed earlier than usual. Helping Max with his brainstorming had been more challenging than she'd anticipated. He'd dismissed every story topic she suggested. Then, after learning that Jiffy was writing about his puppy, Max decided that he wanted to write about his cats – which was the first idea Bella had come up with and promptly dismissed by Max.

At last, she'd tucked him in and crawled into her own bed with *A Tale of Two Cities.* But she'd had a hard time focusing on the book, and when she turned off the light, she'd had an even harder time falling asleep. That damned Beacon Atlantic advert kept jangling through her head. And she kept thinking about the wet footprint she thought she'd seen, the yipping she thought she'd heard, the yowling Pandora claimed to have heard, and the pomegranate seeds spattered like blood.

Nor could she get comfortable in her bed with Chance and Spidey somehow sprawled across every possible spot where her feet could go. Ordinarily, they'd sleep downstairs or prowl the house or whatever it is cats do at night, but she couldn't let them roam free, given Eudora's 'acute ailurophobia'.

Having forgotten to set the alarm, Bella had overslept, and Max missed the bus. She drove him to school without bothering to comb her hair or brush her teeth, wearing the flannel pajama bottoms and bleach-spattered T-shirt she'd slept in. She'd managed to brush her teeth when she got home five minutes ago, but that, and feeding the ravenous cats, were the extent of her pre-caffeinated capabilities.

Drip, drip, drip . . .

'Come on, hurry up,' she says, in case the coffee machine, like Nadine, might heed her voice commands.

She closes her eyes, wishing she could crawl back into bed. This time, alone.

Maybe she could find some time to nap before Max gets home. Pandora is planning to take her visitors out sightseeing, and the weather is cooperating – for now at least. In the wake of last night's storm, the morning air is damp and woodsy and the Dale is wrapped in silvery tendrils of mist.

March really is going out like a lamb, just as I—

'Good morning, Bella!'

She turns to see Eudora – fully dressed, hair combed, and wearing makeup, darn her.

'Oh . . . good morning. You're up early.'

'Rather late, given the time difference, but I do believe I've acclimated. Better than Nigel has, at any rate. He's still snoring away.'

'Well, the coffee's almost ready, if you want some, and then I'll set out your breakfast.' Seized by another yawn, she hides it behind her hand with a muffled, 'Sorry.'

'Set it out? Don't you mean fry it up?'

'What? Oh . . .' Belatedly, she remembers Pandora's request for a full English breakfast. 'Absolutely. Fry it up. Why don't you go relax in the breakfast room? I'll holler when the coffee's ready.'

'I prefer tea.'

'Oh, right! There's a beverage station with an assortment of teabags in there, and a microwave for the water, if you want to—'

'*Proper* tea.'

Oh.

Right.

'Pandora mentioned that I must specify,' Eudora goes on, 'or I'd be given a supermarket brand bag doused in a lukewarm mug.'

'She did, did she?'

'Always looking out for my best interests, she is.'

'Wish I could say the same,' Bella mutters under her breath as Eudora leaves the room. She fills the kettle, plunks it on the stove, and turns the flame to high, then looks for the cats and sees only a pair of empty food bowls on the floor.

Hoping they haven't wandered into the breakfast room, she looks around and her gaze falls on the table. She'd cleared it of clutter and crumbs last night and covered it in a pretty blue and white checked tablecloth, with a mason jar of supermarket flowers as the centerpiece. They aren't lilies, nor English bluebells, but bright yellow daffodils, so cheery even Pandora would approve.

She lifts the tablecloth hem and, sure enough, Chance and Spidey are curled up on the seat of a chair, in a cozy little cave.

'Sorry, guys, but I've got to put you in a safe haven again, just for a little while.'

They squirm in protest when she carries them toward the mudroom. Changing her plan, she brings them back up to her bedroom instead. They'll have more space, more windows, and she won't have to listen to them meowing for their freedom.

She has enough to do this morning without cooking an English breakfast, but the sooner she feeds her guests, the sooner they'll be free to vacate Valley View.

Back in the kitchen, the coffee is ready at last. She fills a mug and takes several satisfying sips. Ah, so much better.

Gazing out at the yard as she waits for the kettle to boil, she searches the bare branches for buds and the muddy bed beneath the window for signs of the crocuses she and Max planted last fall. There are no green shoots, but she does see a series of muddy pawprints.

A dog? That would explain the sound she'd heard last night.

The kettle whistles. She takes out a delicate bone china cup and saucer, prepares the tea, and carries it to the breakfast room.

It's an inviting space, with whitewashed wainscoting and ruffled blue café curtains along three walls of windows. In summer, there's enough seating for a crowd, but the tables and chairs are currently stored in the basement, where Bella intends to refinish them before the summer season. Now, there are only a few stools at one end of the tall counter that holds a Keurig coffee machine, microwave, toaster, and stacked pamphlets and fliers with information about the Dale.

Eudora is browsing through them.

'Fascinating stuff,' she says as Bella sets down her tea. 'People really go in for all of this, don't they?'

'They do.' Though surely she must have known that, being no stranger to the Dale.

'Pandora said you're not a medium, Bella?'

'No, I'm not.'

'You must be the only one in town who isn't.'

'Pretty much. There are sugar packets for your tea right there' – she indicates the countertop dispenser – 'and there's milk in the mini fridge under the counter.'

'Mmm,' Eudora says, intent on the brochure she's holding. 'Have you had a reading?'

'I'm . . . not sure how to answer that.'

'Yes or no will suffice.'

'Then . . . no.'

'But?'

'I didn't think there was room for a *but*.'

'Well, I'm curious. Do tell.'

Like her niece, Eudora is all angles and edges, from her physical appearance to her tone. But Pandora's sharpness softens when she flashes a rare smile. The smile on Eudora's face at the moment strikes Bella as insincere and void of good humor.

'Well, I've never actually sat for an official reading. But a lot of my friends are mediums, and sometimes they share information from . . . uh, Spirit.'

'Meaning dead persons.'

'Trust me, nobody around here uses the word *dead*, unless they're reminding you that there's no such thing.'

'Because the soul endures.' Eudora waves the brochure. 'This explains it, and so very much more.'

'Tip of the iceberg. If you're looking for information, you should talk to Pandora. She's an expert on all of this.'

'Oh, I'm aware. An expert on all of this, and ever so much more. Bluebells, for instance.'

This time, her smile is genuine, if sly, and Bella returns it.

'I *am* thinking of having a reading while I'm here,' Eudora says. '*Not* with Pandora.'

'That's probably wise.'

'How so?'

'My friend Odelia – she lives next door – says that sometimes an emotional connection can interfere with a medium's abilities. She can't always perceive spirit energy connected to her personal life. So if, say, you were hoping to hear from a lost loved one you and Pandora share, you're probably better off going to someone else.'

'My goodness, you seem to know quite a bit about this.'

'Oh, I'm just passing along what Odelia and the others have told me. It's definitely not my area of expertise.'

Neither is cooking a full English breakfast, but she'd better get started. She excuses herself and starts to leave the room.

'Bella?'

'Yes?' She turns back.

'Can you please ask your friend Odelia if she has availability for me today?'

'Sure, I can ask.'

'Brilliant, thank you. And I must say, you're doing a smashing job with the place. The suite is lovely, and the bed is so comfortable. Much better than on board that wretched ship.'

If adventure you're a'seekin' . . .

'Was it uncomfortable?'

'Aye, we had rough seas nearly the entire journey. All that crashing and thrashing doesn't quite lull one to sleep, does it? But now that I'm here, I slept like the d—' She catches herself and puts a finger to her lips. 'Like a soul that's crossed over. How's that? Sounding like a local now, am I?'

Bella grins. 'Absolutely.'

Eudora's not so bad after all. She may look like Pandora, and sound like her, too, but she seems much more laid back, once you get to know her.

'Oh, and luv?'

'Yes?'

'I'd fancy some sugar and cream for my tea, if I may?'

'Right, as I said, there's sugar in that container, and milk in the—'

'I prefer lump sugar to those dismal little packets. And cream, if you have it?'

She forces a smile. 'Sure. Coming right up.'

'It isn't that dreadful nondairy product, is it?'

'Nope. It's cream.'

She keeps it for Chance, who, unlike many cats, isn't lactose intolerant. She's pretty certain Chance wouldn't be any happier about sharing her favorite treat with Eudora than Pandora would be about her aunt going to Odelia for a reading.

Oh well. Who is Bella to deny Eudora cream for her tea, or Odelia the opportunity to bring in some cash?

'And Bella?'

She tries not to clench her jaw as she turns back yet again. 'Yes?'

'About breakfast – it won't be long, will it? I am famished. Last night's supper was most unappetizing and I scarcely touched it.'

'You didn't get the soup, did you? I should have warned you.'

'Oh, the waitress did – Callie, I believe her name was?'

'Calla. She's a friend of mine.'

'She meant well, I know . . .'

Uh-oh.

'. . . but I do wish she hadn't allowed me to order the red snapper. It wasn't particularly fresh.'

'Well, Lily Dale isn't exactly on the ocean, is it?'

She doesn't mean to snap at Eudora, but her patience is wearing thin, and she needs to get back to the cooking, and her coffee.

Tempering the retort, she adds, 'But you know, Eudora, if you're in the mood for something fresher, Cassadaga Lake is stocked with bass and walleye. There are poles and tackle in the shed, and—'

'Oh, I don't *fish*, luv.'

Bella frowns. 'Yesterday, Pandora said you do. Or at least you did, the last time you were here.'

'Did she?'

'Yes, she said you made a fish pie.'

'Aye, she did, didn't she. I'm afraid it entirely slipped my mind – I was knackered from the travel and the gin.'

'It slipped your mind that she said it? Or that you *do* fish?'

'Both, luv. It was *such* a long day. Now then . . .' She gives a pointed nod at the steaming cup of tea.

'Sugar and cream. Coming right up.'

Back in the kitchen, Bella pauses for an uneasy sip of coffee that's grown chillier than Eudora Feeney's eyes.

What is it with her? One minute Bella is convinced that the woman is perfectly likeable, the next that she's eccentric, snobbish and/or insufferable, and now she finds herself wondering if there's something . . . *off* about her.

Based on what?

Nothing. Nothing at all. And if the past nine months in Lily Dale have taught her anything, it's that she's far more comfortable with common sense and concrete evidence than she is with hunches and intuition.

Architecturally, Valley View has little in common with Pandora's ancestral home back in London. Built at opposite ends of the nineteenth century, this is a rambling gingerbread confection, while Marley House is a tall brick Georgian townhouse.

But the moment she set foot in Valley View with Orville all those years ago, she was home again. Yes, she was madly in love with him, and eager to build a life together here. But she fell just as hard for Valley View; its plaster walls, vintage woodwork and period embellishments enveloped her like a hug from a beloved friend or relative.

She'd dreamed of filling the house with children and assumed that was the plan. Wasn't that what people did when they married? Settled down, raised a family?

Orville didn't outright refuse to have children, but he felt no need to rush into anything. That was how he put it after they were married, though she was an older bride and her biological clock was ticking away. As far as he was concerned, if it happened for them, it happened, and if it didn't, he'd be fine. It didn't happen. And when it became clear that it wouldn't happen without fertility intervention he said they couldn't afford, Pandora was forced to accept that motherhood wasn't meant to be.

She made the best of what she had, devoting herself to nurturing her mediumship and this house. And so for her, losing Valley View in the divorce was like losing a loved one – perhaps more devastating than losing Orville himself.

Careful not to jostle Lady Pippa, who shares her pillow, she rolls onto her side and gazes about the room, tucked into a gabled corner of the third floor.

Leona Gatto had chosen the jungle theme and décor, and Pandora found it dreadful – perhaps because Leona loved to talk about her many African safaris, while Pandora's most exotic holiday in years had been an overnight at a budget motel in Ohio to attend a tarot tutorial.

But today, awakening beneath Valley View's sturdy roof, she embraces it all: green frond-patterned wallpaper, jungle print fabrics, framed amateur artworks of animals grazing on grassland and savannah, even the faux fur throw rugs scattered on the hardwoods. The room is pleasantly warm. She'd taken the liberty of turning up the thermostat last night, a welcome respite after a long, chilly winter of conserving heat in her drafty cottage.

When Valley View was their private residence, Pandora and Orville had mainly used the third floor for storage. This room had held several trunks she'd shipped from London, filled with childhood mementos and items from her ancestral home, going all the way back to its first occupants, Theodora and Cornelius Feeney. The contents held no real value, yet Pandora couldn't bring herself to part with any of it. Candlesticks and vases, her father's fisherman's sweater and his pipe, Mummy's costume jewelry, photographs, letters, documents, sheet music, books . . .

Today, she's experiencing a rather odd and urgent curiosity about the Marley House relics. That's likely due to finding herself back in the Jungle Room, gazing at the spot formerly occupied by her trunks. Or perhaps her reunion with Auntie Eudora has ignited a subconscious awareness, or . . .

Had the subject come up last night?

Not at dinner. That conversation had mainly revolved around food, Nigel and Eudora's transatlantic voyage, the Dale and the things they'd like to do while they're here.

They'd lingered long after Calla had cleared the plates, polishing off both bottles of wine as the bill sat in the middle of the table. When it became clear that Nigel and Eudora assumed they were Pandora's dinner guests, she told Calla to put it on her house charge.

To Calla's credit, she didn't point out that there was no such thing – or maybe she didn't know. Walter and Peter would understand. And she'll promise to pay the bill just as soon as she can.

They'd made their way back to Valley View, a journey Pandora hardly remembers, aside from the darkness and rain and guilt over the dinner bill. Against her better judgement, she settled in the back parlor with her guests instead of heading straight up to bed. Nigel poured them each a glass of port, she recalls with a queasy swallow. He'd helped himself from the dining room liquor cabinet – though that seemed a bit impolite.

Perhaps Pandora had told him where to look? There are some pricey bottles stashed away there, left over from Leona's days. They aren't necessarily Pandora's to share, but why should they go to waste? Why shouldn't someone enjoy them?

Yes, she may have said exactly that. She may have said a lot of things, now that she sorts through the evening's end.

Marley House certainly came up in conversation, though the details are lost to her. She remembers Nigel doing most of the talking, asking questions. She'd commented on how lovely it was that he was taking such an interest in her childhood, and her father's and Eudora's, and the ancestral home.

'I adore old things. People, too,' he'd added, putting an arm around Eudora, who'd laughed delightedly.

They'd talked about Valley View, too, of course. Nigel wanted to know all about its past, the bootleggers, the hidden compartments . . .

'Oh, let's have a look!' he'd said at one point.

But it was late, and she'd been far too woozy to lead a house tour. It was all she could do to drag herself up two flights of stairs to bed, leaving the two of them behind.

Really, it had been a delightful evening. Yet right now, she has the vague sense that something, somewhere along the way, had made her uneasy.

She closes her eyes, trying to pinpoint whatever it was, but her head is pounding and she allows sleep to overtake her again.

SEVEN

Odelia bustles into the kitchen five minutes after Bella realized she was in over her head and summoned her. True to her word, she hasn't taken the time to change out of her pajamas. She's wearing red fleece long johns. They're not footy style, and lack a trap door at the derriere, but otherwise look like something a toddler might wear. So do her slippers, fuzzy gold with little lion heads bobbing above her toes. Her purple cat-eye glasses are pushed up in a nest of unkempt orange curls.

'I know, I'm a hot mess, but you sounded desperate.'

'I am. And you know, that's the most amazing thing about you, Odelia. You came running before you even knew what you were getting yourself into.' Bella drops a hunk of butter into a frying pan and reaches for a spatula. 'I mean, it could have been anything. Wrestling a snake, delivering a baby, putting out a fire . . . yet here you are, no questions asked.'

'Always. You call, I come. I don't see any snakes, women in labor or flames, though it does smell somewhat scorched in here.'

'That was the second batch of eggs.' She points at the garbage can, pulled out from under the sink and full of egg shells and blackened sludge. 'I broke the yolks on the first.'

'Is that the emergency, then?'

'Yes. Breakfast. *For them*,' she adds in a whisper, jerking a thumb toward the breakfast room. 'Eudora and Nigel. They're in there having tea, expecting this huge meal any second now, and I just . . .'

'You need a hand. Don't worry. I'll just whip up some pancakes. Do you have gochujang, ginger and kimchi on hand?'

'No, no and no, and – for *pancakes*?'

'Korean pancakes. I've almost perfected the recipe for my cookbook. I'd love a professional chef's feedback.'

'Sorry, but Pandora specified that this has to be an English breakfast.'

Her eyes narrow. 'Where *is* Pandora?'

'Still asleep. But she said—'

'How nice for her, sleeping the day away while she has you slaving in the kitchen serving her guests.'

'It's fine. I thought I had it under control, but . . . I don't. Can you help me?'

'Of course. But just to be clear, I'm not doing this for *them*' – she points at the breakfast room, then the ceiling – 'or for *her*. I'm doing it for *you*. Now, I see you've got eggs, tomatoes and mushrooms. Do you want me to throw together an omelet?'

'No, just keep an eye on the sausages and bacon while I make toast and get the baked beans going.'

'I'm on it. I take it my friend Max was well enough to go to school this morning?'

'Good as new.'

'I'm glad. I've been concerned about him. Must have been all that sugar.'

'I know, and it's my fault. I feel terrible about it.'

'Don't beat yourself up, Bella,' Odelia says, pushing the sizzling meat around the skillet. 'You're such a good mommy.'

Bella goes still, hand on the knob of the cabinet she was about to open.

You're such a good mommy, Bella Blue.

Sam had said those very words, and often, after Max came along, providing reassurance whenever she doubted her own capabilities.

She'd foolishly assumed some kind of maternal instinct would kick in the moment Max was born. It hadn't occurred to her that you have to learn how to be someone's mother, the way you learn how to be a wife. But with motherhood, there was so much more at stake – a helpless being depending on you just to stay alive.

But Sam had been there, boosting her confidence.

You're such a good mommy . . .

She imagined it was the kind of thing her own mother would have told her, had she lived long enough to become a grandmother. But Rosemary Angelo barely had the chance to be a mother. Bella felt her absence more than ever as she made her own way into motherhood, often feeling as though she were navigating a cluttered room in the dark.

You're such a good mommy . . .

Just words, she reminds herself, opening the cabinet. Mundane words that countless people say to countless other people every single day. She's missed hearing them; had assumed no one would ever say them to her again. But Sam isn't here, whispering in Odelia's ear, any more than he was whispering in Pandora's about the sushi sunrise.

And yet . . .

'What makes you say that I'm such a good mommy?' she asks casually, as she takes the can of beans from the cabinet and reaches for the can opener.

'You are. I just don't know how you do what you do every day.'

'You mean, being a single mom? A lot of people are. *You* were,' she points out.

'But I wasn't recently widowed, running a guesthouse *and* renovating it. You're staying strong, just like you promised your husband.'

Bella's hand freezes on the crank handle. She closes her eyes and sees Sam, pale and weak in a hospital bed on that final day. In their final moments together.

She hears his labored breathing, hears him saying, 'You can do anything.'

'Not this. Not alone.'

'You have Max. You have . . . me . . . I'll be with you, even when . . . Promise me you'll . . . stay . . . strong . . .'

She'd promised.

Those were the last words they'd ever said to each other.

She opens her eyes. 'Odelia? Did Sam tell you that?'

'Hmm?'

'Did . . . did Sam say that he wanted me to stay strong? That I promised him I would?'

Turning away from the stove, spatula poised, Odelia considers the question with maddening calm. 'Didn't you tell me he said it?'

'I doubt it. It's definitely not something I like to talk about, or remember.'

'I understand. Then it must have come from him.' She smiles. 'He's always with you, you know, Bella. Even now.'

Yes. Just like Sam had told her.

She nods, swallows hard, and focuses on turning the handle around the can's perimeter as Odelia turns back to the stove.

This wasn't a message from Sam. Yes, she wants to believe that he's by her side right here, right now. And yes, Odelia had echoed Sam's own words as if she were channeling his spirit.

But when Bella removes her wistful emotions and sheer longing to re-examine the exchange from a purely logical viewpoint, it doesn't seem nearly as uncanny. Most deathbed conversations between couples probably involve the dying spouse telling their beloved to be strong.

Lucky guess, that's all it was.

Except it wasn't like that. Odelia wasn't performing a reading. She didn't even seem aware of what she'd said. It was so very . . . incidental. And that's what makes it possible that it was Sam.

Bella pushes the incident from her head – for now, anyway – as she dumps the beans into a small pan and slides it onto a burner alongside the sizzling skillet.

'Odelia, can you—'

'I'll stir.'

'Thanks.' She puts two slices of bread into the toaster and pushes the lever. 'Before I forget, Eudora wants a reading. Can you do it?'

'Me? Why not Pandora?'

'She wants you.'

'Of course I *can*. The question, if she's anything like her niece, is whether I *want* to do it.'

'You need the money, don't you?'

'I never do what I do for personal gain, Bella. My mission is to spread hope and enlightenment for the greater good. You know that.'

'Yes, but I also know what it's like to have bills piling up and to lose sleep trying to figure out how to pay them.'

'If you need a loan—'

'Odelia!' She laughs. 'I'm talking about you. You said you were broke.'

'Oh, money.' She waves a dismissive hand. 'It's meaningless beyond the earthly plane. If I can help you, just say the word and I'll figure out a way.'

'You are helping me. You're frying bangers and stirring beans. But I think you should do the reading for Eudora.'

'Pandora won't like it.'

'All the more reason, right?'

Odelia grins. 'Well, if you put it that way, I suppose I can't refuse.'

As Bella washes the tomatoes and mushrooms, her gaze returns to the disturbed garden bed under the window. 'Odelia, have you seen a loose dog wandering around Cottage Row?'

'No. Why?'

She quickly explains about the yipping and yowling and points out the muddy pawprints.

'I'll bet Blue Slayton's German Shepherd got out of the house,' Odelia says darkly. 'I'll tell Calla to have a word with him.'

There's no love lost between Odelia and her granddaughter's new – old – boyfriend. Bella knows her reasons go back to the high school love triangle and are impacted by her affection for Jacy Bly and her aversion for Blue's father.

Unlike Odelia and her friends, David Slayton has achieved great wealth through his vocation. He hosts the cable television program *Dead Isn't Dead*, and authored a recent book by that title. Meeting him in person last fall when he made a publicity stop in the Dale, Bella found him to be nice enough, but not nearly as slick and charismatic as he appeared on the show.

'It's an act,' Odelia had said. 'The cameras add a sheen that makes anyone appear impressive and larger than life. The real David Slayton is a small, selfish man.'

Once a member of the Assembly, he no longer resides in the Dale, but built a grand, neo-Victorian mansion right outside the gate. It stood empty all last summer, but his son arrived in September, ostensibly to do some work on the house – not that he seemed particularly handy.

According to Calla, he'd walked away from a lucrative but unfulfilling Wall Street career.

'He's just trying to figure out what he wants out of life,' she'd told Odelia once, in Bella's presence.

'Oh, please. Isn't everyone?' Odelia had rolled her eyes. 'At his age, he should spend more time doing and less time thinking, like Jacy.'

'Trust me, Gammy, Jacy spends way too much time doing and not enough time thinking. That's why things didn't work out for us.'

'Well, things didn't work out very well for you and Blue Slayton, either, first time round.'

'That's ancient history. People change.'

Maybe Calla's right about Blue. Or maybe Odelia is, and he's going to hurt Calla all over again.

Either way, it's Calla's life and Calla's decision.

Odelia's strong opinions have been causing friction in her relationship with her granddaughter, just as her insecurity and indecisiveness are taking a toll with Luther. Bella finds it frustrating that someone so intuitive, with such far-reaching omniscience, can't seem to see what's right in front of her, but that's often been the case with her friends here in the Dale. Mediumship doesn't unlock magical powers.

Not always, anyway.

She thinks again of what Odelia had said about her promise to Sam.

Again, she pushes it out of her head, busying herself cracking eggs into a frying pan.

'Whew! Is it warm in here, or is it me?' Odelia looks up from the skillet, puffing out her lower lip to blow her bangs away from her flushed forehead.

'It's warm in here. You know Pandora and her chilblains. She probably turned up the thermostat. I'll go turn it down if you keep an eye on the eggs.'

In the dining room, she sees that the thermostat has indeed crept up ten degrees. Darn Pandora. As she lowers it, she notices that the glass-fronted liquor cabinet door is ajar, and there's a wide gap among the bottles. Pandora and her guests must have polished off one – or two – last night.

That shouldn't bother her, but for some reason, it does. Not so much because of Pandora's proprietary attitude toward Valley View, but because her visitors rub Bella up the wrong way.

As she starts toward the cabinet to close the door, she hears voices speaking quietly in the breakfast room.

'. . . still think that it would be well worth the risk,' Nigel is saying.

'I know, but what if she picks up on something?'

'You'll simply have no idea what she's talking about.'

'That's easy enough for *you* to say. You're not the one—'

'Hush, keep your voice down,' he cautions her, and the conversation becomes inaudible.

Bella turns to go back to the kitchen, but trips over the edge of the rug and flies forward, hands outstretched in front of her. They hit the glass cabinet door full force. Miraculously, it bangs closed but doesn't shatter.

'Bella! Whatever are you doing?'

She turns to see Eudora in the breakfast room doorway.

Nigel comes up behind her, and Bella sees a glint of shrewd suspicion in his expression before it turns benevolent as he asks, 'My goodness, are you all right?'

'I'm fine. I just tripped over the rug. I guess that's better than tripping over my own two feet, which happens all the time.' She's talking too fast, her voice too high-pitched, but she can't seem to help herself, feeling like a cat burglar who'd nearly been caught.

Which is ridiculous.

You live here! You didn't do anything wrong!

'I'm the clumsiest person in town. Ask anyone,' she goes on, then adds, 'I mean, not that you'd ask, and not that you care. Anyway, I was just in here because – I was setting the table, and, well . . . that's clumsy me, for you.'

She sees their eyes go to the table. It holds only a vase of supermarket roses, a pair of brass candlesticks and the jigsaw puzzle, half-complete and surrounded by sorted pieces.

'I was *about* to set the table,' she amends, opening the cabinet and grabbing three china plates. 'Guests usually eat in the breakfast room, but I think a nice sit-down in here seems fitting for a meal like this, and guests like you.'

'That would be lovely.' Nigel's smile seems a little stiff.
So does Eudora's. 'Lovely indeed.'

'OK, well, great. I'll holler when it's ready – it won't be
long, I promise.'

Bella heaves a sigh of relief as they disappear into the
breakfast room and puts the three plates on the end of the
table with a shaky hand.

It's not like she crept in here to *eavesdrop*. She was simply
going about her business and accidentally overheard a discussion they wanted to keep private.

She reruns the snippets of conversation in her head as she
painstakingly moves the puzzle out of the way.

What would be well worth the risk?

What if *who* picks up on something?

Something like . . . *what*?

She can't make sense of it, and really, why bother trying?
It can't have anything to do with her. They must be talking
about Pandora, and Bella is certain their grievance, whatever
it may be, is justified.

She slides the completed portion of the puzzle along the
polished surface to the far end, then looks at the clusters of
loose pieces. She and Drew had separated them by color, with
all the straight edge pieces off to one side. Realizing there's
no easy way to keep them sorted and move them quickly, she
sweeps them all into the empty box and sets it aside.

She quickly sets the table with three places, in case Pandora
materializes. Then, back in the kitchen, she and Odelia put
the finishing touches to the breakfast.

'Baked beans and tomatoes with bacon and eggs . . . and
you think the meals *I* make are wacky?' Odelia shakes her
head.

'I never said that. Maybe I've said . . . creative. And . . .
interesting.'

'It's fine, Bella. To each his own, right? I'll start cleaning
up while you go tell the lord and lady that *breakfast is served*,'
she says in an oh-so-decorous tone.

'The only *lady* around here is Pandora's cat, Lady Pippa.'

'She brought her cat? Knowing that her aunt is terrified of
them?'

'Actually, that was news to her. She seemed to think her aunt couldn't wait to meet her cat. But you know Pandora. Sometimes she can be a little too wrapped up in herself and miss details about other people.'

'*Sometimes? A little?*' Odelia snorts. 'And where are Chance and Spidey?'

'In the Rose Room. I'm keeping them out of the way for Eudora's sake.'

'*They* live here. *She* doesn't. And neither does Pandora, for that matter.'

'Shh, they'll hear you.'

'Bella, I don't know why you're going along with this charade.'

'I don't either, to be honest. It's just . . . you know how Pandora is always so blustery and haughty?'

'And snooty and highfalutin and pretentious and pompous.'

'Don't those words all mean the same thing? Anyway, when it comes to this situation with her aunt, there's something so . . . I don't know, almost vulnerable about her.'

'Bella, she's asking you to lie for her. It's wrong.'

'Not lie. Just . . . cover. And just until she tells them the truth. She wants to explain in person.'

'Well, when she does, she can pack up her stuff and her cat and her visitors and head for her own house.'

'I don't think that's the plan. They really like it here, and it might be more trouble than it's worth to move them. They had a pile of luggage.'

'It just bothers me that in the meantime, you're going out of your way for these people – and your poor cats are locked up like prisoners.'

'I'm just trying to keep everyone safe. It's not the first time I've had to hide them away while someone was here. Remember that little girl last September?'

'The holy terror who kept pulling Chance's tail and trying to ride on her?'

'Exactly. Chance was relieved when I put her and Spidey in the laundry room. She knew she was better off.'

'Well, if Eudora Feeney is the sort of woman who goes around tormenting innocent creatures, then I might want a private moment with her breakfast plate before you serve it to her,' Odelia says darkly.

'She isn't, and don't you dare touch her plate, Odelia. I'll be right back.'

Walking toward the breakfast room, Bella goes out of her way to step on the creakiest floorboards so that Eudora and Nigel won't think she's sneaking around, trying to eavesdrop and spy on them. Which is ridiculous, because why would she?

Peeking into the breakfast room, she finds them mid conversation, this time in regular tones.

'. . . and I do think I'd prefer Bella's friend to a total stranger,' Eudora is saying.

'Ah, speak of the devil,' Nigel says, spotting her in the doorway. 'We were just talking about you, my dear.'

'Nice things, I hope?'

He's jovial and nonchalant. 'I can't imagine anything but.'

Is he maybe a little *too* jovial? *Too* nonchalant?

There you go again! What is it about these two that has you looking for trouble where there's none?

'Breakfast is ready. Thanks for being so patient. Come on into the dining room.'

'We were just discussing my reading today,' Eudora tells her as she leads the way. 'Have you spoken to your friend Odelia?'

'Not only have I spoken to her, but she's here.'

'Splendid!' Nigel says. 'I see that she's joining us for breakfast?'

'Oh – no, I set the third place for Pandora.'

He gives a little shake of his silvery head. 'I'm afraid we kept her up well past her bedtime. I doubt she'll make an appearance before noon. But I hope your friend Odelia will dine with us, and you as well, of course, Bella.'

'Aye, we don't stand on ceremony, Nigel and me,' Eudora adds. 'We're perfectly comfortable communing with the staff. Do set a fourth place and join us.'

'Well, thank you, Eudora. How very civilized of you.'

Bella would have preferred a few more cups of coffee and maybe a bowl of Lucky Charms in the kitchen, but she finds herself seated in the dining room, facing a massive plate of food. Eudora is seated to her right, Nigel opposite, and Odelia across the table.

'This is delicious, Bella,' Odelia says, digging in and adding a pointed, 'Really, it's so good. *So* good.'

Nigel takes the hint. 'Yes, you've outdone yourself. I don't even miss the black pudding, do you, darling?'

Eudora shrugs. 'Well, of course I *miss* it, but this will have to do, won't it?'

It's fine, Bella silently tells Odelia, who catches her eye. *Don't say anything.*

Odelia says something. 'I hear you're a talented chef, Eudora. Maybe you'll do the honors tomorrow? I'd love to watch you in action. I'm writing a cookbook.'

'A cookbook!' Nigel echoes. 'I thought you were a medium.'

'I am. I'm just—'

'Splendid! Eudora's never had a reading, and she was hoping you might be willing to take her on?'

'Oh, uh . . . sure.'

'Brilliant! When can you do it?'

'Let's see . . .' Odelia pauses as if pondering an insanely busy schedule. 'I think I have an opening this afternoon at three-fifteen, if that's convenient for you, Eudora?'

'It is, it is. I've so many questions to ask the spirits, I don't know where to start.'

Odelia clears her throat. 'You can ask questions, but remember that Spirit may not give you all the answers you're seeking.'

Drowsiness is starting to creep over Bella again. She sips her coffee and half-listens as Odelia describes how she works and offers pointers, most of which she's heard before.

Arrive prepared to receive information with an open mind . . .

You may not hear from the spirit you expect . . .

If you don't immediately recognize the energy that touches in, its earthly identity might become clear later . . .

Remember that free will impacts prophecy . . .

Elbow resting on the table, Eudora jostles Bella's arm as she uses her knife to cut into a sausage. 'Sorry,' she says around a slick mouthful.

Bella hasn't known many – *any* – renowned culinary experts in her life, but she's watched plenty of cooking shows on TV, and the chefs tend to be more refined than Eudora. Then again . . .

The cameras add a sheen that makes anyone appear impressive and larger than life.

Eudora's lapse in table manners shouldn't bother Bella, but she finds herself irked by the sound of her open-mouthed chewing.

It's because you're cranky and overtired and overheated.

She'd adjusted the thermostat, but the old cast iron radiators don't cool down instantaneously.

'Always seek truth from a reading,' Odelia is saying. 'And always expect it.'

Plate forgotten, Nigel sets down his fork and pushes back from the table to face Odelia on an angle, his bent elbow propped on the back of his chair. 'What does that mean, exactly?'

'It means that the message will be honest. What you get may not be what you expect or want to hear, but my guides will always deliver what you *need* to hear. We're all on this earthly plane to learn certain lessons and accomplish specific things.'

'Interesting. But surely your guides get some things wrong? After all, no one is perfect.'

'Well, *I'm* not,' Odelia agrees, 'and I'm the middleman in the process. My role is to deliver the messages as I receive them, and sometimes as I interpret the symbols I'm given.'

'What do you mean?'

'Every medium works differently, but most of us develop our own form of shorthand. For instance, if I see a pink helium balloon, it means my guides are bringing in a little girl. A blue balloon is a boy. A shiny black car coming toward me means someone is going to cross over.'

Eudora shudders. 'That's rather macabre, isn't it?'

'Not if one grasps that death is merely a transition from a soul's existence on one plane to another.'

'But why can't a black car just be a black car? What if

that's the vehicle the person drives?' she asks. 'Why can't a balloon just be a balloon?'

'It might be, for another medium. But after all these years, when my guides show me specific symbols, they have a unique significance.'

'What happens if you get a symbol that doesn't mean anything to you?' Nigel wants to know.

'Then I simply relay what I've been given to the sitter, and I leave it to them to interpret. It isn't just symbols,' she adds. 'All my senses are involved. Sometimes I hear something – a melody, or an unusual turn of phrase. Sometimes I experience a physical sensation – for instance, someone who passed due to a heart attack might announce himself by causing me to feel a tightness in my chest.'

'How utterly terrifying.'

Odelia shrugs. 'Sometimes. But you get used to it. And some readings take more out of me than others.'

As if to prove the point, she bows her head and closes her eyes.

Nigel looks at Bella and asks in a low voice, 'Has she dozed off?'

'I don't think so.' But Bella is about to. She swallows a yawn and reaches for her coffee.

'I'm awake,' Odelia murmurs, rubbing her palms against each other. 'Someone just touched in, and I'm trying to . . .'

She falls silent again.

Eudora turns to Bella. 'What on earth is she doing? What does she mean, someone touched in?'

'Spirit.'

'Where?'

Bella shrugs. '*Here.*'

'But *where*?' Eudora looks around the room, as if expecting to see someone.

Odelia murmurs something unintelligible to someone invisible, then opens her eyes and looks directly at Nigel. 'Did you want a reading, too?'

'Me? No, I'm afraid it's really not my cup of tea.'

'I'm being told to encourage you.'

'Told by whom?'

'Spirit.'

Taken aback, Nigel also glances around the room, then at Eudora. She shrugs.

Odelia reaches for the salt shaker and sprinkles some over a wedge of tomato. 'There's a persistent female energy that seems eager to communicate with you, Nigel.'

'Who is she?'

'It's hard to say. She's crossed over rather recently, I believe. As I said, if you'd like a reading—'

'No, thank you.'

Bella sips her coffee, noting Nigel shifting his weight, obviously uneasy. Most people would be, if someone mentioned a supernatural presence hanging around who wanted a word with them. She's well accustomed now to how things go around here, but even she's feeling a little unnerved. Somehow, the room no longer feels warm. There's a palpable chill in the air.

Eudora, sawing another piece of sausage, bumps Bella's arm again. Coffee sloshes over the rim of her cup, spattering her hand, the tablecloth, her clothes.

'Oh, so sorry. How very cack-handed of me. Got you good, didn't I.'

'Are you all right, Bella?' Odelia asks.

'I'm fine, I'm just going to go clean up.' She sets down the cup and stands, wiping her hands on a white linen napkin. 'I'll be right back.'

'The meat is a bit tough, you see,' Eudora tells Nigel, 'and it takes some effort to hack through it.'

'It does, doesn't it.' He lifts his teacup. 'Bella, if you're going to the kitchen, would you mind bringing more cream?'

'No problem.' Her jaw clenches. 'Can I bring anyone else anything? Orange juice, maybe, or—'

'Perhaps bacon,' Eudora says.

'Bacon? Didn't you just say it was too tough?'

'Only the sausage. The bacon is adequate.'

'Well . . . great.' She heads toward the kitchen. 'Really great. I'm so glad to hear it.'

Nigel clears his throat. 'As you were saying, Odelia . . .'

Hearing a high-pitched sound behind her – a yowl – Bella stops in her tracks and whirls around.

It seemed to come from the table, or . . . beneath it? Somewhere above?

The others are unfazed. Odelia and Nigel have resumed their conversation, and Eudora is sopping up egg yolk with toast crust.

Bella scans the room, hoping to see Blue Slayton's wayward German Shepherd.

No such luck.

She retrieves her cup from the table and slowly exits the room, telling herself she just needs more coffee. Yes, that's all it is.

But in the kitchen, she finds herself remembering last night's pomegranate seed debacle. She'd assured Odelia – and herself – that the bag hadn't jumped out of the freezer on its own, but now she isn't so sure. And why had Odelia been so interested in what kind of fruit it was?

Oh, come on. You know why.

She grabs her phone, opens a search engine and types in *pomegranate symbolism.*

The first hit that comes up reads: '*Fruit of the dead.*'

Heart pounding, she clicks on the link and is taken to a site that explains that ancient civilizations believed that the pomegranate represents power, blood and death.

Bella quickly closes out of the screen and puts the phone aside.

She shouldn't have looked. She doesn't even believe in this stuff. It's just . . .

There were no pomegranate seeds in the freezer when she'd searched it last week for the pint of Triple Fudge Fusion. She'd quickly solved the mystery of the missing ice cream, thanks to Max and Jiffy's transparent cover story, but how had a bag of frozen fruit appeared out of nowhere?

EIGHT

As Bella dries the last of the breakfast pans, her phone, lying face up on the counter, lights up with a text. Leaning in, she smiles when she sees who it's from.

Dr Drew Bailey: *Want to try for that walk this afternoon?*

She still has to make up the guestrooms and tend to the laundry and a few other chores, not to mention catch up on her book club reading. She probably shouldn't say yes, but she's going to. And now that she finally has a free moment, she's also going to change his contact information to just 'Drew'.

She puts the skillet into the cupboard, flips off the overhead light and grabs her phone, eager to escape the kitchen at last.

'Good morning, Isabella,' Pandora says, framed in the doorway. She's wearing one of her signature floral frocks, and her hair is braided, same as always, but in a slightly lopsided fashion. Her complexion is even paler than usual, with dark circles beneath her eyes.

'Good morning,' Bella replies, then glances at the stove clock. 'Just about afternoon, really. Are you hungry? There's leftover sausage and baked beans in the fridge, if you—'

'No!' Pandora pauses to swallow audibly. 'No, thank you. I'll just have some tea and toast, please. Earl Grey. White bread. And please, no . . .' She swallows again and sinks into a kitchen chair. 'No butter or jam.'

Bella hadn't been offering to serve her. But this rare glimmer of vulnerability in the indomitable Pandora moves her to say, 'Sure. I'll get it for you.'

'Thank you.'

Bella turns on the light. 'I take it you had a nice time last night?'

Pandora winces. 'I'm right here, Isabella, no need to bellow. And that overhead fixture is blinding. I feel as though I'm in the midst of a garish and cacophonous carnival.'

Bella flips the switch off and lowers her voice to a near whisper. 'How was your evening?'

'It was lovely, thank you.'

'I heard you saw Calla.'

'Yes. She was waiting tables, poor lass.'

'I don't think she minds helping out at the café,' Bella comments as she takes a loaf from the breadbox.

'Well, it's certainly not good for her image.'

'Her . . . *image*? How so?'

'One can hardly take her literary accomplishments seriously when she's slinging hash at a canteen.'

Bella shakes her head and reaches for the kettle.

'Isabella, please just boil the water in the microwave.'

'What? I assumed you wanted "proper" tea.'

'I've a bit of a headache and I'd prefer to avoid the shrieking whistle. Where are Eudora and Nigel?'

'They went for a walk around the Dale.'

'*What?*'

'Yes, Odelia told them about the Fairy Trail and they wanted to see it.'

'*What?*'

'Odelia told them—'

'Isabella! Do moderate your volume.'

'I thought you couldn't hear me. You keep saying "what?"'

'Not because I'm impaired, but because I'm astounded. How on earth is Odelia involved in any of this?'

'She was here earlier. She helped me make breakfast.'

'You allowed that woman, with her bizarre culinary skills, to prepare a meal for a world-renowned culinary genius? Are you mad?'

'I needed a hand. Since you were sleeping, I called Odelia.' Bella *thunks* the tin of tea onto the counter.

Pandora cringes. 'Well, you should have woken me. We had plans to drive down to Chautauqua Lake this morning and stroll about the Institution. Nigel is fascinated by the Second Great Awakening, and this area played a vivid role.'

'The Burned-over District.'

'Precisely.'

Like Lily Dale, Chautauqua Institution is a gated lakeside

colony established as a religious camp in the 1800s. Chautauqua, too, draws visitors from around the world to this rural southwestern corner of New York State. Its season also extends from late June through Labor Day. And like Lily Dale, it has evolved into a world-famous destination devoted to a singular pursuit – not spiritualism, but the arts.

Everything in Chautauqua is on a grander scale, from the lake itself to the Victorian homes, gate fees and scope of events. The Institution's season calendar features international superstars, acclaimed speakers, literary geniuses, global religious leaders and sitting presidents. It has its own symphony orchestra, opera, ballet and theater company.

The front door opens. 'Bells? Hey, are you home?'

'In here, Misty!'

'Are you busy? I need you to tell me the plot of this godawful book before—' Popping into the kitchen clutching *A Tale of Two Cities*, she stops short, spotting Pandora, who gives her a withering once-over.

Poor Misty. She's thrown together as always, wearing baggy sweats, her coppery hair flyaway with static.

'That "godawful book" is among the greatest works of *literature* in our time,' Pandora says, accentuating each syllable's consonants.

'Maybe in *your* time. Not in mine.'

'Poppycock. Charles Dickens is timeless, unlike that . . . absurd Real Housewife who authored *your* book club read.'

Bella intercedes. 'Ladies, remember, the whole point of our group is to appreciate a wide range of books.'

Pandora sniffs. 'Precisely. I suffered through *her* selection. It's only fair that she suffer through mine.'

'See? Even *you* know it's the worst book ever. Plus, mine was a quick read. This *tome* would take me a year to get through.'

'I understand that some things are more difficult for you, Misty, but don't you think it's wise to challenge yourself intellectually?'

'I'm not an idiot, Pandora. I'm just super busy these days with my Zodiac and cryptozoology classes, and Keith is driving me nuts, and I don't believe in wasting time on things that aren't worthwhile.'

'Cryptozoology? Now *there's* something that isn't worthwhile.'

'What is it?' Bella asks.

'The study of mythical creatures,' Pandora says.

'Oh, like the . . . okapi? They're a cross between a zebra, deer and giraffe. Odelia said she and Leona saw them on their African safari.'

That earns an eyeroll from Pandora.

'Cryptozoology isn't really about *mythical* creatures,' Misty corrects. 'More like mysterious and elusive creatures, like dragons and yeti.'

Pandora rolls her eyes again. 'Talk about a waste of time.'

Bella has noticed that most mediums here in the Dale have a surprising intolerance for at least one area of parapsychology. Apparently Pandora disdains cryptozoology while being passionate about aura and chakra cleansing. Odelia dabbles in past life regression but rolls her eyes at astral projection. And Misty seems to buy into just about everything except telekinesis, having failed miserably at spoon-bending and table-turning despite repeated attempts.

'Getting back to Keith,' Bella says. 'Who is he?'

'He's a drummer.'

'In Doris Henderson's circle?'

Misty laughs. 'No! He's Spirit. Keith Moon, the drummer in The Who. You know how I tend to attract musicians. He's been hanging around lately.'

'Oh, *that's* what Jiffy was talking about! When he brought up "the moon" yesterday in the car, I thought he was talking about . . . you know, the moon, moon. Not Keith Moon. We had a little "Who's on first" exchange.'

'A what?'

'You know – the old Abbott and Costello routine. I probably wouldn't know about it either if Odelia weren't always telling me about Bud Abbott. You get the musicians, she gets the comedians. Bud, Mae West, Charlie Chap—'

She breaks off when the toaster pops up at precisely the same moment as the microwave *beep-beep-beeps* to a halt and Pandora emits an agonized cry, as if a drum corps just marched through the kitchen, cymbals clashing.

'Pandora?' Misty asks. 'Are you all right?'

'Quite.' She closes her eyes for a moment.

Misty looks at Bella, who mouths *hangover*.

'Ohhhhh . . . Hey, Pandora? You know what you need?'

'Yes. Some blessed quiet. *And* strong tea and dry toast,' she adds, with a pointed glance at Bella.

'Coming right up, Pandora.'

Misty shakes her head. 'I know this sounds crazy, but trust me, I've got plenty of experience in this area. I'll be right back.' She drops the heavy book on the table with a thud and disappears, letting the front door close with a bang behind her.

Pandora scowls. 'Experience with *what*? I don't trust her, and she *is* crazy. Makes a terrible din, as well.'

'Maybe you should go back to bed and spare yourself this . . . garish cacophony,' Bella suggests, setting the tea and toast in front of her.

'I wish I could, Isabella, but as I said, we've plans to go to Chautauqua.'

'You can always save that for another day. You won't have much time down there before—' She catches herself, not wanting to bring up Eudora's afternoon reading with Odelia.

Pandora doesn't seem to notice, brooding in silence as Bella wipes down an already clean countertop. Eager as she is to escape and respond to Drew's text, she's reluctant to leave Pandora alone right now. She seems burdened by something more than a hangover, but Bella can't think of a tactful way to ask if she wants to talk about it. For someone who over-shares about so many things, Pandora can be exceedingly reserved when it comes to emotional topics.

The front door bangs open again. 'I'm baa-ack,' Misty trills.

'Bloody hell,' Pandora mutters. 'I guess we know where the lad gets it.'

'Jiffy? Where he gets what?'

'The uncanny ability to create a rowdy disruption wherever he goes,' she says, and Bella can't disagree with that.

Misty bursts into the room, carrying a white plastic shopping bag. She dumps several plastic bottles onto the table with a rattle and roll, catching one just before it goes over the edge.

'I'm going to fix you right up, Pandora, see?' She holds up

the bottle. 'This is borage oil, and I'll mix it with this' – she plucks a vial from the table – 'prickly pear, plus two different varieties of ginseng. I also need chervil. Odelia has some and she's going to bring it right over.'

Pandora scowls. 'I'm quite all right, Misty. I don't need you or Odelia Lauder to "fix me up", thank you very much.'

'Oh, you're welcome. It's really no trouble at all.'

'It's most troubling to me,' Pandora says under her breath.

'Here, rub some of this into your face, especially under your nose.' Misty thrusts a tube at her. 'It's an aromatic cream infused with cardamom and fennel oil. You won't believe how much it will help.'

'I don't believe any of this, really. Help *what*?'

'Your hangover. Believe me, I've been there, so many times. I'm on the wagon these days, because I realized I had a problem. It all started when I was a kid. I used to drink to help tune out all that exhausting spirit energy before I knew what it was and what to do with it. And even when I figured it out, there were so many times when I was just overwhelmed, you know, by everything just coming *at* me all the time.'

Pandora tightens her lips, but says nothing.

'Now that I've given up drinking, I'm finding other ways to deal with it. Staying super busy helps. Here comes Odelia,' she adds, and shouts a cheery, 'We're in here!'

For the second time today, Odelia arrives in the kitchen announcing, 'Odelia to the rescue!'

She's still wearing her lion-head slippers, but has changed into orange corduroy overalls, with a headful of sponge rollers. Her mauve lipstick clashes with her hair, her outfit and her glasses – behind which her left eye appears to be bruised.

'Oh no! What happened to you?' Bella asks, and then, leaning closer, sees that it isn't a black eye at all. It's just made up with shadow, liner and mascara, all the more dramatic as the other eye is completely unenhanced.

'I was in the middle of my beauty routine when Misty texted. It seemed urgent, so I rushed right over with the chervil. I'm sorry you're under the weather, Pandora.'

Pandora murmurs something unintelligible and presses her thumb and fingertips into either side of her forehead.

'Don't worry. You'll be good as new in no time.' Misty takes the green sprigs from Odelia. 'You know, chervil does wonders for inflammation. When I was pregnant, I had the worst cankles until someone told me to try a chervil smoothie.'

'Cankles?' Odelia echoes.

'Swollen ankles,' Bella explains. 'I had them when I was expecting Max.'

'So did I, with Stephanie!'

'Well, I would have made chervil smoothies for you both if I'd known you then. That's what friends are for, right? If we don't take care of each other, who will?'

Misty's flippant remark seems to strike a chord with Pandora. The angular lines of her face seem to soften, like an artist's sketch strokes smudging ever so slightly.

'I mean, think about it,' Misty goes on, opening a cabinet and digging through the contents. 'One way or another, all four of us wound up alone here in the Dale. Pandora and Odelia are divorced, Bella's a widow, and I'm married, but Mike is never around. What would we do without each other?'

Touched, Bella says, 'You're right, Misty. It's nice to know we have each other's backs.'

'It is, isn't it?' Odelia smiles.

Pandora says nothing, but gives a thoughtful nod and takes a long sip of her tea.

Misty finds a whisk, closes the drawer and opens a cabinet. 'Every time I think of how helpful you all were when Jiffy went missing in December, I wonder how I'll ever be able to repay you. Hey, Bells, do you happen to have any turmeric?'

'No, sorry.'

'Hmm, I'll figure out a substitute.' She browses the shelves. 'Oh, M&M's! Mind if I grab a few?'

'Sure, but that's a strange substitute for turmeric.'

'Oh, they're for me. I've got such a sweet tooth.'

And now we know where the lad gets that, Bella thinks, grinning as Misty takes an enormous handful.

Odelia turns to Pandora. 'So I met your Aunt Eudora and her friend Nigel this morning. Nice folks.'

'Yes. About that . . .' Pandora clears her throat. 'I'm afraid I need to request a small favor of you. And you as well, Misty.

You see, my aunt and Nigel are under the impression that I still reside here at Valley View, and I would like to keep it that way.'

Misty shrugs, crunching her candy. 'Fine with me. I won't say anything.'

But Odelia, feigning surprise and dismay, asks Pandora, 'You mean, you're asking us to *lie* for you?'

'Of course not!'

'Good. Because we both know that truth is the foundation of our spiritualist beliefs.'

'Of course it is.'

'Good,' Odelia says again. 'So what *are* you asking?'

'Just that you keep the details of my living arrangements to yourself until I have a chance to clarify things with Auntie Eudora. Please, Odelia. Certain things are very . . . difficult for me, you see.' She shakes her head and reaches for her teacup. Her hand is trembling.

Bella looks at Odelia. She, too, seems to have noticed – or maybe she's noticing something over Pandora's shoulder.

Most likely Spirit. She gives a little nod, as if in response to something someone just did or said behind Pandora, then pulls out a chair and sits opposite her. 'What kinds of things are difficult for you?'

It's the kind of question Pandora would ordinarily deflect. Instead, she takes a long sip of tea, sets down the cup, and hesitates before saying, 'When I was growing up, Auntie Eudora was the only connection I ever had to my father – I mean, aside from my mum. But my parents were true opposites, while Dad and his sister were two peas in a pod, as Mum always said.'

'I can relate to that,' Bella says. 'I felt the same way about my godmother.'

'Your Aunt Sophie?' Odelia asks, and Bella nods.

'Right, only she's not really my aunt. She was my mom's best friend from the time they were in kindergarten. In some ways, Aunt Sophie knew her better than my father ever did, because they grew up together, you know, and told each other everything. After my mom died, she was really there for me. She tried to do all the things mothers do for their daughters, even though she had no children of her own and she wasn't always very good at it.'

She smiles, remembering the First Communion veil Aunt Sophie had made for her even though she didn't know how to sew, and the birthday cupcakes she'd baked despite not knowing a spatula from a measuring spoon.

'Nor does Auntie Eudora have children,' Pandora says. 'She never wanted them, and doesn't care for them.'

'Doesn't care for them?' Misty echoes. 'What kind of person doesn't like kids?'

'Might I remind you that *I* don't have children myself, Misty. Not everyone chooses to be a . . . a *breeder*.'

'Well, there's nothing wrong with being a breeder, Pandora!'

'There's nothing wrong with being childless, either, Misty,' Bella says hastily. 'Plenty of people choose not to have children.'

Though . . . *Is* that the case with Pandora? Something about her posture, and the way she avoids eye contact, makes Bella wonder whether she might have had maternal stirrings at one time. If so, it didn't happen for whatever reason, and she clearly doesn't want to discuss it.

Misty, oblivious, goes right on talking. 'I know! Of course there isn't. And at least Pandora likes kids.'

'What makes you think I do?' Pandora asks with a dangerous gleam in her eye.

'Jiffy tells me. He says a lot of the Dale kids think you're a mean old lady, but that you're really a very nice . . . um . . . lady.' With a nervous laugh and belated self-awareness, Misty turns back toward the counter and picks up a measuring cup.

'Yes, well, unlike your Sophie, Isabella, my aunt never attempted to nurture me as a parent would,' Pandora says. 'She doesn't believe in coddling and silly play. Rather, she treated me as an equal, even when I was a lass. That gave me tremendous respect for her. I sought her approval and wanted to be just like her. I suppose, in some ways, I looked up to her as I would have my father, if he'd lived. He thought so highly of her, and I just . . . well, I wanted – I *want* – her to think as highly of me.'

'I'm sure she does, Pandora. She seems to have great

affection for you,' Bella says, though from what she's seen so far, Eudora seems almost indifferent to her niece. To everyone, in fact, but Nigel.

But in this moment, Pandora needs reassurance more than she needs truth.

'She has *affection*, yes,' Pandora says. 'But affection isn't admiration, is it?'

'Well, no.' But who wouldn't prefer affection over admiration?

The high and mighty Miss Feeney, that's who.

'The last time I saw Auntie Eudora, she was so very impressed with all . . . this.' Pandora waves a hand around the room.

'You mean, Valley View?'

'Everything. Valley View, the Dale, my life here. And now . . . actually, she's still impressed, I suppose, but only because she believes that I triumphed in a bitter divorce when in fact . . .' She shakes her head.

'But you *did* triumph,' Odelia tells her. 'Trust me. No one knows that better than I do. You kicked that lousy ex-husband to the curb and you built a new life without him.'

'But it isn't a better life, is it? I'm positively skint.'

Misty puckers an over-plucked brow. 'What the heck is skint?'

'Penniless!'

'Aren't we all,' Odelia mutters as Pandora continues her soliloquy.

'Orville left me with nothing but a mountain of debt. The wanker sold our home out from under me and moved into that trollop's La La Land estate while I was forced to set up house in a hovel.'

Bella understands Pandora's frustration, but it isn't like her to feel sorry for herself, or air her private troubles. 'Come on, Pandora, Cotswold Corner is hardly a hovel.'

'Ah, so the name *is* catching on.' Pandora brightens, then dims. 'But it's no Valley View, Isabella.'

Odelia shakes her head. 'Look, no one knows better than I do what it's like to be in your situation, but maybe you should just—'

'I shouldn't and I *shan't*! You can't possibly understand my situation! You *have* family. One of your granddaughters lives right here in the Dale. All I have is Auntie Eudora. She's finally here after all these years, and I want this holiday to be spot on. She's traveled so far, expecting to stay in a lovely old manor, not . . . on a leaky air mattress in a drafty cottage.'

'She traveled that far to see *you*, Pandora,' Bella reminds her. 'I really don't think it's about the accommodation.'

'Bella's right,' Odelia says. 'But for what it's worth, I won't be the one to tell her you don't live here anymore, Pandora . . .'

'Thank you, Odelia.'

'. . . unless she asks. If she comes right out and asks me, "Does Pandora really still live at Valley View?" I'll have to tell the truth.'

'Fair enough.'

Misty sets a glass in front of Pandora. 'Presenting Misty's Magical Miracle Elixir! I know it doesn't look very yummy, but I guarantee it'll make you feel better.'

Pandora seems to gag just looking at the foamy liquid. It's the color of over-cooked cabbage, and smells even worse.

'I really should bottle this stuff,' Misty says, packing the ingredients back into the plastic bag.

'That's one option,' Odelia agrees, wrinkling her nose at the glass.

'I bet I could make a fortune. Ooh, Odelia, I know! You can include the recipe in your cookbook. We'll talk, OK? I'd better get back home. See you later, ladies. And don't worry, Pandora. Your secrets are always safe with me,' she adds, as she sails out of the room.

'She really is a breath of fresh air,' Odelia comments. 'I'd better go, too. I've got a busy afternoon ahead. Did your aunt tell you, Pandora?'

'Tell me what?' she asks, pushing away the glass of elixir and reaching for her tea.

'She made an appointment for a reading.'

'An appointment! With *whom*?'

'With *me*.'

Pandora lowers the cup. '*What?* Did you talk her into it?'

'Of course not! It was her idea.'

'Impossible.'

'Come now, nothing is impossible,' Odelia says, just as she once advised Bella about bearing her burden of grief.

Pandora shakes her head vigorously, though it obviously pains her to do so. 'She's a *Feeney*.'

'So are you,' Odelia points out. 'What does that have to do with anything?'

'My father's side of the family has always been skeptical, to put it mildly, of anything remotely paranormal.'

'Wasn't your mother a medium?'

'She was indeed, and my father was willing to overlook her gifts when they married.'

'So was my ex-husband,' Odelia tells her. 'Only, he changed his tune right afterward. He expected me to give it up. Instead, I gave him up – and good riddance.'

'Ah, yes. But my own parents were otherwise well suited, and my mum certainly didn't practice mediumship while my father was alive. After he passed, of course, he was just fine with it, and she never let him hear the end of that. Mum always did enjoy a good *I told you so*.'

Bella says, 'Wait, your father got through to your mother after he . . . crossed over?'

'Of course. They were in touch for the rest of her life.'

'But . . . Odelia, didn't you tell me once that you couldn't channel your daughter's spirit after she died because you were too close to her?'

Odelia nods, taking on the sorrowful expression that always comes over her when she thinks of that difficult loss. She'd been estranged from Stephanie, her only child, when she died.

'It can be difficult to receive a loved one's energy, especially in the months or even years after the person passes,' Odelia confirms. 'Grieving takes up so much energy, it doesn't really allow you to do anything else.'

'But in time, it can happen. My mum eventually heard from my dad,' Pandora says, 'and now I'm regularly in touch with both of them.'

'That's interesting,' Bella murmurs. Maybe it's just too soon for her to hear from Sam.

You're not a medium, remember?

But if it's true that everyone is capable of tuning in to spirit energy, and if anything is possible, then there's still a chance that she might.

There are so many things she wants to say to him, and ask him. Then again . . .

With a twinge of guilt, she realizes there are other things she'd prefer to keep to herself. Well, one thing: *Drew*.

'I guess my work here is done,' Odelia says, heading for the doorway. 'Holler if you need anything else, Bella. You, too, Pandora. Maybe you should go lie down for a while. Bye!'

In her absence, the kitchen seems preternaturally still. Bella looks at Pandora, both hands clasped around her cup. She clears her throat. 'Uh, Pandora? When your father finally came through to your mother, how did it happen, exactly? Was she meditating and trying to channel him? Or was there . . . you know, something specific that triggered it? Like an anniversary, or she wasn't feeling well, or—'

'Oh, no, nothing like that. It's a rather amusing story, really. One of my father's old school chums had come by the house that evening to visit Mum and see if she needed anything. They got to talking, and he invited her to the pub, and she was going to say yes, as she'd been so lonely, you know . . .'

Yes. Bella knows.

'And in that instant,' Pandora goes on, 'she heard my dad's voice clearly say "No!". Rather forcefully, she told me. And so she didn't go. Later, my father informed her that his chum had always been quite the cad. He didn't want her getting involved with him.'

This was hardly what Bella had wanted or expected to hear, but it was probably, as Odelia had said earlier, what she needed to hear.

'I really am quite knackered.' Pandora gets shakily to her feet. 'Do summon me when Auntie Eudora and Nigel return.'

She nods, lost in thought as Pandora leaves the room.

Drew. She has to do something about Drew, because . . . well, how would Sam feel about Bella's involvement with another man?

Oh, come on. How would anyone feel?

Maybe she's better off not hearing from Sam. Or . . . no, maybe she should be taking a step back from Drew, just in case he's the reason her husband isn't getting through to her. What if Sam's been trying, and Bella's been too distracted to notice?

She'd convinced herself, after a full year without him, that it was time to move on.

She grabs her phone again and opens the text from 'Dr Drew Bailey', as she's now decided to let him remain in her contacts list. She quickly types a reply to his text about trying for that walk this afternoon.

Sorry, can't.

She reads and rereads it. It sounds so cold and terse.

She adds, *It sounds great, but I just have a lot to do around here. Raincheck?*

No. Now it's as though she's just too busy, and not as though she's . . .

What *is* she doing?

Just distancing herself. At least for now. She deletes the whole reply and starts again.

Thanks, but I can't today.

Better. After a moment's consideration, she deletes the last word. This isn't about the timing. It's about what she needs to do until she can figure things out with Sam.

Wait, figure things out?

With Sam? Sam, who's crossed over?

Wait, crossed over? Not dead?

Has Lily Dale finally gotten to her? Does she believe she can talk to spirits now? Is she really going to buy into this whole dead isn't dead thing? Is she going to put aside science and logic and . . . and *Drew Bailey*?

But what if there's a chance, however slim, that Sam can get through to her? Doesn't she owe it to herself to try?

More importantly, she owes it to him. Because if it was the other way around – if Sam was here with Max and Bella was on the Other Side – she'd be trying to reach him. And if he was blind and deaf to her efforts, caught up in a new life and new people – a new person – well, she'd be utterly destroyed. Her *soul* would be destroyed.

She rereads the text she's written to Drew one last time.

Thanks, but I can't.

The message is cold, yes. Terse, too. But at least it's the unembellished truth.

She hits Send before she can change her mind.

NINE

A wakening to pale sunlight filtering through the drawn bamboo roller shades, Pandora finds that her nap seems to have eased her headache and queasiness.

But when she rolls onto her back, she isn't so sure. Should she have tried Misty's magical miracle elixir after all?

No. The girl means well, but she's really quite mad, what with her lotions and potions and . . . and *cryptozoology*, of all things.

Cryptozoology always brings Orville to mind. Many things do, but this memory is particularly irksome.

When they first met, he'd told Pandora that as a child on a Highlands holiday, he'd glimpsed a strange creature rising from the depths of Loch Ness.

'I'm quite certain it was the monster.'

'Oh, Orville, you can't be serious!'

'Well, perhaps it was a floating log,' he admitted. 'One that looked very much like Nessie to a child's eye.'

But after taking a cryptozoology workshop, he was not only convinced he'd seen the legendary monster in Scotland, but he began to spot it quite regularly . . . right out behind Valley View, lolling about in Cassadaga Lake.

'Look! Right there! Do you see it?' he'd ask Pandora, gesturing out the window at the water.

Of course she never did, though she often humored him back in the days before his betrayal.

Now, she rather enjoys imagining the creature rising out of his Southern California swimming pool to devour him whole.

Hearing footsteps coming up the stairs, she sits up, jostling Lady Pippa. The cat emits a disgruntled *meow* and burrows under the fake fur throw that covers them both.

There's a knock on her door. 'Pandora, luv?'

'Do come in, Auntie Eudora!'

Her aunt opens the door and peers into the room. 'Ah, there you are. Bella said you were feeling rather poorly.'

'Much better now, thank you.'

Pandora hoists herself out of bed, still fully dressed, if limp and rumpled compared to Eudora's starched white blouse, slim black trousers and houndstooth duster. Her aunt smells of light perfume and fresh air, blue eyes bright and alert, face prettily flushed as if from an invigorating workout.

'Look at you, fresh as a daisy despite all that travel and such a late evening!' Pandora says. 'How on earth do you do it? You had quite a bit more wine than I did. Gin, too. And port.'

Eudora was never a teetotaler, but Pandora doesn't recall her ever tossing back as much liquor as she had last night. Maybe it was Nigel's influence. He isn't the sort of man Pandora would have envisioned for her aunt, knowing her as she does. Or rather, as she *had*.

She'd anticipated changes after all these years apart. Expected to see that Eudora had aged, naturally, and slowed down. But if anything, the woman seems revitalized. Pandora can only assume it's because she's finally fallen in love. Romance does have a way of rejuvenating the soul.

'Oh, I'm perfectly fine, luv.'

'And you certainly look it. Which moisturizer do you use? You're positively glowing.'

'That's kind of you. It's a new brand. Not available here in the States, I'm afraid. But I shall send you a tube as soon as I'm back home.'

'Thank you, that would be lovely.' She covers a yawn. 'My goodness, I've never been one to indulge in a leisurely kip, but I've done a bang-up job of it today, haven't I? What time is it?'

'Nearly half past one. I'm afraid we'll have to save our Chautauqua jaunt for tomorrow. I've made an appointment for a reading with your chum, Odelia.'

'Right. Not a *chum*, really. She's . . . Isabella's neighbor.'

'And yours.'

'Ah, yes, of course. And mine. I just meant . . .'

Bloody hell.

Now would be the ideal time to confess the truth to her aunt. How to begin? She clears her throat. 'Auntie Eudora . . .'

'I do hope your feelings aren't hurt, luv, that I'm not having a reading with you. Bella said I'd be better off going to someone with whom I don't share a personal connection.'

'Oh?'

'Aye, she said a medium's emotions can muddle the energy.'

'*Did* she?'

'A lie, is it?'

'Well, no, but Isabella is hardly an expert in that regard. I do hope you'll get a good reading, though I'm gobsmacked that you're even giving it a go. You never had much patience for this sort of thing.'

'People change.'

'I suppose they do, but this is rather drastic, isn't it?'

'When in Rome, luv. I thought it would be fun, just for kicks, really. And I'm sure you do appreciate us spending our first day right here in town instead of chasing off to sightsee, particularly as you're under the weather.'

'Just a bit knackered, really. I can't remember the last time I've been up into the wee hours, or had so much . . .' About to say *to drink*, she changes it to, 'fun.'

'Aye, it *was* a rousing good time, wasn't it?'

Aye . . .

Again, Pandora is caught off-guard. She's been away from London for many years, but she hasn't forgotten the local vernacular. Her aunt's rather posh inflection seems to give way, now and again, to phrases that are more in-keeping with northern England – phrases Pandora herself picked up during her time at uni. Maybe that's where Nigel is from . . . although, no, his own dialect is pure London.

Still trying to come up with a segue into her confession, Pandora bends to retrieve her lug-soled Oxfords and bumps her head on the low slanted ceiling as she straightens.

'My goodness, Pandora!' Her aunt rushes to her side. 'Are you all right?'

'Yes, quite.' She sinks onto the window seat and rubs the spot, head throbbing once more.

'Oh, luv . . . this room.'

'What about it?'

Eudora shakes her head, gazing about. 'It's inferior. Why

would you give the Rose Room to the help and resign yourself to such close quarters?'

'I find it cozy, and Isabella needs to be near her son.'

'Then why not put the two of them way up here in the top of the house like orphans in a garret? It's so dreary.'

'I cherish my privacy,' Pandora says stiffly. 'And I don't like anyone walking about overhead.'

'I suppose. But surely there are other rooms to choose from. Those zebra print throw pillows behind you are rather dreadful, aren't they? Clashing with the leopard-spotted cushion as they do.'

'Indeed, they're the height of fashion!' Pandora snaps. 'This is New York, after all. The global epicenter of design innovation.'

In truth, the pillows *do* clash, and this corner of New York State is much closer to the Midwest in proximity and sensibility than it is to New York City. But she's feeling peevish and can't help but defend the Jungle Room décor she so loathes in the face of such rude criticism.

Whatever has got into Auntie Eudora? She's always had impeccable manners and in fact had attended one of the finest finishing schools in Switzerland, though it's not something she likes to discuss.

Perhaps she's gone a bit senile in her dotage. Lost her filter, as people do.

Pandora finishes tying her shoes and sees that her little Scottish Fold has poked her flat-eared tufted head from beneath the throw.

'Ah, there's my darling Lady Pippa. Auntie Eudora, I'm so pleased to introduce you at last!'

'Lady Pippa?' She looks about the room. 'Is she a . . . ghost?'

'Of course not! She's my cat. A Scottish Fold, just like dear Dodger. You were so looking forward to meeting her,' she adds, seeing her aunt flinch and move quickly back to the doorway.

'I know I *was*, but in the interim, I seem to have been stricken with a terrible case of . . . er, catophobia.'

Pandora raises an eyebrow. So it's just as Isabella had claimed.

'How very peculiar. Did it come on without warning, or did something trigger it?'

'Out of the blue, really. Now then, Nigel and I were wondering if you'd like to join us for lunch before my appointment. Our treat, of course.'

'Oh, that . . . yes, that would be lovely, thank you.' She is indeed famished.

'Splendid! We never did get a chance to finish our conversation last evening and I can't wait to hear more.'

'I'm afraid it's all rather fuzzy. Do refresh my memory – what were we talking about?'

'Books, and Marley House, and food . . . oh, all sorts of things, really.'

'Oh, yes, yes.' Pandora nods as if she remembers. 'Where shall we go for lunch? We'll have to stay close by if you're to get back on time. Or you might want to postpone the appointment for another day?'

'That won't be necessary. We're eager to try the local cuisine, and there's a delightful establishment just a few miles down the road, in Fredonia. It's called Applebee's. Do you know it?'

About to respond, Pandora spots a blur of ectoplasm in the hallway behind her.

Nadine, drifting morosely.

It's hardly unusual. She's never been Blithe Spirit. But after what happened yesterday with Nigel and the knife, the presence and proximity to her aunt strikes Pandora as rather ominous.

'Shall we, luv? Nigel is already in the car.'

'Mmm, I'll be right there. Oh, and do watch your step, it's a steep flight!' she calls, as her aunt's footsteps retreat down the hall and stairs.

Then she hisses, 'Nadine! Stop it this instant! Whatever you're up to, you must stop!'

Sensing the spirit has already moved on, she closes her eyes for a brief meditation, breathing deeply, summoning white light protection from her guides.

Yet something is amiss.

She opens her eyes and sees her reflection in the bureau mirror. Stepping closer, she examines the haggard woman. Her braids are askew, and her pale face is trenched with exhaustion and worry, with a faint red mark on her forehead where she bumped it on the ceiling.

Is it any wonder she's feeling so ill at ease in her condition – in pain, under-nourished, and still feeling the effects of having over-imbibed last night?

And maybe . . .

Yes, maybe she'd felt the *need* to over-imbibe because of this vague unsettledness. Increasingly, she feels as if she's dragging herself about, draped in a dark, weighted cloak.

Her own return to Valley View must have something to do with it, though she's spent plenty of time in her former home over the years. It isn't always easy. Being in this house dredges up resentment that the house no longer belongs to her, along with residual anger over a failed marriage and memories that are better left obscured.

Yet this pervasive pall doesn't seem to involve Orville.

What is it, then? Why is she feeling so uneasy when she should be joyful, reunited with her beloved aunt? She should be basking in the familiar warmth and feeling well loved again at last.

She does not.

Has too much time passed? Is it Nigel's presence? Has he somehow obstructed the flow of positive energy between Pandora and her aunt? Is she simply feeling like a third wheel, wishing she had Eudora all to herself?

It feels larger than that. Deeper.

Perhaps she's simply feeling guilty over her charade, and preoccupied with her own lack of disclosure. Of course, that must be it. Living a lie would drag anyone down, particularly a woman of great character, such as herself.

'You must tell Auntie Eudora the truth,' she informs the woman in the mirror. 'Without further delay. You must—'

No!

The word screams into her brain.

Spirit does not approve. But that makes no sense.

'Why not?' she whispers. 'Why not tell?'

Her guides are nagging at her, trying to tell her something. Trying to make her *feel* something.

Flooded with foreboding, she closes her eyes, breathing, meditating.

Turn about . . .

Something is terribly wrong.

Turn about!

She pivots slowly away from the mirror like a blindfolded child at a party game, sensing spirit hands on her shoulders, rotating her into position.

There. Right there.

She opens her eyes and her gaze settles on a framed painting above the bed. It's done almost entirely in shades of gold – a pride of lions, an arid landscape, a gilded sky.

She focuses on it, opening her mind to Spirit's message. Gradually, she zeroes in on a pair of black pinpricks lurking in the painting's background. Stepping closer, she spots a beady-eyed creature camouflaged in the tall grasses. It has tawny fur, a canine face and tall, pointy ears. Rather like a wolf, or a fox, though not quite.

'Pandora?' Eudora calls from below.

She remains motionless, staring at the animal. Is it stalking the lions, or hiding from them?

'Luv, we really must go if I'm to be back in time for my reading!'

Her aunt's distant voice seems to mingle with other unintelligible voices whispering all about her, the hot wind rustling the African savannah, and the lions' low, rumbling growls.

The canvas ripples and stirs to life. She sees the grass swaying and the lions grazing, then the sky darkens and the sun morphs into a moon. The lurking creature rises, tilts its head back and emits a piercing, familiar yowl.

Pandora gasps and squeezes her eyes shut.

When she opens them, the painting is back to normal, and she hears only her own pulse pounding in her ears.

Bella is sitting in the back parlor rereading the same page in *A Tale of Two Cities* for the third or fourth time when her phone buzzes with a text.

Chance, curled up by her side, lifts her head expectantly.

'I know,' Bella tells her. 'Uh-oh.'

She takes her phone out of her pocket, bracing herself for *Dr Drew Bailey*.

He has yet to reply to her earlier response to his invitation. She wants to think it's because he's just busy with his furry and feathered patients. She wants to think *he* doesn't think her curt reply meant what it implied. Actually, she doesn't want to think at all, but her thoughts have been flying in an exhausting flurry ever since she hit Send.

But this text isn't from Drew. It's from Calla Delaney, asking, *Are you busy?*

She exhales a breath she didn't know she'd been holding, and Chance settles back to sleep against her leg as Bella types, *No, what's up?*

Three dots wobble in the message window as Calla types, and then her reply appears: *Can I stop by?*

Bella smiles. *Sure, when?*

She waits for the three dots. The message window remains blank.

Then she hears the front door open, and Calla calls, 'How about right now?'

Grinning, Bella tosses the book aside and hurries to the front hall. Of all the friends she's made in Lily Dale, Calla is the most like-minded. That might be because she's the closest in age, just two years younger.

Or it might be because her own introduction to the Dale was so similar, in some ways, to Bella's.

She, too, was grief stricken and recently bereaved when she arrived. She, too, was oblivious to the Dale's Spiritualist roots, and wound up here with her until-then estranged grandmother because she had nowhere else to go. She, too, was skeptical when she discovered that the town was populated by people who talk to the dead.

But of course, Calla's family, via Odelia, has a long local lineage and a strong genetic tendency toward clairvoyance, and she eventually embraced her gift, though she isn't a registered medium with the Assembly.

Flushed and windblown, Calla is kicking off her sneakers on the mat and hanging her jacket on the coat tree.

'Hi! Shouldn't you be home writing?' asks Bella.

'I've been at it since early this morning. I needed a break.'

Trying to finish her second novel, Calla holds herself to a rigid schedule and spends long days tucked away in her rented cottage with her phone in Do Not Disturb mode and a *Go Away* sign taped to the front door. It doesn't stop Odelia, but everyone else knows to give her space.

Spidey scampers in from the parlor to investigate and skids to a stop on the hardwoods at Calla's feet.

'Hey there, little guy.' She scoops him up and nuzzles his fur. 'I thought you and your mommy were locked up in the laundry room.'

'Wow, word gets around,' Bella says. 'I sprang them the moment I had the house to myself. Come on in.'

'Where is everyone?'

'They went to lunch. But, *shh*.' She points up the stairway.

'Lady Pippa's naptime?'

'Wow, you *are* psychic.'

'Not that I'm not, but pretty much everyone in the Dale knows that cat's daily schedule, thanks to Pandora. And of course Gammy mentioned Pandora's staying here while her aunt's in town.'

'Did she also mention that we're not supposed to let on to Eudora and Nigel that she doesn't live here?'

'Yes. I'm not sure I get it, but whatever.' She shrugs. 'I hope I'm not interrupting anything. I know you're busy.'

'Nope, I'm just sitting around reading *A Tale of Two Cities*.'

'I finished it last night. I can't believe I've never read it before, since I was an English major and such a bookworm kid, and I loved *A Christmas Carol*. The Dickens' story, I mean. Not the gazillion film and television renditions.'

'Same here,' Bella says. 'I reread it every Christmas Eve.'

'Same here!'

'Did you know that Dickens traveled through this area the year before he published it?'

'What? Charles Dickens was *here*?'

'Well, not here, but he passed by on his way from Cleveland to Niagara Falls, according to Nigel. Maybe he soaked up some energy vortexes or something,' Bella says with a grin, leading the way to the back parlor. 'Do you want some coffee?'

'God, no. I drank an entire pot this morning.'

'Tea, then?'

'No, thanks. I don't need a thing, Bella, but if I did, I know my way around this place and I'd get it myself. Just sit and relax while you can. I hear Pandora has you waiting on her hand and foot.'

'Who told you that?'

'One guess.'

Like any small town, Lily Dale has a local gossip mill, and Odelia does her share to keep it churning.

Calla plops herself down on the Chesterfield with Spidey on her lap and props her sock-clad feet on the tufted ottoman. 'Gammy's worried about you, Bella.'

'Is that why you're here? Because you can see that I'm fine.'

'Not really.'

'Yes, really.' Bella returns to her seat beside a still-snoozing Chance and puts her own feet up on the coffee table. 'I am.'

'No, I can see that you're fine. I meant, that's not really why I'm here.' She pauses. 'I know how you feel about these things, but I was home writing, and I kept getting the sense you needed me.'

'Because of Pandora? I'm OK with it, Calla, truly.'

'No, I didn't know what was up with Pandora until I stopped by Gammy's just now on the way over. She gave me an earful. But I don't feel like whatever is going on has anything to do with her taking advantage of you.'

Bella shifts her weight. 'Uh . . . what *do* you think it has to do with?'

'Now that I'm here, I think I'm getting some idea.' Calla gets up, walks over to the doorway, leans out and listens for a moment. 'I'm going to close this, just in case.' She presses a hidden button to release a small brass pull, tugs it, and a vintage wood-paneled pocket door glides out of the wall and across the opening.

She turns back to Bella. 'So I met Eudora and Nigel last night at the café.'

'I heard. What did you think?'

'I'd rather hear what *you* think.'

'Me? I'm the only one around here who can't read people's energy.'

'Sometimes I think you're the only one around here who notices important details the rest of us miss while we're trying to receive energy.' Calla sits again. 'Tell me your impressions of them.'

'For the most part, they're perfectly pleasant.'

'But . . .'

'But yeah, a few things are bothering me. And it isn't just that Chance seems to dislike them – which is mutual – and she's a really good judge of character, aren't you, sweetie?' she adds as the cat, hearing her name, stirs from sleep.

'Of course she is. She chose you and Max to be her family.' Calla reaches out to pet her. 'What else is bothering you about these people, Bella?'

'You know how Pandora likes to be such a proper lady? Well, there are times when Eudora seems a little . . . coarse. Not that there's anything wrong with that, but it isn't all the time, you know? It's like she's pretending to be someone she's not, and then she slips up.'

'I noticed that, too. It's like she has a fancy British accent like Pandora, and then it changes.'

'Right. And I get that. I grew up downstate, and sometimes I hear that creeping into my own voice.'

'Like when you offered me *caw-fee*?' Calla asks with a grin.

'Oh, no, did I? See?'

'Yeah, it happens. I grew up in Florida until I was seventeen. Sometimes, my inner Scarlett O'Hara comes out, sugar,' she says in an exaggerated drawl.

Bella laughs. 'Speaking of coffee . . . I wound up wearing mine this morning thanks to Eudora's elbow. She doesn't have the best table manners for a chef.'

'She doesn't, does she? Not only that, but when we were talking about the menu, it was like she was trying to seem sophisticated about food, asking questions, you know . . . and one of them was, "Is the red snapper caught locally?" I'm not sure if her culinary skills are lacking, or if it's her geography.'

And while we're on the subject of fish, she drank like one, and so did Nigel.'

Bella tells her about the afternoon gimlets and the vacant spots in the liquor cabinet. 'I get the impression the two of them are old hands at it, but Pandora had a nasty hangover this morning.'

'Not surprising. It was almost like they wanted to get her wasted. I saw Nigel kind of casually refilling her glass while she wasn't looking.'

'Why would they do that?'

'Maybe so they could stick her with the bill? Because they did.'

'Oh, no.'

'Oh, yes. She told me to put it on her nonexistent house charge, and when I told Peter about that, he said her financial situation must be even worse than she's letting on.'

'That would explain why she seems so troubled.'

'Yes, and . . . well, I didn't get the sense that she was very comfortable with her aunt.'

'Pandora's always a little stiff. And her aunt is, too.'

'No, I know, but the energy flow between them wasn't what I'd expect.'

'Wouldn't that be the case if someone was hiding something? Because Pandora is pretending she still lives here.'

'Yes, a lie would explain the reason I felt like they weren't connecting.'

'Maybe she's not being truthful with the rest of us, either,' Bella says. 'She's been known to embellish the truth. The way she described her aunt before she got here made me expect an elderly, genteel, sophisticated woman, so I was taken aback.'

'What do you know about Eudora's career?'

'Only what Pandora told me,' Bella realizes, pulling out her phone. 'Let's look her up.'

But a quick search results in a long list of links confirming that Eudora Feeney is, indeed, a respected British chef and restaurateur.

'She looks so much like Pandora here, doesn't she?' Bella shows Calla a smiling black and white headshot of Eudora holding a knife poised over a partially diced onion.

'Yes, they're Feeney women! Genetically gifted with a remarkable youthful countenance, you know.'

She laughs at Calla's grandiose impression. 'She told you that too, huh?'

'Oh, yes. So I guess she is who Pandora says she is. That's good.'

'She has to be the only chef in the world who'd drive right past the Culinary Institute of America without stopping for lunch when she had a reservation.'

'What? That's crazy!'

'Yeah. She said she was too excited to get to Lily Dale. Maybe she's just burnt out on restaurant cuisine after all those years working so hard in the industry.'

'So burnt out she forgot that red snapper isn't a lake fish?'

'Well, she's getting up there in years. I'm, what, forty years younger? And I forget things, too.'

Like those pomegranate seeds she can't recall buying.

Fruit of the dead.

'According to this article, her Covent Garden eatery went bankrupt in 2008. Pandora didn't mention that, did she?' says Calla.

'No, I got the impression Eudora was just retired. I guess you can't blame her if she wants to forget about the restaurant business.'

'What about Nigel? What's his story?'

'Let's find out.' Bella enters *Nigel Spencer-Watson* into the search engine. She scrolls down the list of hits with Calla looking over her shoulder at the phone screen. None of them fit.

'That's so weird. Maybe try it without the hyphen,' Calla suggests.

'Oh, right. Good idea.'

She removes it and tries again.

Nothing.

'How is it possible,' Calla asks, 'for a man who supposedly had a long and illustrious career as a professor of English Literature and a Dickens scholar to leave no imprint on the internet?'

'Either he's kept a low profile or we've found another lie.'

'He told me he has articles in print. Publish or perish.'

'How can he have done that without leaving some kind of trail online? I guess it's a lie.'

'But which part of it? Do you think Pandora made up his esteemed background, or that Eudora did?'

'I guess either could be possible,' Bella muses. 'But there's also a good chance they don't even know. He wouldn't be the first opportunist to prey on an elderly widow.'

'For her money?'

'But how wealthy can she be if her business went bankrupt?'

'True. It doesn't make much sense. What else could he want from her?'

'Or from Pandora? She's barely scraping out a living.'

'But they think she lives here, remember?'

Bella stares at her. 'You're right. Whatever he's after has something to do with Valley View. But what is it?'

TEN

'You're awfully quiet back there, luv,' Auntie Eudora comments from the passenger seat as they head home after lunch. 'Did your meal give you a tummy upset?'

'No, not at all,' Pandora assures her, though she can't even recall what she'd ordered. She'd gone through the motions of chewing and swallowing, and attempted to follow the conversation. Nigel had guided it along like a classroom discussion, posing questions to Pandora about inconsequential topics, mostly involving the past, Marley House, Charles Dickens, food . . .

Her answers had been vague and perhaps a bit testy at times, especially when he'd asked about her wedding.

'I'd prefer not to talk about it, please.'

'I'm sorry. Just yesterday, you seemed eager to reminisce about it. Eudora's visit, and her gift – the bluebells . . .'

'Yes, well, yesterday is not today, is it?'

Apprehension had followed her to the restaurant like a tethered storm cloud, and her malaise mounts with every mile that flies past on their way back.

'My burger was delightful,' Nigel says, one hand on the wheel, the other fiddling with the car's audio system.

'My salad was as well.' Eudora has her seat tilted back and the window rolled halfway down, the warm breeze billowing in. She looks like a contented cat basking in the sun.

'Really? I'm astonished that a chef of your stature would relish a hum drum meal at an American chain restaurant,' Pandora finds herself saying.

Eudora doesn't turn to meet her gaze, but her face is reflected in the side mirror outside the car. Her eyes are masked by large black sunglasses, but her jaw is taut as she replies, 'Come now, I didn't say I *relished* it, did I? I was merely . . . pleasantly surprised. And ravenous.'

'And keeping things in perspective after that dreadful fish

last night,' Nigel puts in over the staticky radio as he continues
to jab at dashboard buttons. 'Blimey!'

'Why not just turn it off?' Eudora asks.

'Because it was working perfectly yesterday. I'll need to
call the car hire company to file a complaint.'

'Well, we *are* in the middle of nowhere, Nigel,' Eudora
points out. 'Maybe there are no radio stations in the area.'

'Try 1410, Nigel,' Pandora suggests. 'That's the local
station, WDOE. It always comes in for me when I drive this
route.'

He presses buttons and the speakers crackle. 'I don't think
there's any such station.'

She sighs. 'There is. It's just Spirit.'

In the rear-view mirror, she sees Nigel's eyebrows rise.
'What do you mean?'

'Interference with electromagnetic technology is quite
common,' Pandora explains.

'Are you saying that a . . . a *ghost* is responsible for this
broken radio?'

'I'm saying that it isn't broken. Spirit is an energy current
and quite capable of disrupting other energy currents. It
happens all the time.'

'How so?' Eudora props her sunglasses above her forehead
and turns to look at Pandora.

'Lights flicker. Television channels turn on on their own.
Phones ring and no one is on the line.'

'But why do the spirits do it?'

'It depends. Sometimes, it's to get our attention, let us know
they're here. Or they might be trying to deliver a message.'

As if on cue, the radio suddenly comes in loud and clear
– not with a song, but a familiar commercial.

'If adventure you're a'seekin' . . .

You can't go wrong with Beacon . . .'

Nigel grins. 'Did the spirits do that, Pandora? Because we
sailed over on that cruise line.'

'Of course not. The bloody advert is omnipresent. Do lower
the volume.'

'I'll just turn it off. We're almost home.' Eudora silences
the radio as they make a right turn off Route 60 onto Dale

Drive. 'If you'll drop me at Odelia Lauder's doorstep, Nigel, I'll be right on time.'

'I shall, I shall.'

'It's hardly a long walk,' Pandora points out. 'Right next door?'

'Oh, I know, but it's on the way and I'm eager to get there, and it will give you and Nigel a chance to get to know each other.'

In the distance between Odelia's house and Valley View? What an odd thing to say.

Pandora ponders the comment as they wind along the lake-side road past winter-worn year-round houses with barren gardens, some with forgotten holiday light strings and yards dotted with forlorn lawn ornaments.

Residents are out and about, and of course she knows them all. Harold Maxson stands on a low pier with a fishing line suspended in blue-gray water. Mrs Remington, the Slaytons' long-time housekeeper, sweeps the neo-Victorian's wraparound porch. Teenaged brothers Dylan and Ethan Drumm bicycle past wearing shorts, no jackets and helmets.

'Silly lads,' Eudora comments.

'Yes, they should have protective headgear.'

'They should have trousers and parkas. It's much too chilly for summer clothing, don't you think?'

'In Lily Dale, *summer* is often too chilly for summer clothing,' Pandora points out. 'And it is a lovely day for a change, with April round the corner.'

Nigel nods. 'True. Tomorrow is the last day of March. Going out like a lamb, is it? The meteorologists are calling for another warm, sunny day.'

'Don't count on it. Not in Lily Dale.'

Lamb . . .

Lion . . .

She thinks of the painting Spirit showed her earlier. Perhaps it was in reference to the March weather. Were her guides warning her that a storm is imminent?

She looks at the sky. The sun has slipped behind a swathe of gray, but it's a soft shade and not the oppressive gloom that threatens snow. That could change in a matter of seconds, and often does. But would she be feeling such an insidious dread over inclement weather?

Hardly.

Lion . . .

Odelia Lauder had been wearing ridiculous slippers with lion heads. Perhaps the vision had something to do with her.

Lion . . .

Lamb . . .

Lamb . . . sheep . . . shepherd . . .

Duncan.

Leeds.

Northern England.

For some reason, that chapter in her life keeps poking at her consciousness. It would make sense if Auntie Eudora had played a prominent role in it, but Pandora hadn't seen much of her aunt during the years she was away at uni.

They're back in the Dale now, jostling along muddy, rutted lanes.

Nigel pulls up in front of the rickety-looking cottage adjacent to Valley View, and Eudora hops out.

'Off I go. Wish me luck, darling.'

'Good luck,' Nigel says.

'Sithee!' With a wave, she makes her way toward Odelia's rickety front steps.

Nigel turns to Pandora in the back seat and tips an imaginary hat. 'It's my pleasure to chauffeur you home, Lady Feeney.'

She watches Eudora disappear inside, that unexpected *sithee* ringing in her ears – a regional farewell she'd often heard during her years in northern England. But Auntie Eudora is a Londoner.

'Why would you wish her luck, Nigel? Is she hoping something specific will come through?'

'Isn't everyone?'

'I don't know, I thought she was doing this for kicks. And anyway, luck has very little to do with it. Often it's the loudest, pushiest spirit who gets the message across, not necessarily the one the sitter hopes to hear from.'

'Yes. That's what your chum Odelia said.'

'She isn't my— never mind.'

He parks beside a tall stone planter in front of Valley View. A wind-battered pinwheel spins slowly above dried-out plant stalks. It had been a shiny red and blue when young Max had stuck it into the dirt on the Fourth of July, but the foil has since flaked off.

'Who *does* Auntie Eudora hope to hear from, Nigel?'

'Oh, I don't think she's interested in connecting with the dead as much as she is the medium's psychic abilities.'

'How so?'

He climbs out of the car and opens her door for her. 'Of late, Eudora has been . . . misplacing things.'

'What do you mean?'

'She tends to lose track of her belongings. Isn't that an area in which a psychic would be able to provide assistance?'

'Yes, I've had a number of clients over the years attempting to locate everything from missing persons to a winning lottery ticket.'

He turns to regard her with a gleam in his eye. 'Do you mean you were asked to choose the winning numbers? Can you do that?'

'If I could, do you think I'd be living . . .' She catches herself, and gestures at Valley View. 'Here? No, this man already *had* the numbers, on a ticket that had won a hundred thousand dollars. After the draw, he'd put it away overnight for safekeeping and then couldn't remember where it was when he was ready to claim the prize.'

'And you were able to find it?'

She nods. 'My guides showed me something rather . . . vulgar. It turned out he'd taped the ticket to the underside of the toilet tank.'

'How distasteful! I do hope he gave you a generous reward?'

'*I* didn't have to fish it out, Nigel.'

'But *you* told him where to look.'

'Yes, well, he did call to thank me profusely after he'd cashed in.'

'The bloke won thousands, and offered nothing more than his gratitude? Perhaps the vulgar image was in reference to his character, then. Oh, dear, I nearly forgot to lock the car.'

'No need. This is the safest place in the world.'

'I wouldn't be so certain.' He aims the key fob at the sedan and it emits a double chirp as the locks click into place. 'Eudora and I saw some rather unsavory characters out and about this morning.'

'I beg your pardon?'

'Yes, and we were taken aback as we, too, believed the Dale to be safe. But a pair of suspect chaps appeared to be loitering outside a home that appeared unoccupied. It was as if they were casing the place.'

'Perhaps they were workmen?'

'They weren't dressed as such. And when we came along, they made a hasty retreat.'

Pandora frowns. 'That is most unusual.'

'I'm afraid crime occurs everywhere, my dear. Even in this charming place.'

'Which home was it?' She casts a furtive glance across Melrose Park, hoping it wasn't her own.

'Small, old-fashioned and a bit shabby,' Nigel says. 'But then, they all look alike here, don't they?'

They most certainly do not. Cotswold Corner is painted a smashing shade of pink, with bright red window boxes. The vibrant splotch in this dreary setting is like a coloring book page that someone started, then set aside for later.

Pandora is overcome by an unexpected longing for June, when it will all be filled in again, the world reborn lush and alive after an endless Lily Dale winter.

'Pandora.' Nigel puts his hand on her arm at the base of the front steps. 'May I have a private word with you?'

'Of . . . of course.' Had he caught her looking at Cotswold Corner and figured out the truth?

'It's about your aunt.'

Oh dear. Judging by his somber expression, it's a serious matter.

'Is she unwell?' Pandora asks, reminding herself that Eudora is the picture of vitality.

'Her physical condition is remarkably healthy for a woman of her age. But I'm afraid her memory is rather spotty these days, as I said.'

'Is that all? Why, Nigel, even *I* occasionally find myself

walking into a room to get something and promptly forgetting what it was.'

'It seems a bit more serious than that. One minute, she's astute, and the next, well . . .' He shakes his head. 'I've urged her to consult a physician, but she refuses to acknowledge the problem. So I've been hoping this visit might jog her cognitive awareness.'

'I see.'

With grim recognition, Pandora finds everything falling into place. No wonder she's experienced a profound emotional disturbance connected to this visit. No wonder her aunt's energy seems so unfamiliar. No wonder Eudora seems to have lost her grasp on things that happened, and details she should know. No wonder her behavior is out of character, her filter has grown flimsy, and . . . and she doesn't eat bread.

'Is this the reason you've brought up so many questions about our familial past?' she asks Nigel.

'Yes, of course. I'm hoping to stimulate the part of her brain that's lapsed.'

'I shall do my best to assist. Though it's funny . . .'

'Yes?'

'I always believed senility had more of an impact on short-term memory than long.'

'Oh? Well, I suppose it's different with everyone.'

'Yes, I suppose it is.'

'Shall we go in?' He starts up the porch steps. 'I'm planning to browse your bookshelves to find something to read in the suite until Eudora returns.'

'That sounds like a splendid idea. Perhaps you'll start with Calla Delaney's novel? Remember, she promised to autograph it for you.'

'Ah, yes.'

Nigel's face, as he glances back over his shoulder, has become Orville's. What on earth . . .?

She squeezes her eyes closed, aghast.

'Is something amiss, Pandora?'

'No, I . . .'

She forces them open. Ah, he's Nigel again.

'Are you feeling faint?'

'No, still recovering from last night's merriment, I'm afraid.' She forces a smile. 'I believe I shall linger out here for a bit.'

'Splendid idea. Fresh air will do wonders, I'm certain.'

He disappears inside the house and Pandora sinks onto the steps.

Spirit clearly wants her to see that Nigel has something in common with her ex-husband. She reminds herself that it isn't necessarily a negative trait. Orville was a fellow Englishman. He, too, was a bibliophile. Like Nigel, he enjoyed a good burger and a fine port. Perhaps that's all it is.

Nigel is clearly concerned over her aunt's deteriorating memory – enough to have made this arduous journey to reconnect Eudora to her only living relative. Would Orville have gone to such lengths for Pandora? Would he have cared so deeply about the details of her past? Her ancestral home, relatives alive and dead, tangible and intangible relics collected over the years – stories and recipes, memories and keepsakes . . .

No. Orville was a minimalist, didn't have a sentimental bone in his body, and had no patience for such things.

Her heavy sigh mingles with softly tinkling wind chimes in the eaves, gravel crunching beneath tires on a neighboring lane, and faint rock music spilling from the approaching car's open windows.

Pulsing synthesizer, clashing cymbals, electric guitar . . .

Pandora looks expectantly toward the street. An SUV rolls into view, with a familiar black man behind the wheel. Ah, then the music is coming from somewhere else. Not that Luther Ragland wouldn't listen to rock and roll, but his taste runs more to jazz and American songbook, and anyway, the windows are rolled up.

He parks in front of Odelia's house and turns off the engine.

Pandora can still hear the music. Lyrics now, too. Something about fighting in the streets. How dreadful. But the tune is catchy and vaguely recognizable.

Luther gets out and starts toward the house next door. He's wearing a camel-colored overcoat and polished dress shoes, and is careful to avoid the puddles along the walk.

My, but he *is* a fit chap. Tall, broad-shouldered and

clean-shaven, he exudes a commanding presence, despite being several years into his retirement from law enforcement.

Pandora herself had rather fancied him before he and Odelia had transformed their long-time friendship into something more . . . although it isn't clear exactly what that is. She doesn't know what he sees in the woman, really, and hasn't given up hope that he might come to his senses one of these days and turn his interest toward Pandora.

Luther stops short on the path, spotting the 'Reading in Session' sign on Odelia's door.

'She's got a client, luv,' Pandora calls to him.

He turns and spots her. 'I see that. I thought she was free this afternoon, but I guess business picked up. Oh, well. I'll just call her lat—'

'I'm sure she won't be long. Do come join me.'

'That's all right, I'll—'

'Luther? Please. I'd like a word with you about a rather pressing issue.'

He obliges, but must not have heard that last part over the blasting music, because he takes his time, retracing his steps down the path and along the road rather than cutting across the yard.

Watching him, Pandora nods her head along with the drum beat.

What *is* this song? It's so familiar, from the distant past. Her younger days, when she was just a lass, studying music at Leeds.

Luther comes up the walk on a waft of woodsy aftershave. 'Are you waiting for Bella? Or babysitting Max?'

'What? No! Do you take me for a governess?'

'I just thought maybe—'

'*No.*' She pats the step beside her. 'Do sit down, Luther.'

He eyes the worn tread, flecked with dried leaf fragments and a film of ice-melt salt. 'That's all right, I'll stand.'

'This issue is quite confidential.' She casts a quick glance over her shoulder to make sure Nigel isn't afoot. The front parlor windows are open a few inches. If he's lurking beyond, he'd be able to eavesdrop through the screens.

It's a peculiar idea, and one that would never have entered

her mind if Spirit hadn't superimposed Orville's features over
his. Now the two seem intertwined in her brain, Nigel trig-
gering doubt and mistrust, most likely unfairly.

Or perhaps not.

'Might I have some assistance rising, Luther? I'm a bit
stiff.'

'Oh, sorry. Sure.' He holds out a hand.

She grabs it in both of hers like a lifeline and pulls herself
up, delighting in the masculine warmth of his grasp. It's been
so very long since she held a man's hand. It would be even
nicer to feel his arms about her, but he releases his grip as
soon as she's steady.

'Ah, much better,' she says. 'Now I can look into your eyes
as we converse.'

'Yeah, Pandora, uh . . . what's going on?'

'Let's step a bit further away from the windows, shall we?'
They do, and she lowers her voice. 'I'm in the midst of a
sojourn here at Valley View while my aunt and her friend are
visiting from abroad. Her mental health is declining, poor dear,
and she's under the impression that I remain in residence, so
I've opted to go along with it.'

'You mean, you're pretending to live here?'

'Of course. You'll play along with our little charade, won't
you? For Auntie Eudora's sake?'

'Uh, sure. I guess.'

'Splendid.'

'But I don't think I'll be seeing her, or—'

'I wanted you to be in the loop, just in case.'

'Got it. Well, thanks for including me.' He looks back at
his car. 'If that's all you wanted to talk about, I guess I'm
going to—'

'No, of course that wasn't all. It's come to my attention
that unsavory characters have been spotted here in the Dale.'

'Oh?' Luther folds his arms and rocks back on his heels.
'Are they alive, or dead?'

That gives her pause. It hadn't even occurred to her that
Nigel and Eudora might have glimpsed apparitions. But it isn't
likely, especially as they'd both seen them, and neither
professes to be sensitive in that area.

'They're quite alive,' she concludes. 'And I'm afraid they appeared to be planning some kind of heist.'

'A . . . *heist*?'

'Yes, they were reportedly casing the joint.'

'Which, uh, joint?'

'It remains unclear. But it's my civic duty to make law enforcement aware. Can you call in a patrol?'

'Well, I'm retired these days, so—'

'That hasn't stopped you from sniffing about for criminal activity, Luther. Do you require a notebook and pen to write down this tip?'

'No, thanks, I'm good.' He points at his temple. 'I keep it all right here. These unsavory characters who were casing the joint, plotting a heist . . . is this a, uh . . . a vision you had?'

'No, no, my aunt and her gentleman friend literally saw this unfolding.'

'Your aunt who's suffering from mental illness?'

'She is, but it's not as if she's gone *mad*. She's just a bit senile, and really, Nigel seems quite sane, although . . .'

He does have a way of morphing into her ex, and Nadine seems to have no use for him, and . . .

The music has grown louder. Pandora bobs her head in time to the drumbeat.

'Luther, what *is* this song?'

'What song?'

'The one that's playing . . .' She notes his frown. '. . . in my head. You can't hear it, can you?'

'I cannot.'

'I see. It seems to be about a revolution.' After listening to more lyrics, she adds, 'And religion, it seems . . . yes, kneeling and praying are involved.'

'Is it a hymn? Gospel music?'

'No, it's rock and roll. You're certain you can't hear—'

'One hundred percent positive.'

'Then it must be Spirit. There's a message in the song. What is it?'

'Guess you'll have to figure it out, Pandora.' He looks at his watch, and then his car. 'I'd better get—'

'Oh, I do love a musical challenge. Did you know that back in the eighties, I—'

'The nineteen-eighties?'

'Yes, of course. How old do you think I *am*?'

'Come on, this is Lily Dale. Do you know how many times Odelia has shared an anecdote about something that happened to her centuries ago?'

'Yes, well . . . *Odelia*. In any case, I was once a contestant on *Name That Tune*. Do you know it? The gameshow on the telly? It was the UK version, of course. And I—'

The door opens behind her and she turns to see Isabella stepping out onto the porch, accompanied by Calla Delaney.

'Pandora! Luther! What's going on?'

'I just stopped by to see Odelia, but she has a client,' he says. 'Pandora called me over to tell me about the revolution song that's in her head and the unsavory characters who are *not*.'

'Not . . .'

'In her head, like the song. The song is in her head.'

Pandora nods. 'Yes, it's Spirit. There seems to be something rather foreboding about it. Calla, can *you* hear it?'

Calla listens for a moment, then shakes her head. 'All I hear is my inner taskmaster telling me to get home to my manuscript, and a very hungry Li'l Chap telling me it's time to feed him.'

Li'l Chap is the Russian Blue kitten she'd adopted last fall, yet another Lily Dale stray who'd fortuitously turned up in the right place at the right time.

'Oh, Pandora – it was nice to meet your family last night. How's your visit going?'

'Splendidly, thank you,' she tells Calla.

'And is everything . . . alright? With you, and your aunt, and Nigel?'

'How so?'

'In the beginning – before all that wine – I just felt as though the energy was a little tense. Like . . . maybe you'd had an argument or something?'

'No arguments. Auntie Eudora and I haven't seen each other in many years, and I'm just acquainted with Nigel. Perhaps that's what you sensed.'

'Must be,' she agrees, but Pandora sees a look pass between her and Isabella.

She wants to ask about it . . . or does she? Again, she glances at the open screens in the parlor.

'Well, I've got to go back to work. See you later, everyone.' Calla hustles down the porch steps and cuts across Melrose Park toward home.

Watching her go, Pandora notices that the sun has poked out again, sending streamers of golden light over Cotswold Corner, setting the little pink cottage aglow like a beacon.

If adventure you're a'seekin' . . .

You can't go wrong with Beacon . . .

'I'm waiting around to talk to Odelia so that I can book that Beacon cruise before the deadline tomorrow,' Luther is telling Isabella.

'How very peculiar!' Pandora blurts, and they turn to look at her. 'They seem to be everywhere these days, don't they?'

Luther raises an eyebrow. 'Unsavory characters?'

'No, no, the cruise line! Beacon Atlantic.'

Isabella rolls her eyes. 'The commercial is definitely everywhere.'

'Auntie Eudora and Nigel sailed over on a Beacon Atlantic vessel. And now, Luther, you've brought it up as well.'

He nods. 'I'm trying to convince Odelia to join me on a cruise to Bermuda, but she keeps stalling. I guess her guides aren't really on board with it – excuse the pun.'

'You, uh . . . you haven't had any visions about it, have you, Pandora?' Isabella asks. 'Nothing about sinking ships, or anything like that?'

'No, of course not,' she says, and yet . . .

She closes her eyes briefly and sees the image of an ocean liner pushing through the night sea. Dark sky, dark water. Enormous waves, churning white foam, *blood*—

A phone rings, and the image dissolves.

'Sorry, I've got to grab this call. I'll take it in my car.' Luther strides away.

'The bus will be here soon,' Isabella informs Pandora. 'I'm going down to meet it.'

'I thought the lad forbade you to do so.'

'He did. But your foreboding trumps his forbidding.'

Watching her stride away down Cottage Row, Pandora is once again aware of the rock song.

The lyrics have given way to throbbing synthesizer, punctuated by blasts of percussion. Her brain remembers the song's structure. It's building to something big. She squeezes her eyes shut in anticipation of what's coming, and when it does – when the vocalist erupts in a primal scream – a new vision appears before her.

It's the pointy-eared canine from the painting upstairs.

ELEVEN

B ella sits on a low stone wall across from the bus stop. Today, the area is far from deserted. People are enjoying leisurely drives and strolls along the lake. There are cyclists on the bike trail and joggers on the footpath. Fishermen dot the water's edge, with ducks bobbing on the ice-pocked surface and chatty birds perched overhead.

Still no buds on the bare tree limbs, though.

Still no Sam.

Still no Drew.

But Bella has other concerns.

When she and Calla emerged from the back parlor, Nigel was in the nook off the dining room, standing on a chair browsing the upper bookshelves.

'Just looking for a copy of your novel, Ms Delaney,' he told them with a jovial wave.

'Oh . . . there's a whole row of them right there.' Bella showed him. Calla's book was the only one in the library with all the copies positioned with the front cover facing forward instead of the spine. It was accompanied by a hard-to-miss 'Local Author' shelf-talker.

Yet Nigel had missed it, or so he claimed. He seemed flustered as he climbed down from the chair and plucked a copy from the shelf.

'I'll autograph it for you,' Calla offered.

'That would be lovely. Later, when Eudora is back. I know she wouldn't want to miss such a momentous occasion.'

'Oh, it's not a big deal. I was just going to grab a pen and scribble my name.'

'Yes, yes, looking forward to it,' he said, and beat a hasty retreat up the stairs.

Unsettled, Bella had rounded up Chance and Spidey and closed them into the Rose Room before she and Calla stepped outside.

If Nigel Spencer-Watson doesn't exist, then who is the man who's taken up residence under her roof, and what is he looking for?

What about Pandora, and the foreboding song playing in her head?

What about the jingle looping, once more, in Bella's?

If adventure you're a'seekin' . . .

You can't go wrong with Beacon . . .

It's far more likely the result of an infuriatingly infectious advertising campaign than some dire spirit warning. But for Odelia's sake, she opens a search window on her phone and quickly types in *Beacon Atlantic*.

The first thing that comes up is the company's website. And beneath, she sees links to several news articles that are, at a glance, about some mishap . . . on the *Queen Jane*'s maiden voyage.

Nigel and Eudora were on that ship.

Before she can click on a link, the yellow school bus rounds the bend.

With reluctance, Bella returns her phone to her hoodie pocket. It will have to wait. She can't afford distractions when it comes to the boys.

The doors creak open and backpack-toting kids pile out, cheerful and chatty, reveling in breezy sunshine that isn't quite warm, but for a change isn't bone-chilling, either.

As usual, Max and Jiffy are the last two to disembark, trailing along after the others and engaged in animated conversation. Or in today's case, song.

It's The Who's 'Magic Bus'. Bella smiles. Maybe Jiffy, too, is channeling Keith Moon.

'Hi, Ms Jordan,' a second-grader says, and turns to holler over his shoulder, 'Hey, Max, your mom's here again!'

Max and Jiffy halt as if a ferocious lion has reared in their path.

'Mom! What are you *doing*?'

'Bella, this is really bad for us!'

'Especially me!' Max says. 'It's *my* mom.'

'And especially me, too, because I'm with you!'

Gone are the days when their reaction to her presence might

have hurt Bella's feelings. She knows better than to take it personally.

Yet she also knows what it's like to be embarrassed by a parent in front of your friends. In her own childhood, Frank Angelo was always the only father on the playground. While the other kids' mothers stood around and gossiped, he sat on a bench and kept an eye on her. She wished he'd bring a book or crossword puzzle or something, but he told her he wasn't there to read.

'I'm here to watch my Bella Angel,' he'd say, and that was what he did. He watched her.

One day, she overheard a couple of girls laughing about it. About him. About Bella. And that was the last time she ever went to the playground.

Now, seeing Max and Jiffy's dismay, Bella regrets allowing Pandora's foreboding and her own misgivings about Nigel to get to her.

'You're such a good mommy, Bella Blue,' isn't the only comment Sam ever made about her parenting skills. He'd also said, more than once, *'You're being over-protective.'*

He'd said it when she'd balked at leaving Max with a babysitter so that they could have date night.

He'd said it when Max was taking his first steps, and she'd encased every hard edge in their apartment in cushioned bumpers.

He'd say it now. The boys would have been fine walking up the street, especially with so many people out and about.

'Don't worry, guys. I'm not here to walk you home. I just strolled over to check out the lake. Wow, it's so beautiful today, isn't it?'

They glance at the water, at each other, and warily at her.

'I'm just going to hang around here and enjoy the scenery. See you later!'

They continue on toward Cottage Row, shooting glances over their shoulders every few steps to make sure she's not following. Pretending to ignore them, she takes out her phone and auto-dials Luther.

He picks up on the first ring. 'Hey, Bella.'

'Oh, good, you're off your call. I hope everything's OK?'

He laughs. 'That was a robot reminding me I have a dentist appointment. Sorry. I just needed an excuse to get away from Pandora Feeney. You know how it is.'

'Do I ever. Listen, I'm down at the gate. Max and Jiffy are about to walk up the street. They don't want to be seen with me, so can you just keep an eye out for them?'

He laughs. 'Sure. We can't have a mom cramping their style in front of the big kids, can we?'

'I know, I was just worried . . . what did you say about unsavory characters?'

'Pandora said it. Well, her aunt and uncle did.'

'Oh, Nigel isn't her uncle, he's Eudora's gentleman friend. The boys just went around the corner,' she adds, as Max and Jiffy disappear from view.

'And here they come up Cottage. Eyes on.'

'Thanks. Tell me what Nigel and Eudora said, Luther.'

'They seem to think there's a group of thieves plotting a heist.'

'*What?*'

'I know.' He sighs. 'And Pandora told me this right after she said her aunt is suffering from dementia.'

'She's . . . I didn't know that.'

Bella wonders whether it's true, or another lie. But whose? Pandora's? Eudora's? Nigel's?

'Luther, before you dismiss it, I thought someone was creeping around Valley View last night, so . . . I guess I'm a little paranoid now.'

'What happened?'

She explains quickly, leaving out the *fruit of the dead* and the disembodied yowl.

'You know, maybe there's something to this,' Luther says. 'It *is* the off-season, and there are a lot of empty houses here that might be targeted for burglary. I'll take a drive around and check things out, make sure there are no signs of break-ins anywhere. And I'll have a word with Pandora's aunt and her friend and find out exactly what they saw.'

'Right, about that—'

'What's shaking, fellas?' she hears him say.

The boys are with him. She swallows her concerns about

Nigel, saying instead, 'Just don't let them go inside before I get there, OK? I'm on my way.'

She hangs up and heads toward home.

The filmy afternoon sunshine and glimmer of springtime in the air have stirred the Dale's year-round residents from dormancy. People are running errands, chatting in front of the post office and library. Neighbors wave at her from porches and yards. One teenaged boy is even washing his car, as though they've seen the last of the season's mud, slush-splatters and road salt.

Rounding the corner onto Cottage Row, she sees Luther leaning against his SUV and laughing about something with Max and Jiffy.

'And then he drank it!' Bella hears him say, and the boys explode with laughter.

'All of it?' Max asks.

'Almost – until my mom said, "April Fool."' He shifts his gaze to Bella. 'Oh, hi, Bella. I was just telling these guys about—'

'No! Don't tell her!' Jiffy says.

'Tell me what?'

Max giggles. 'Just about the crazy trick Luther's mom played on his dad for April Fool's Day.'

'She got him good, and not just that once. She did it every single year.' Luther shakes his head. 'You'd think he'd have learned to see it coming, but he never did.'

'I can't believe he thought it was coff—'

'Max! If you tell your mom, then you can't do the trick on her, plus she might tell my mom and then I can't do the trick on her.'

'You're right. Mom, we can't tell you.'

Jiffy turns to Luther. 'You can't say it either.'

Luther mimes pulling a zipper across his mouth with a muffled, 'Lips are sealed.'

Bella's no psychic, but she foresees a fake-coffee incident in her very near future.

'How much homework do you guys have?' she asks the boys.

'We just have to work on our stories. Mine is about me and

my puppy. The title is called, "The Adventures of Jiffy and Jelly".'

'Oh, I love it!' Bella turns to Max. 'Did you think of a title for yours, yet?'

He nods. '"The Adventures of Max and Chance and Spidey".'

'Hey, no fair! That's 'xactly the same as my title.'

'No it isn't,' Max shoots back. 'Yours is called "The Adventures of Jiffy and Jelly", not "The Adventures of—"'

'Oh, Isabella!' Pandora trills.

Bella turns to see her beckoning from the foot of Valley View's front porch steps.

'Be right there!' She sighs, the day's weariness catching up with her again.

'You OK, Bella?'

'I'm fine, just tired, thanks, Luther.'

'You've always got your hands full, but especially now, apparently.' He indicates the boys, and then Pandora.

She nods. 'Yep. I guess I'd better . . .'

'Right. And I'd better . . .'

'Right.'

'What are you guys talking about?' Jiffy doesn't miss a thing.

'Is it about an after-school snack?' Max asks. 'Because my stomach feels a lot better and it also feels starving.'

'So does mine. Only I didn't even barf yesterday. I felt like I was going to but I held it in.'

'How?' Max asks.

'Like this.' Jiffy clamps his mouth shut, freckled cheeks bulging.

Luther shoots a questioning look at Bella.

'Too much sugar,' she explains, even more exhausted at the memory of that ordeal.

He gives a thoughtful nod and turns back to the boys. 'You know, I'm going to take a short drive around while I'm waiting for Odelia, and—'

'Oh, can I come?' Jiffy asks. 'I like to take a short drive around. And sometimes I like a long drive. Like when I moved here from Arizona last year, we had to drive almost all the way from sea to shining sea.'

'Me too,' Max chimes in, 'when I moved here last year.'

'You only went from sea to shining lake, and my drive was a lot longer, and by the way, we got to stop a lot of times for food and snacks.'

'Sometimes you get to do that on short drives, too,' Luther says. 'If you two want to tag along with me, it might even happen on our drive today.'

'Can the food and snacks be chocolate cupcakes?'

'I think we'd better stay away from sweets today,' Bella says quickly.

'Are you coming on the short drive with us, Bella?' Jiffy asks.

'No.'

'Are you sure? Because you said *we*.'

'Nope, Bella is staying here,' Luther says, 'and you guys are coming with me, as long as we get Jiffy's mom's permission.'

'We don't have to. My mom always permisses me to do stuff at Bella's because it's not dangerous.'

'Let's go ask her anyway.' Luther puts a firm hand on each boy's shoulder and steers them toward Misty's.

'Thanks, Luther. Have fun, guys.'

She heads toward Valley View.

Pandora is gazing up at the house. Her back is to Bella, but her posture indicates that her feeling of foreboding hasn't disappeared.

'It's the most peculiar thing, Isabella,' she says, without turning as Bella approaches. 'Do you see that turret where the Teacup Suite is located?'

She nods. The windows are open up there. Nigel might very well be able to hear the conversation.

'For a moment, it was the Bastille.'

'What?'

'The Bastille is a landmark vestige of the French Revolution, and—'

'I know what the Bastille is, Pandora. I just don't get what you're saying.'

'As I gazed upon Valley View in meditation, my spirit guides transformed the turret into the Bastille,' she explains – sort of – with her usual dramatic flair, rolling the 'r's.

'Why, uh, would they turn the turret into the Bastille?'

'To deliver a message through a symbolic image.'

'What's the message?'

'I haven't a clue.'

Bella might, but chooses her words carefully, conscious about being overheard. 'I'm no medium, Pandora, but your aunt and Nigel are staying in the turret room. Do you think it has something to do with them?'

'I don't know.'

'Well . . . you mentioned that Eudora went to culinary school in Paris.'

'Le Cordon Bleu.'

'Exactly.' She waits for Pandora to grasp the obvious, but is met with an exasperated sigh.

'Isabella, when my guides refer to Paris' – pronounced *Parrrrree* – 'they show me *la tour Eiffel*.' Pronounced with such an exaggerated accent that it takes Bella a moment to translate.

'Oh, the Eiffel Tower. Right. But the Bastille is also in Paris, so I was just thinking—'

'That isn't how I work.'

'Spirit shorthand?'

'Precisely.'

'So what does the Bastille signify in your spirit shorthand?'

Pandora shrugs. 'I've never seen it before.'

'Maybe it's about book club. We're reading *A Tale of Two Cities*, and it's about the French Revolution.'

'Ah! The revolution! Like the song!'

'You mean the one Luther couldn't hear?'

'Yes, I couldn't place it, but it was so familiar. Classic rock and roll. The band is from the UK.'

'The Beatles! Revolution!' Bella blurts, like a *Name that Tune* contestant.

She braces herself to hear Pandora's tale of appearing on that show, but Pandora shakes her head.

'Not the Beatles. Not that "Revolution". It isn't the title. It's in the lyrics.'

'Maybe I know it. Can you sing it for me?'

'I'm afraid not. That dreadful cruise line advert is now ringing in my head.'

'Mine, too.'

Bella stares up at the house, thinking of Nigel, wondering where he fits in, if at all, and trying to piece things together in a logical way.

'Is there a connection between Beacon Atlantic and the Bastille, Pandora? Let's think about it. I mean, they both start with a B.'

'That isn't it,' Pandora says flatly.

'Well, Beacon Atlantic sails to Europe. The Bastille is in Europe.'

'The Bastille is in France. The cruise line's only European port is in the UK.'

'All right, well, let's keep thinking.'

There must be some connection between Pandora's vision and *A Tale of Two Cities*. It's set during the French Revolution, and one of the main characters is imprisoned in the Bastille.

'The cats!'

Pandora's eyes snap open.

'I've had Chance and Spidey imprisoned because of your aunt's phobia,' Bella reminds her. 'Imprisoned . . . like Charles Darnay in the Bastille. And—'

'That isn't it.'

'Wait, yesterday, Drew – Dr Bailey – dropped off their monthly prescription medication. It's called Revolution.'

She waits for Pandora's eyes to widen with recognition, but they narrow and she shakes her head. 'No.'

'Yes! It makes perfect sense.'

'Not to me, and not to Spirit.'

'OK, so maybe it's not about the cats . . .'

Or Drew Bailey.

Even though he prescribed the Revolution, and he's been on her mind.

'You're the one who's always saying there are no coincidences, Pandora.'

Well, not just Pandora. Everyone here in the Dale says it. *'There are no coincidences'* is as ubiquitous a Lily Dale catchphrase as *'Nothing is impossible.'*

'And,' Bella goes on, 'you're the one who chose *A Tale of Two Cities* for book club. Why?'

'Because the club needs to appreciate classic literature.'

'Yes, but why *that* book?'

'Because Dickens is my favorite. He knew my ancestors, you know. Cornelius and Theodora Feeney were his—'

'Neighbors, right. But you could have picked any Dickens title. I think Spirit might have influenced your choice. And I think *A Tale of Two Cities* holds the key to the message.'

Pandora stares at her for a long moment.

'You may be correct about that, Isabella. If you'll excuse me, I'm going to walk over to the Stump and meditate there.'

'All right. Good luck.'

'I do wish people would stop saying that in regard to Spirit. This has nothing to do with luck, as I told Auntie Eudora. She's hoping her reading will help her recover lost belongings. But it doesn't work that way.'

Bella watches Pandora walk away and then turns back to look at the turret. It's just a turret. She sees a shadow move across the window. Nigel is there. Has he been listening?

And if Eudora is searching for lost belongings . . . does she expect to find them here in Lily Dale? At Valley View?

She thinks of Nigel standing on the chair, searching the high bookshelves, claiming to have overlooked all those copies of Calla's novel.

Two doors down, Luther emerges from Misty's house with Max and Jiffy. They race ahead and jump into the back seat of his SUV. Luther glances up at Odelia's house. The 'Reading In Progress' sign is still on her door.

He sees Bella and waves. 'We'll be back in a bit. Enjoy your down time!'

'Thanks, Luther. I will.'

She watches them drive away.

If adventure you're a'seekin' . . .

You can't go wrong with Beacon . . .

She sits on the porch step with her phone and opens the search window again. This time, she clicks a link to a news story about the *Queen Jane*. It's a video segment from a cable news network, with the tagline *Maiden Voyage Mystery*.

Bella clicks play and lowers the volume, just in case Nigel is around.

On screen, a female reporter is standing beside a cruise terminal sign, talking into a microphone.

'The *Queen Jane*, the glistening crown jewel of new cruise line Beacon Atlantic's fleet, set sail from Southampton, England, last week amid much fanfare. Six days into the transatlantic crossing, the ship experienced rough seas. That's not unusual at this time of year in the North Atlantic. What happened in the dead of that night, according to one concerned passenger, most definitely *is*.'

Bella tilts her phone for a better view as the scene shifts to an interior. A man sits on a couch. He appears to be in his mid-sixties, with a slight build and sleek silver hair. A chyron identifies him as *Harold Yarosh, Queen Jane Passenger*.

'The Wi-Fi on board was spotty, so I stepped out onto the balcony with my laptop to see if I could get a better signal,' he says, in what Bella recognizes as a Long Island accent. 'I was trying to load a website and that little icon just kept spinning and spinning, you know . . .'

'And what happened?' The same reporter is sitting across from him, asking questions in an earlier taped interview.

'I heard a noise on one of the balconies overhead. Not right overhead, but up there somewhere. There was some movement, like a thump – and then something just went . . .' He gestures with his hand. 'Whoosh, overboard.'

'When you say "something" . . .'

'Something big and heavy.'

'Did you get a look at it?'

'Like I said, it flew past. Not right in front of me, off to the side, but . . .' He pauses to swallow. 'I know what it looked like to me.'

'And what is that?'

'A person.'

'A person . . .'

'Yes.'

In voiceover, the reporter interjects, 'Harold Yarosh is now almost certain he saw someone fall or jump overboard. But at the time, he dismissed the idea.'

The man shifts his weight on the couch. 'It was dark. And, you know, it happened so fast. I couldn't tell where it came from.'

'But it was somewhere overhead?'

'Well, yeah, I mean, when someone – when *something* falls past you, it has to come from overhead, right?'

'Did you look up after it fell?'

'I looked *down* after it fell. I . . . you know, I leaned over the railing.'

'What did you see?'

'Nothing. There was nothing to see. We were barreling through the ocean at high speed in the dark.'

'And you didn't look up to see where it had come from?'

'It could have been anywhere. The ship is massive. Our cabin was on a lower deck. And I couldn't wait to get back inside. The waves were rough.'

'Did you report the incident?'

'No. I mean, I mentioned it to my wife, and then, to be honest, I put it out of my head.'

The camera angle widens to show a woman sitting beside him on the couch. She looks a little like Cleopatra, if Cleopatra were an aging suburbanite with bifocals perched on the end of her nose. Her chyron reads *Linda Yarosh, Queen Jane Passenger.*

'To be honest, when he told me he'd just seen someone go overboard, I said, "Harry, you're drunk."'

'I wasn't drunk.'

'He was not drunk.'

'We'd had a glass of wine with dinner.'

'Two glasses of wine,' his wife says, 'but he was perfectly sober.'

Again, the voiceover: 'The Yaroshes forgot about the incident until they got home and realized they'd left an item on board the *Queen Jane.*'

'Linda was unpacking and one of her bracelets wasn't there. She asked me to call the cruise line and see if the housekeeping staff had found it. I got online to search for the contact information and the first thing I saw was a news item about someone who'd gone missing.'

The scene cuts back to the reporter standing at the cruise terminal, this time alongside a paper flier taped to the wall behind him, the edges flapping in a brisk wind.

'Tilly Morton, a housekeeper on board the *Queen Jane*, was reported absent from her scheduled shift shortly after the ship's arrival in New York Harbor. A thorough search of the vessel confirmed that she was not on board. Rigid monitoring procedures make it virtually impossible for anyone to disembark the ship without detection. All passengers and crew are required to pass through security checkpoints at disembarkation.'

Bella squints at the flier, trying to make out the details. The word 'MISSING' is printed above a photo of a middle-aged woman with long red hair and glasses. Her phone screen is much too small for her to make out the woman's features.

Harold and Linda Yarosh are back on screen, looking somber.

'As soon as I heard about this, I remembered what I'd seen on the balcony that night, and I wondered . . .' He shrugs. 'I just wonder, you know? Whether that was her falling, or . . .'

'Jumping,' Linda says. 'She could have jumped. We just don't know what happened to her.'

'Or if what Harold Yarosh saw that night was, indeed, the missing woman.' A dramatic voiceover wraps up the segment over an image of a ship disappearing on a gray horizon. 'One thing is certain. Tilly Morton boarded the *Queen Jane* in England, and failed to disembark in New York a week later. It's as if she vanished into thin air.'

TWELVE

Inspiration Stump is the most sacred ground in Lily Dale. A legendary tree charged with powerful vortexes once stood in this clearing along a woodland path in Leolyn Wood. Its remains are now preserved in concrete with three steps.

During the summer season, it serves as a stage of sorts, or a pulpit, as mediums gather here to channel energy for visitors who crowd the benches. Largely deserted the rest of the year, the shrine has been buried beneath a frozen white shroud for three months. Last week's thaw melted all but a few gritty patches of snow.

On this late March afternoon, Pandora has this peaceful, primordial spot to herself. Sitting on a bench, clogs caked in mud, she surrounds herself in protective white light and meditates.

Or rather, she attempts to.

But there are too many troubling thoughts on her mind – about Orville, the divorce, and what a fool she's been. She's out of money, out of options, out of time and out of luck. She can't bear to speculate about what will happen to her when she loses Cotswold Corner. And it's no use dwelling on how she ended up in this situation.

In the end, it was all about misplaced trust. She'd trusted the wrong man. When he betrayed her, she'd trusted her own instincts and fled to a spiritualist sanctuary in the Canadian mountains.

She hadn't intended to leave Valley View for good. She'd just needed to get away from Orville, from everything.

A ghastly mistake. When she returned, the locks had been changed and the house was emptied and vacant, an estate agent's sign posted in the yard. Orville had placed her belongings in storage. There they remained for the duration of the divorce proceedings and a long while after. She didn't have the heart, nor the energy, to face the remains of happier days.

Being back at Valley View, with Nigel's endless questions about Marley House and the old days on Doughty Street, has dredged it all up again. His efforts to jog her aunt's memory have succeeded in jarring Pandora's.

She'd thought she might be able to meditate here, away from it all. Unfortunately, there are times when coming to the Stump, even alone in the off-season, is like searching for a friend in a crowded arena. Bombarded with spirits all needing to be heard, she asks her guides to clarify the message she needs to hear.

'The song,' she whispers. 'That's all I need right now. Just send the song.'

In uni, she'd learned that music, unlike spirit voices, is organized sound that the brain can anticipate and interpret.

Ah, there. It's playing faintly, whispering in the bare tree branches . . .

Electric guitar . . . Drums . . . Synthesizer . . .

The vocals . . .

Fighting . . . a revolution . . . kneeling to pray . . .

Synthesizer again, building, building, building . . .

She becomes aware of a rustling in the undergrowth at the edge of the clearing. She turns toward it, and the bare-branched shrubs become tall, sun-parched grasses. Goosebumps prickle the skin on the back of her neck. She struggles to keep her breathing slow and steady as the music builds and the lurking creature looms closer.

And when it happens – when the scream, the *yowl*, reverberates through the woods – an animal leaps from the shadows. It isn't a dog, or a wolf, or a coyote, but . . .

A jackal?

The jackal!

Impossible. They aren't found in New York State. Not even in North America.

Yet it's here, yowling, hurtling toward her, mouth gaping, fangs bared, claws outstretched . . .

In the last second before the beast is upon her, it vanishes. Alone once more, Pandora hears her own ragged breathing, and the music playing on.

Drums.

Guitars.

Synthesizer.

Lyrics.

All at once it hits her: the name of the band, and the title of the song . . .

And now it makes sense. The jackal. The Bastille. Orville. Nigel . . .

Auntie Eudora.

A terrible, dreadful logic seeps over her.

Bella returns to the back parlor to read one more chapter of her book before Luther returns with Max.

She knows it's the efficient thing to do. It's the smart thing to do. As opposed to, say, sitting down at the computer in her study to search for more information about Tilly Morton, who vanished from the *Queen Jane*. Or Nigel Spencer-Watson, who's managed not to leave a trace on the internet.

This time, she isn't curled against the deep cushions with the open book propped against her knees. She's perched on the edge of the couch, feet on the floor, book on her lap, alert as a passenger waiting on a station bench. Her ears are trained, not for a boarding announcement, but for the slightest creak indicating that Nigel is on the move.

This is far from the first time she's found herself alone in the house with a virtual stranger. Nor is it the first time she's had qualms about a guest's true identity.

Part of her wants to believe that it's plausible for an elderly Englishman to exist without a digital footprint. It might be easier to swallow if he were a recluse, or someone whose livelihood hadn't involved academia. But even if he'd stretched the truth about having been published, aren't faculty listed on college websites and in course catalogues?

Another part of her – the part that's growing more apprehensive with every tick of the mantel clock – is certain that Nigel is up to no good.

. . . it was the epoch of belief, it was the epoch of incredulity . . .

Dickens again, with the enduring theme of duality in *A Tale of Two Cities*.

Belief, incredulity.
Light, dark.
Best, worst.

At best, Nigel might be taking advantage of Pandora's aunt. At worst . . .

What if Tilly Morton hadn't fallen, or jumped, from the *Queen Jane*?

What if Nigel had something to do with it?

Seriously, Bella?

She wishes someone, other than her sensible inner voice, would say exactly that. Because in this moment, even her sensible inner voice is wavering.

She toys with her phone, wishing she could call Drew Bailey, and trying to remember exactly why she can't.

She rereads the brief text exchange that concludes with *Thanks, but I can't.*

Is what she'd said, and how she'd said it, really so finite? He's usually quick to reply to her texts. Is the fact that he hasn't a sign that he's interpreted it to mean she no longer wants to see him?

Oh, come on. Maybe he's just busy!

And even if that's not the case, isn't it precisely what she'd wanted him to think?

Why is she second-guessing herself now? She can't have it both ways. She can't push Drew away when she's feeling strong, and turn to him for support when she isn't.

She snaps the book closed and tosses it aside. If Sam were alive, none of this would be happening. If she could just talk to him – no, if she could just hear him – he'd tell her what she should do. She leans her head back and closes her tired eyes, her left thumb feeling for the rings that are no longer on her fourth finger.

'I need you,' she whispers.

The words are meant for Sam.

The voice she hears in her head is Drew Bailey's.

If ever there was a woman who didn't need rescuing, it's you.

That was . . . when? Just yesterday?

Hearing a sound, she tenses. Nigel? Nadine?

The front door opens, then closes. Footsteps clack along the hardwoods.

Eudora.

Bella jumps to her feet, hurries into the hall, and spots her, halfway up the stairs.

'You're back! How did it go?'

'The so-called reading?' She turns to regard Bella through narrowed eyes. 'It was utterly abysmal. A complete waste of time.'

'What do you mean?'

'She's a charlatan. She got nothing. Nothing at all.'

'You mean Odelia couldn't read you?'

'That woman couldn't read the ABCs if they were illumin-ated in neon right in front of her,' Eudora snaps in an accent that sounds nothing like Pandora's prim and proper aunt.

She continues on up the stairs and closes the door to the suite with a resounding click.

Bella stares after her, wondering what went wrong. Were her expectations too high? Too specific? Pandora had mentioned that Eudora was hoping Odelia could help her find something.

Isn't that what everyone who comes to Lily Dale wants? To find something – or someone – they've lost? Often it's a loved one, but not always. Many visitors have lost their health, and seek healers to restore it. Many have lost their way, and ask the psychics to help guide them to the right path.

But it sounds like Eudora is looking for something more tangible, a personal belonging that's gone missing. It's not unusual for someone her age to misplace something. Just yesterday, Drew mentioned that his elderly father is always losing his drugstore reading glasses. But something tells Bella that whatever Eudora lost must be far more significant and valuable – and that Nigel is helping her search. Why else would he have climbed on a chair to comb the top book-shelves when there were hundreds of titles well within reach?

But if they're expecting to find it here in Lily Dale – *here* at Valley View – what can it possibly be?

It must be something Eudora left behind on her one and only visit, many years ago for Pandora's wedding. Or it could be something Pandora had in her possession when she lived here. So why not just ask her about it?

Because they don't want her to know.

Maybe that's what Pandora's spirit guides are trying to tell her – if one believes in spirit guides. If one doesn't believe, then maybe Pandora's subconscious mind is responsible. Either way, she obviously senses that—

Bella gasps as something nudges the back of her legs.

It's only Chance. The cat walks around her, bumping and rubbing her shins as she does when she's happy to see her.

'Hi, sweetie. It's OK. I was just – wait! What are you doing down here?'

She'd closed both cats into the Rose Room earlier, before heading to the bus stop. The house does have hidden passageways, including one in Bella's closet that leads to the basement. But she couldn't have gotten to it unless she'd managed to open the closet door, and the panel hidden behind the hanging clothes, and then the basement door in the kitchen.

Could there possibly be another tunnel Bella doesn't know about?

Nothing is impossible.

Ah, the Lily Dale credo. But in this case, it might actually be the case. Valley View's walls conceal well over a century's worth of secrets.

Bella scoops up the cat and hurries upstairs. The door to the Rose Room is still closed. When she opens it, she sees Spidey asleep on the bed. Relieved, she steps over the threshold, closes the door, and sets Chance on the floor.

'How the heck did you get out of here?'

She looks around the room. The first time she set foot in here, she'd felt as if it had been created just for her, with its antique furniture, lace curtains, creamy bedding, white woodwork, wallpaper imprinted with cabbage roses in her favorite color, the splashy shade that's somewhere between pink and orange and red . . .

Sushi sky.

She thinks of Sam, and her left thumb goes to her bare ring finger.

She walks over to the bureau. One of the bottom drawers

isn't closed all the way. She'd learned the hard way, back when Chance was nursing her litter in this room, never to leave a drawer open even a crack. One of the kittens had gone missing and after a frantic search, Bella had found him snuggled among her socks.

She's been careful to close drawers and cabinets ever since. But she'd overslept this morning, been in such a flurry . . .

Still, she hadn't taken anything from this drawer today, or in a long while. It holds stacks of sweaters from her teaching days – certainly nothing special, and not something she'd wear around the house on an ordinary day.

About to push the drawer closed, she pulls it open instead.

The sweaters are no longer neatly folded. They aren't in a crumpled heap, but it looks as though someone went through them. If it had been a cat burrowing into a cozy nest, there'd be telltale dark fur shed on her nicest sweater, a creamy white cashmere at the top of the stack.

She closes the drawer and opens the one above it. Her folded jeans and leggings, too, show signs of having been disturbed.

Remembering Pandora's unsavory characters, and Luther's admission that burglars might very well be hanging around the Dale at this time of year, Bella turns to survey the room again.

This time, she notices jarring details.

At the foot of the four poster bed, a corner of the dust ruffle hem is lifted, caught on the box spring. Opposite, the window seat cushions are askew. The spines along the built-in bookshelves are no longer aligned.

Her heart races. Chance didn't escape the room through a secret passageway. She slipped out when someone opened the door.

Bella turns quickly back to the bureau and opens the jewelry box.

Her gold wedding band, diamond engagement ring and the tourmaline necklace are right on top, just as they should be. So is the folded note Luther had given her, with the Einstein quote: *Everyone who is seriously involved in the pursuit of science becomes convinced that a spirit is manifest in the laws of the Universe.*

Trembling, she puts the rings on her fourth finger and, after several tries, fastens the pendant around her neck for safekeeping.

There isn't a doubt in her mind that someone has been in this room, going through her belongings . . .

Or that a burglar would have pocketed the most valuable things in it.

She spots something, almost camouflaged, among the floral printed window seat cushions.

She steps closer, staring in disbelief at the round, rosy-colored fruit.

It's a pomegranate.

THIRTEEN

Pandora checks over her shoulder one last time before slipping round to the back door of her cottage. The front entrance would be plainly visible from Valley View, should someone happen to glance across Melrose Park. But the rear is secluded, and there's a key hidden under a terra cotta planter on the low concrete step.

She uses it to let herself in, closes the door behind her, and heaves a sigh of relief. Cotswold Corner may be a shabby little cottage, but it's home and she's grateful to have it, precarious as her ownership may be.

She takes in the cookbooks lining an open shelf above the stove, the silk English bluebells in a vase on the table, the old electric Metamec wall clock that once hung in the kitchen at Marley House . . .

According to the hands, it's just past noon. Or . . . midnight?

She stares at the motionless clock, realizing that the house, too, is preternaturally still. The refrigerator isn't humming.

Pandora flips a light switch. Nothing happens. Her gaze falls on the tall rubber-banded stack of unpaid bills on the counter, countless utility bills among them.

The temperature feels well below the fifty-five degrees she's been forced to keep the thermostat set to this winter, and she knows that Spirit has nothing to do with the chill.

'Yes, well . . . get on with it,' she mutters, stepping out of her muddy clogs.

She goes into the adjacent parlor, rustic hardwoods creaking beneath her stocking feet. Today, she has no critical eye for the room's small size and flea market furniture. Today, it's nothing but cozy and homey. She aches to turn on the lamps, turn up the heat, and curl up on the old chintz sofa with a mug of tea, a book and her cat.

But Lady Pippa is waiting at Valley View, and she really

does need to get back to her. And, of course, to Eudora and Nigel.

She looks at the gallery of framed photographs on the wall above the sofa. Family, mostly. Pandora and her parents together and separately, her mother as a young woman and a matronly one; her father as a child, a young man, an older young man, but never old. There's one of him with Auntie Eudora, snapped in the late 1950s.

Dad was a young husband and perhaps already a father, wearing a wedding band and an overcoat. He has a protective arm across Auntie Eudora's shoulders. She's still a teenager carrying a bit of baby fat, round-faced with short bangs, dark lipstick, and a full-skirted sleeveless dress revealing fleshy arms.

They're posing in front of a brick wall. There are two large suitcases at Dad's feet, as though he'd just set them down. A Scottish Fold kitten peers out from behind Auntie Eudora's bobby socks and saddle shoes.

A few years after her father died, Pandora stumbled across the photo in a family album. Mum had confirmed that the kitten was indeed Pandora's own Dodger. He'd originally belonged to Auntie Eudora. The photo had been taken when Dad delivered her to her finishing school in Switzerland, apparently with Dodger along for the ride.

Pandora turns to the built-in cabinet that holds her vinyl record collection. She hasn't played the albums in years, doesn't even have a turntable, but she keeps them for nostalgia's sake.

They're alphabetized, beginning with Abba and ending with The Who.

She pulls out the last album in the row. 'Who's Next' was released back in '71 when she was just a lass, living with her mother at Marley House. She'd sit beside the hi-fi stereo listening to music for hours, singing along.

'You're splendid, luv,' Mum used to say. 'The next Petula Clark.'

Pandora wanted to sound like Petula, but Auntie Eudora looked like her – a sleek blonde in go-go boots and miniskirts, the baby fat long melted away.

Though she's maintained her svelte figure, her aunt bears little resemblance to the young woman she once was, or even the middle-aged woman she'd been when they last met here in the Dale.

Ah, but who does?

Pandora thinks of the haggard stranger she'd glimpsed in the mirror earlier. Everyone grows older. Some – Feeney women – more gracefully than others, but time does snatch one's looks as it marches on, along with other spoils.

Saddened as she is by Nigel's revelation about her aunt's cognitive struggles, Pandora finds herself relieved, as well. Senility would seem to explain the strange sense that the Eudora she'd known and cherished has vanished from her life, even though she's right here, right now.

It would seem to, but does it, entirely?

Pandora has known people – friends, clients – who have dealt with mental illness. As an empath, it's something she can often perceive. Though she's intellectually aware that her aunt may be suffering from dementia – not just because Nigel told her but because of the personality and behavioral changes – she hasn't been psychically aware. It may be that she's simply too emotionally invested in the relationship, and yet . . .

Something is wrong. Something is off. She can't help but feel that Eudora – her own flesh and blood, her family, her champion – is no longer an ally.

She looks down at the record album. Spirit has sent a song – the lead single and closing track, 'Won't Get Fooled Again' – to warn Pandora about Nigel.

She'd seen him as Orville for a reason. Her guides are warning her not to let Nigel fool her as Orville had. She can't trust him, because he, too, might blindside her. Not romantically, of course.

She supposes he could be two-timing Auntie Eudora. But this warning feels more ominous.

And then there's the jackal.

The moment she'd seen the creature in the woods, she'd known that Isabella had been right about Pandora's vision of the Bastille. It must have something to do with *A Tale of Two Cities*, because there's a jackal in the book. Not an animal,

merely a narrative nickname for barrister Sydney Carton, the
jackal to his law partner's 'lion'. Carton works hard behind
the scenes while his partner gets the glory when a case is won,
much like the lowly jackal assists the mighty lion with a kill.

Pandora fails to see what this has to do with Nigel Spencer-
Watson. She doesn't doubt that he, like Carton's jackal, has a
brilliant mind. Perhaps he, too, has led an unsung existence
in the shadow of more esteemed literary scholars. Or . . . did
he vie with another suitor for Auntie Eudora's affections, as
Carton does in the novel's love triangle?

She supposes any or perhaps all of those scenarios might
contribute to the cryptic message. But none would explain
Pandora's growing sense that doom is encroaching on the Dale.

'Bella! Is everything OK?' Odelia asks, opening the door.

'I'm . . . not sure. Can I talk to you?'

'Of course. Come in. Is it Max? His stomach?'

'No, it's not Max. He's out with Luther.'

'Luther!'

'Yes, he stopped by to see you, and since you were busy
he took Max and Jiffy for a drive to give me a break.'

'Well, good for him. You need one. Only you don't look
like you're taking one. What's going on?'

Bella follows her into the house. It's small, homey, and cluttered with books and magazines, bric-a-brac and framed photos.
The walls, trim and ceilings are painted – none of it white, and
not always in coordinating colors. But for the most part, the
mishmash seems to work in the same way Odelia's wardrobe
and recipes do. Unique, wildly creative, and pure *her*.

'Come on into the kitchen,' Odelia says. 'Would you like
some lemonade? Or a cup of hot cocoa?'

'Cocoa, please . . . something hot sounds perfect right now.'

'And something hot you shall have. Have a seat. I'm working
on a couple of new recipes.'

The kitchen is a fragrant shambles, with ingredients spread
all over the countertops and a pair of pots simmering on the
stove.

'This is the cocoa. That's lamb stew,' Odelia says. 'I'm
hoping Mother Nature takes the hint.'

'Well, the forecast is for a beautiful day tomorrow.'

'I know, but this is Lily Dale, Bella. March always comes in like a lion and goes out like one, too.'

Lion . . .

Something nags at the edge of Bella's consciousness. Something about a lion.

'You were wearing lion slippers this morning, Odelia,' she points out, though that isn't it. 'I hope Mother Nature didn't take that as a hint.'

'Oh, dear. You're right.' She takes two mugs from the cabinet. 'You have such a good eye for small details, Bella.'

She remembers what Calla said, about how she catches the details the others miss.

Great, then do your thing.

Lion . . . what is it about lions?

'I just need to make two quick calls,' she tells Odelia, sitting at the table and taking out her phone.

She dials Misty's number. It rings . . . rings . . . rings . . .

'Hi, Bells! What's up?'

'Are you busy?'

'I was trying to do an online assignment, but Keith keeps interrupting me. Never channel a drummer!'

'I'll keep that in mind, Misty. Hey, can I ask you a favor?'

'Anything, as long as I can ask one of you, too.'

'Of course. Can I have Luther drop Max and Jiffy with you for a little while when he gets back?'

'No problem, Bells. And when you come over to pick him up, you can stay for a minute and tell me about *A Tale of Two Cities*!'

'Um . . . sure,' she agrees, as if condensing a nineteenth-century historical novel into a minute will be a breeze.

She dials Luther as Odelia ladles cocoa into the mugs.

He picks up right away. 'Hi, Bella. We're almost back. We've had a nice drive. Saw lots of trees, houses, a few deer, a few birds . . . nothing else, if you know what I mean.'

'Oh, good. I'm at Odelia's.'

'Are you trying to talk some sense into her about the cruise?'

'No, I'm . . . can you just come over? Drop the boys with Misty first. She's waiting for them. And make sure you watch them go inside, because they wander and I don't want them wandering today.'

'Got it. See you in a few.'

She hangs up as Odelia sets a steaming mug in front of her. It says, 'World's Best Psychic.'

About to sip, Bella peers into it. 'Is that . . . what *is* that?'

'A giant marshmallow.'

'Not that . . . *that.*'

'Oh, it's a slice of jalapeño pepper. As I said, it's *hot* cocoa. The jalapeño gives it a nice kick. Try it.'

Bella sips, swallows sweet liquid fire.

'Just the thing to get you through the late day slump, isn't it?' Odelia asks, settling across from her.

'That . . . it . . . is,' she manages in a scorched voice.

Recovering a bit, she tells Odelia that she's certain someone rummaged through her personal belongings and planted a pomegranate in her room.

'And before you say it's Spirit,' Bella says, 'it could have been Max, playing a trick on me. He might have overheard me talking to you about the mess in the kitchen last night. And I know he and Jiffy are plotting April Fool's tricks.'

'Where would Max get a pomegranate?'

'I have no idea, and I'm planning on asking him about it. I'd rather think he's responsible, than that someone's been prowling around Valley View.'

'Or that Spirit is manipulating objects to deliver a message.'

'That, too. Anyway, I know something went wrong when Eudora was here. What happened?'

Odelia's red-lipsticked mouth tightens into a straight line above her mug. 'I couldn't read her. It happens sometimes. Some people just can't open themselves to spirit energy even when they think they're trying. I couldn't get anything at all. She was completely closed off. And she kept asking questions, interrupting my meditation . . . it was very distracting.'

'What was she asking?'

'She wanted me to ask Spirit to help her find something she'd lost.'

'What was it?'

'She wouldn't tell me. She said if I was psychic and Spirit

was real, I wouldn't need to ask her that. She got very testy with me. I finally told her I wasn't going to get anything and that we needed to end the session. Naturally, I wasn't going to accept money anyway, but before I could mention that, she said she wasn't paying me, called me a scam artist, and stormed out of here.'

'I'm pretty sure there's a scam artist involved in this, and I know it's not you, Odelia.'

'Pandora's aunt?'

'Or Nigel.'

'Interesting. A spirit was attempting to make contact with him this morning at breakfast. Female energy, recently crossed over, and I sensed she had a bone to pick with Nigel. She made me wonder if he might be some kind of grifter, like Levi Joe Hicks.'

Bella's eyes widen. She, too, has been thinking of the career criminal who'd checked into Valley View last fall under an assumed name. She'd discovered his true identity after conducting an image search online using a candid photograph she'd snapped.

Before she can comment, the front door opens and Luther calls, 'Special delivery for Odelia Lauder!'

Odelia quickly smooths her hair just before he pops into the room, holding a bouquet of orange tulips.

'Luther! These are beautiful.'

'And so are you, my dear.'

Odelia blushes and heads for the small sunroom she uses for her readings. 'I'll just go get a vase for these.'

Bella smiles at Luther. 'Look at you, all sweet and smitten.'

'I have a feeling a special guy in your life might have some pretty spring flowers for you, too.'

'You saw Drew?'

He laughs. 'I meant Max. The boys and I stopped at the store for a healthy snack and when we saw the spring bouquets, we decided to buy them for you two and Misty.'

'Oh . . . that's . . .' Bella feels her face grow hot. 'That's so sweet, Luther. Thanks so much.'

'I wouldn't be surprised if Drew brought you flowers, too, though.'

Yeah, well . . . she would be.

She changes the subject. 'You didn't find any evidence of outsiders prowling around the Dale, then?'

'Not a one. Pandora is prone to exaggeration. Must run in the family.'

'It must,' she murmurs. 'But—'

'Look what I found!' Odelia returns with a vase and a long houndstooth duster. 'This is Eudora's coat. She ran out of here so fast she forgot it. Can you take it to her when you head home, Bella?'

'Sure.' She smells the woman's perfume clinging to the fabric as she hangs it over the back of a chair. It isn't unpleasant scent-wise, but Eudora is becoming increasingly so.

Bella brings Luther up to speed while Odelia busies herself arranging tulips and talking him into a mug of *hot* cocoa. He agrees that Bella's plan is a good one, but cautions her to be careful.

'You don't know who or what you're dealing with, Bella. I'm not saying this man could be dangerous, but you never know.'

She nods. That's why, before leaving Valley View, she'd hurried up to Pandora's room to collect Lady Pippa and settled her into the Rose Room with Chance and Spidey. She'd locked the cats in. Just a precaution, until she could figure out what was going on.

'There's something else,' she says, pulling up the link to Tilly Morton's disappearance and handing him her phone.

He reads it in silence, with Odelia looking over his shoulder.

'I knew it!' she says. 'I knew my guides were warning me about Beacon Atlantic!'

'But what does a missing housekeeper on the *Queen Jane* have to do with us going to Bermuda?' Luther asks.

'I don't know, but Spirit wouldn't be warning me if it didn't have meaning.'

'Pandora seems troubled by something, too,' Bella says.

Odelia raises an eyebrow. 'It's called a hangover.'

'No, I mean she was hearing music about a revolution and seeing visions of the Bastille.' Bella also explains her own theories – that it has to do with the cats being locked up, or with *A Tale of Two Cities*.

'I'd like to think that Spirit is criticizing her book club selection,' Odelia comments, 'but somehow, I doubt that's it. Have you told her what you found online about Nigel?'

'You mean, what I *didn't* find about Nigel? Not yet.' She turns to Luther. 'Do you think I should wait until I know more?'

He nods. 'Since nothing's been stolen, and no real harm done, there's no sense in telling her that her aunt's boyfriend is a nosy old snoop. I hope that's all there is to it.'

She nods. 'I just keep thinking about Leona Gatto, you know? Her accidental drowning was no accident. What if Tilly Morton's fall wasn't an accident, either?'

Dusk has fallen when Pandora returns to Valley View, having lingered in the cold darkness of Cotswold Corner for as long as she could stand it. She was mulling over the scrambled Spirit message, yes, but she was also steeling herself to return to her former home and all that has unfolded beneath its roof, both past and present. If not for Lady Pippa, she might have stayed away a while longer.

How many times has she gazed wistfully across Melrose Park at this towering house, with porch and landscape lights glowing and lamplight spilling from the windows, with regret that it no longer belongs to her? Tonight, as she hurries toward it, she finds herself looking over her shoulder at the dark, deserted little cottage she's leaving behind.

How will she bear losing Cotswold Corner? Where will she go from here, destitute and forsaken? She's never felt so alone, or so frightened, in all her life.

Opening the front door, she hears voices and sees Auntie Eudora's houndstooth duster rather carelessly draped over the newel post. She begins to tiptoe toward the stairs, hoping to escape to the Jungle Room to compose herself before joining the others, but Isabella pokes her head in from the front parlor.

'Pandora, I'm glad you're back. We're just . . .' She gives her a closer look. 'Are you all right?'

'Of course. Why do you ask?'

'You just look as though you've been . . .'

Mercifully, she doesn't utter the dreaded word.

Pandora Feeney does not *cry*. Occasionally, wayward tears may fill her eyes and perhaps one or two may spill down her cheeks, but she's never allowed self-pity to consume her, and she won't start now.

Hearing a burst of laughter from the next room, she asks, 'Whatever is going on here?'

'It's cocktail hour, and Calla stopped by. She was just about to autograph a copy of her book for your aunt and Nigel.'

'Bella? Are you coming?' Calla calls.

'Yes, and Pandora's back. Here we come!'

There's nothing for her to do but follow Bella into the parlor. Her aunt and Nigel are sitting on the velvet sofa holding gimlet glasses. Calla is seated in an adjacent chair with a book and a pen.

'There you are, luv. We've missed you,' Auntie Eudora says.

She certainly looks like her usual self, gray hair neatly styled, wearing a black sweater dress and boots with heels that are impressive for a woman her age, or any age, really.

Nigel is dapper as always in tweeds and a tie.

Pandora has swapped her muddy clogs for a pair of rubber wellies, suitable for mucking about the Dale. She fits right in with Isabella and Calla, both of whom are clad in jeans and trainers.

'Sit down and I'll pour you a gimlet,' Isabella tells her.

Pandora shudders at the thought of gin. 'No, thank you.' She sinks into a chair opposite the sofa. After a moment, sensing a presence, she spots a filmy shadow drifting above Eudora's shoulder. Nadine?

'All right, how should I make this out?' Calla asks, pen poised over the open page.

'Just your name and the date will suffice,' Nigel tells her.

'Oh, I'm happy to personalize it.'

'That will only diminish its value.'

She looks up, startled by the comment, as is Pandora.

'Are you planning to sell it?' Calla asks, with a teasing note in her voice, but not in her eyes.

'Of course not,' he quickly assures her. 'I'm just accustomed to collecting rare books, you know . . . it's rather a hobby.'

'Trust me, this isn't a rare book. But if all you want is my name and the date, I'm happy to oblige.'

'Wait!' Isabella says, pulling her phone out of her pocket. 'I'd love a photo of this. It's our first Valley View book signing.'

'It is, isn't it? Great idea.' Calla leans toward the sofa, posed and smiling. 'Can you get all of us?'

'Yes.' Bella snaps a few pictures. 'Pandora, do you want to get in, too?'

'No, thank you.'

'How about just Pandora with Nigel and Eudora?' Calla suggests, leaning back.

'Oh, no, thank you,' Pandora says quickly, not wanting to be captured in her disheveled state.

'Yes, plenty of time for that later.' Nigel shifts as if he's equally uncomfortable with the impromptu photography session. 'Pandora, your aunt and I were discussing dinner plans. We've developed a fierce craving for Cornish pasties, haven't we, darling?'

'We have, we have.'

'What's a Cornish pasty?' Calla asks.

'A delicious little meat pie in a crimped pastry crust,' Eudora explains.

'Unfortunately, you won't find them here,' Isabella tells her.

'Oh, I'm quite aware. I thought I'd just whip them up, if you'll allow me to use the kitchen?'

'Sure, that's fine, but I'm not sure I have the ingredients on hand.'

'Let's take a look at the recipe and find out, shall we?' Nigel turns to Pandora. 'Now, then, where is it?'

'A recipe for Cornish pasties? I'm afraid I don't—'

'Yes, luv, you do,' her aunt says. 'It's in the Feeney family collection I gave you as a wedding gift.'

Right – the little book that resides on a shelf above the stove in Cotswold Corner.

Now would be an ideal time to confess the truth about where she lives. But as before, when Spirit clearly told her 'No,' she feels an overwhelming need to keep it to herself.

'Auntie Eudora, you're on holiday. We can't have you slaving away in the kitchen. We'll order takeaway – yes, chicken wings!' She gets to her feet. 'Now, if you'll all excuse me, I'm going to freshen up before dinner and—'

The shadow behind the sofa is taking solid form. And it isn't Nadine.

'Pandora?' someone asks, sounding far away indeed.

She stares. The jackal she'd glimpsed in the woods is floating just behind her Aunt Eudora. Its amber eyes bore into Pandora's, transforming into a familiar shade of blue as the creature's golden fur fades to a sleek gray.

'I'm going to . . . I have to . . . to tend to Lady Pippa.' She hurries from the room, dismayed when Isabella follows her.

'Pandora, wait. She's in the Rose Room.'

'What? Who?'

'Lady Pippa. She's with Chance and Spidey. I thought she could use some company. And I didn't want to let them roam around the house, with your aunt's ailurophobia.'

'I'll collect her on my way to my room.' She hurries up the stairs.

Again, Isabella is at her heels. 'The door is locked. I'll open it for you.'

'Why would you lock the cats in your room?'

'I just . . .' In the upstairs hall, Isabella touches her arm and whispers, 'Pandora, I—'

She breaks off at a sound below.

Pandora turns to see Orville at the foot of the stairs, and gasps.

But no, it's merely Nigel.

'Apologies for interrupting, ladies,' he says, 'but I wondered whether there might be another bottle of gin stashed away on the premises? We're running low, and I didn't want to be presumptuous and snoop about for it.'

Something in his tone, and his expression, rubs Pandora the wrong way.

'I'll come help you look,' Isabella says.

'Thank you.' Nigel smiles and makes no move to leave his post at the foot of the stairway.

Pandora sees Isabella's finger tremble a bit as she quickly enters the code on the keypad. Moments later, she's on her way up to the third floor with Lady Pippa in her arms, wondering what Isabella had been about to say, and why she'd seen the jackal morph not into Nigel, but into her Auntie Eudora.

After locking Chance and Spidey into the Rose Room again, Bella descends the stairs. Nigel is patiently waiting below, like a lion stalking its prey.

She can't read his expression as she descends, but his comment rings in her ears.

I didn't want to be presumptuous and snoop about.

A blatant lie.

Does he know she's aware that he's been doing exactly that?

'Why do you keep your bedroom door locked, Isabella?'

She shrugs, keeping her reaction casual. 'You never can be too careful.'

'No, I suppose not.'

Nigel's scrutiny is palpable. Not only was she unable to have a private word with Pandora, but she hasn't yet had a moment to text Luther the photos she'd snapped in the parlor. She needs a few minutes alone without tipping Nigel off to her suspicions. She can't even excuse herself to check on Max, because Misty had called earlier while they were all together in the parlor.

'Hey, Bells, the boys are having a great time playing with Jelly, and Max wants to stay for dinner. I'm making mac and cheese.'

'But . . . what about homework? Max has to work on his short story.'

'I'll help him, don't worry. I have a great imagination. And I promised they can watch *Ninja Zombie Battle*, too, so you've got a couple of hours to do whatever you're doing.'

Misty isn't exactly soft-spoken, and her message was clearly audible to the others, along with the puppy's gleeful barks and the boys' laughter.

'How lovely,' Eudora commented. 'Now you can relax and enjoy your cocktail.'

'Yes, but I really can't sit around for too long. I have a million things to do, and I need to find a menu and order your wings.'

'Yes, and I need to get back to work,' Calla said.

But Nigel and Eudora had urged them to linger until Pandora's return. Maybe now that she's back—

At the bottom of the flight, Bella's foot catches on Eudora's long coat.

'Careful, there!' Nigel reaches for her.

Instinctively, she twists away from him, grabbing for the railing. Her hand instead lands on the duster as she falls forward. It comes loose and she lands hard on the floor, clutching it.

'Oh, my. I tried to break your fall.'

'I know, thank you. I . . . sorry.'

She avoids Nigel's gaze. She knows he was only trying to help her. Of course he was. But in that instant, he was a lion and she was desperate to escape his claws.

Breathing hard, she realizes that Eudora's perfume isn't all that clings to the houndstooth fabric bunched in her hands.

In disbelief, she stares down at a single long red hair.

FOURTEEN

Bella could find no more gin in the dining room cabinet, and the bottle she'd bought yesterday was empty, so Calla ran next door to borrow some from Odelia.

That left Bella alone in the parlor with Nigel and Eudora, keeping up her end of the conversation while thinking about the long red hair clinging to Eudora's houndstooth duster.

There may be a logical explanation that doesn't involve Tilly Morton. But this is Lily Dale, where there are no coincidences. Weighing the possibilities, Bella wants to dismiss the one that seems simultaneously to be the most obvious and the most far-fetched: that the strand of hair is Tilly's.

Calla is back, with a bottle of gin and a large pot of lamb stew.

'Gammy insisted. She made enough for an army, as usual. Now you don't have to order out.'

'That's so nice, thank you.'

'Gammy!' Eudora shakes her head. 'There's that nickname again.'

'Apparently, back in England, "gammy" means she has a bad leg or that she's clumsy or something like that,' Calla tells Bella.

'Then it would be my nickname there. Let's put that stew on the stove and keep it hot until Pandora comes down.'

'Good idea.' Calla heads for the kitchen with Bella close behind, assuming Eudora and Nigel will stay put.

Nigel, however, grabs the large cocktail shaker from the coffee table and tags along. 'I'll whip up another batch. I do wish I had the Feeney family recipe. These aren't quite right, are they?'

'Actually, I think they're perfect,' Calla says, setting the pot on the stove and turning on the flame beneath it.

'Ah, then you'll have another?'

'I'd better not. I have a long night of writing ahead of me, and there's no telling what my characters might do if I'm loopy on gimlets.'

'You should probably head home,' Bella tells her, feeling guilty for having taken her away from her manuscript twice in one day.

Calla shoots her a questioning look, as if to ask if she'll be OK here alone, and Bella gives a little nod.

They'd got the photos they needed. And it's not as though she's in danger, right? Especially not with Luther right next door, having promised he won't go anywhere until they've figured out what's going on.

She walks Calla to the door, conscious that the others are within earshot.

'Thanks for coming over to sign the book!'

'My pleasure!' Calla mouths *good luck* before disappearing into the night.

Bella closes the door after her, pulls out her phone and swiftly opens her photo file.

'Bella? Is everything all right?'

She turns to see Eudora in the parlor doorway.

'Yes, why?'

'You seem a bit edgy.'

'Oh, I was just going to text Misty and make sure Max isn't overstaying his welcome.'

'My goodness, she just called a short time ago to say he was fine.'

'Yes, but he really shouldn't be out so late on a school night.'

'*Late?*'

'Well, it isn't late yet, but it will be.'

'Bella. Far be it from me to interfere in your parenting, but you do seem a tad over-protective of the lad, don't you think?'

'No. I don't think,' she snaps.

'Well, I'm certain you're doing your best, but—'

'I am, and I appreciate that you won't be interfering in my parenting.'

Holding her phone so that Eudora can't see the screen, she quickly selects the photos and sends them to Luther before turning toward the stairs.

'Now, if you'll excuse me, I'm going to go up and check on your niece.'

'I'm sure she's quite all right,' Eudora says, with a dismissive gesture of her left hand. She's holding a gimlet glass and liquid sloshes over the rim.

'Careful there, darling.' Nigel appears holding a tray with more drinks. 'Perhaps we should be calling you "*Gammy*".'

'Oh, you.' Eudora puts her nearly empty glass on the tray and takes a napkin to dab at the minuscule splash on her dress, ignoring the spatter on the carpet.

Bella thinks of the spilled coffee this morning, and a detail jars her brain.

'You've forgotten to lock the deadbolt, Bella.'

She blinks and looks at Nigel.

'You can't be too careful, with unsavory characters afoot.'

'I'm sure they're only interested in the deserted homes in the Dale. There are plenty of those at this time of year.'

As she watches Eudora trade the crumpled napkin for a fresh glass, she remembers something.

Wait, that can't be right . . . can it?

'That stew smells good, doesn't it?' she asks, perhaps a little too brightly. 'I'll go get Pandora so that we can eat.'

'No rush, luv,' Eudora tells her. 'We had a late lunch.'

'That's great, but I actually missed lunch. I'm starved. I'll be right back.'

Hurrying upstairs with her phone in hand, Bella rounds the landing and out of the corner of her eye, sees movement below. Eudora is at the door, her left hand on the deadbolt. Bella hears it turn with a click and sees her pocket the key.

Keeping her panic at bay, Bella reaches the second-floor hall and goes directly to the Rose Room. Her hand is shaking so badly that she fumbles the keypad combination twice before the door unlocks. She opens it inch by painstaking inch so that it won't creak, slips inside, and locks it behind her.

Curled up together on the bed, Chance and Spidey don't stir.

She hurriedly opens the search engine on her phone, brings up the history, and clicks on the site she needs.

For the second time today, she finds herself looking at the photo of a youthful Eudora Feeney. Her smile reaches her eyes, unlike that of the Eudora downstairs. She's holding an onion on a cutting board with her left hand, and a chef's knife in her right.

The woman downstairs had jostled Bella's coffee cup while using a knife with her left hand. She'd held her gimlet glass and reached for the napkin with her left hand. She'd just locked the door with her left hand.

That means—

Bella sees Chance jolt awake, going from deep slumber to high alert in a flash as two sets of quick footsteps come up the stairs.

'Bella? Where are you?' calls the woman who can't possibly be Eudora Feeney.

Sitting on the bed with Lady Pippa on her lap, Pandora stares at the painting of the African savannah.

Why would Spirit show her Auntie Eudora, and not Nigel, as the jackal?

What would an elderly spinster possibly have in common with a predatory wild animal?

I'm missing something.

Pandora closes her eyes, struggling to focus on the problem at hand and not on the many that await when her sojourn is over and the visitors depart. But her brief detour to Cotswold Corner was a bittersweet reminder that the life she had built for herself after her divorce is lovelier and more precious than she'd grasped. Now it, too, will be lost.

In her mind's eye, she sees the shelf above the stove in her kitchen. It holds the Feeney family cookbook so frequently referenced by Nigel. Pandora understands why he believes it might jar some sentimental cognition in Auntie Eudora, especially as a chef.

It's more a journal than a book, begun by Theodora Feeney nearly two centuries ago and filled with handwritten recipes contributed by subsequent mistresses of Marley House, right up to Pandora's paternal grandmother, Isadora Feeney. Some of the historical dishes – fried calves' ears and sparrow stew

– are better relegated to the distant past, though the accompanying anecdotes and notes are entertaining. And there are other treasures tucked among the pages – household lists and ledgers, letters, scraps of poetry, even a short story Theodora had written.

It's been years since Pandora opened the book, or even thought about it.

Tomorrow, perhaps, she'll retrieve it and show it to Auntie Eudora. It might be nice to go through it together.

Or it might have been, if Auntie Eudora were her old self.

Ah, well, people age. People change.

Pandora thinks of the pudgy teenager in the framed photo above her sofa. How unlike her to wear so much *dress*, even if it was the style of the day. It's hard to believe she'd matured into a svelte Petula Clark doppelganger in the space of—

Doppelganger.

The Jackal.

Her eyes snap open.

In *A Tale of Two Cities*, the jackal – barrister Sydney Carton – is a mirror image of defendant Charles Darnay, and nobly switches places with him to take his place on the guillotine.

Pandora thinks of her Auntie Eudora, so familiar, and yet not.

The strange lapses in character and behavior could be attributed to age and senility.

But can the same be said of her sporadic slips into dialect and phrases tied to a geographic area where she's never resided?

Or her willingness to consult Spirit after a lifetime of skepticism?

Or her sudden fear of cats after a lifelong affection for Scottish Folds?

Again, Pandora recalls the framed photo of her teenaged aunt, with Dodger playing at her ankles, and this time she hears Misty's voice.

When I was pregnant, I had the worst cankles . . .

Pregnant.

Cankles.

Spirit expands the photo's backdrop like a camera panning

out on a shot. She recognizes, in the distant background, not the Swiss Alps but a massive building with distinct gothic domes and spires. Kirkgate Market in Leeds. On the brick wall behind her father and Auntie Eudora, a painted sign reads 'Hornbeam Avenue Mother-and-Baby Home'.

Auntie Eudora didn't leave London to attend a posh finishing school. She left because she was pregnant.

Another idea follows, so preposterous that it slams into Pandora like a physical blow.

Standing absolutely still inside the Rose Room as the knob jiggles from the other side, Bella hears Nigel's voice.

'Bella? Are you in there, luv? Is everything all right?'

She holds her breath and says nothing, watching Chance. She's staring at the door, fur standing on end and tail twitching with the awareness that there's a predator in their midst.

The voices on the other side of the door are muffled, but she hears snatches of conversation.

'. . . she said she was . . .'

'. . . but why would she . . .'

'Shhh! Keep your voice down, in case . . .'

She hears nothing at all for a few moments, but Chance is still twitching and they're still out there.

'Bella?' Nigel croons. 'Are you playing a little trick on us?'

She can tell he's trying to sound jovial, but there's a sinister note in his tone.

Her phone, clutched in her hand, vibrates with a text. The sound seems deafening.

It's from Luther. No message, just a link. Bella clicks on it.

The man in the photo is unmistakably Nigel, looking a decade or so younger above a caption that reads: *Special Collections Archivist Hubert Twill Suspected in Rare Book Theft.*

'Bella?' The doorknob jiggles again. 'Come out, come out, wherever you are.'

'Why don't you just shoot the bloody lock off the door?'

'Now darling, we don't want to disturb your *niece* upstairs, do we?'

His emphasis on the word confirms what Bella already

knows. This woman isn't Pandora's aunt, yet somehow resembles her closely enough to fool her own flesh and blood.

But it's another word that sticks in her mind.

Shoot.

He has a gun.

Her mind races. She should call 9-1-1.

No. By the time help arrives, it will be too late.

She should call Luther, right next door.

But the front door is locked and she suspects the back is as well. And even if he could find a way inside, he's unarmed.

So are you. And Pandora.

Pandora, somewhere upstairs, unsuspecting and so vulnerable.

Chance leaps off the bed and paces in front of the closed door. Any second now, she might hiss or leap at it.

Bella springs into action. She scurries to the closet, making as little noise as possible. Feeling blindly behind her hanging clothes, she finds the hidden latch that releases a section of wall.

Beyond the panel lies a nook she'd stumbled across last summer. It had once been a part of the bedroom, with ornate wood moldings, strips of peeling wallpaper from a bygone era, and a cobweb-shrouded gaslight fixture identical to an electric-converted sconce on the bedroom wall just outside the closet door. Hardwood floors extend seamlessly from the bedroom into the closet, but here they end at the edge of a vertical tunnel.

Bella hurries back to grab the sleeping kitten from the bed and tuck him into the front of her shirt. He's startled, releasing a barely audible mew, and then snuggles against her bare skin.

All is still now out in the hallway beyond the Rose Room. Have Nigel and Eudora moved on? Or are they lurking, listening too, poised to burst into the room?

She turns to Chance. The cat is still agitated, but allows Bella to pick her up in a swift, silent movement.

Then she's back in the closet, quietly pulling the door closed after her and ducking into the nook. There, she fumbles to illuminate her phone's screen before setting Chance on the dusty floor and swiftly pulling the panel back into place so that even if they get into her room and look into the closet, they won't suspect it isn't a dead end.

Chance disappears over the drop-off, scampering down the steep, crude wooden stairway that ends in another hidden nook concealed behind a basement wall.

Our turn, she silently tells Spidey, holding him more securely against her pounding heart.

There's no railing. One misstep could be deadly. She holds the phone like a flashlight, running through her options as she starts to descend, step by precarious step.

From the cellar, she might be able to escape the house without detection – but when she's dealing with an armed enemy, *might* could be a lethal risk.

She could stay in the hidden room with the cats and call or text for help, but that would mean being trapped and vulnerable until they arrive. And for all she knows, Nigel's snooping might have led him to discover the hidden tunnel. He could already be lying in wait below.

Bella feels Spidey squirm, as if sensing that they might be heading into a trap. Tiny claws needle into her skin, startling her. She wobbles on the step, flinging her hand against the clammy wall to steady herself.

As she does, her phone – her lifeline – slips from her grasp and lands with an echoing clatter on the dirt floor far below.

Pandora paces the Jungle Room, stepping around Lady Pippa, who's befriended a tuft of fringe dangling from a footstool.

This entire situation makes no sense.

Or does it make perfect sense?

If the woman downstairs is not, in fact, her Auntie Eudora, then she looks so much like her that she can only be a close biological relative. An illegitimate daughter?

That makes perfect sense.

Yet really, it makes no sense. Why would Auntie Eudora send someone in her place?

She would not.

But the woman has Auntie Eudora's cell phone – she'd used it to text Pandora upon her arrival – and her credit card. Pandora had seen it when she used it to pay the bill at lunch.

Perhaps it's all an elaborate prank. Yes, right, for April Fool's. It makes perfect sense.

It makes no sense.

Back home in England, such a trick would be played only on the first of April, and only until noon. Anyway, such frivolity isn't in the Feeney family nature.

It makes no sense.

It . . .

No. It does not. No matter how she sorts it, she knows the charade simply cannot have unfolded with Auntie Eudora's knowledge and blessing. With growing dread, she must therefore acknowledge that—

She hears swift footsteps coming up the stairs. A knock on the door.

'Pandora, luv?' calls the woman who sounds so very much like her aunt that Pandora might be wrong about this after all.

'Yes?'

'Is Bella there with you?'

'No, she's not.'

'Right, well . . . if I might have a word with you?'

'I apologize, but it's not a good time. I'm not feeling well.'

There's no immediate reply. Yet nor do the footsteps retreat.

After a moment, the knob turns and the door opens. A gray head pokes in. 'Ah, there you are. Quite alone here, are you?' Her flinty blue eyes take in the room and come to rest on Lady Pippa, batting the fringe with a fat paw.

Pandora waits for the woman to recoil in terror.

She does not.

She stoops and picks up the cat.

Pandora gasps. 'I beg your pardon!'

'I'll need you to join me downstairs, please.'

'Unhand Lady Pippa this instant!'

'Downstairs. *Now*.' Her voice is deadly calm.

'Darling?' Nigel calls from below.

'Yes, yes, I'll be right down.'

'With both?'

'I'm afraid just the one, darling.' She turns back to Pandora. 'Now.'

Pandora opens her mouth, then closes it when she sees that the woman's right hand is clutching the Scottish Fold, and her left has a firm grip on a gun.

At last, Bella steps down onto solid ground at the foot of the steep staircase. The space is closet-sized and pitch black, built into a corner of the basement, with stone walls along two sides and rough wood on the others. A latch embedded into the wall will release a hidden door and allow her to exit into the basement.

But she can't. Not yet. Maybe not at all.

She hears a faint mew in the darkness. Chance, at her feet, rubbing against her ankles. Bella sinks to her knees, sets Spidey beside his mama, and feels around the dirt floor for her phone.

Finding it, she presses the home button and the touch screen lights up with a network of fine cracks. It's completely shattered, rendering it useless as anything but a flashlight.

She can see two glittering sets of cat eyes in the dark, watching her.

'You two will have to stay in here, where it's safe,' she whispers, her voice barely audible. 'I'll go get help and I'll be back for you, I promise.'

She presses the latch. The release sounds deafening. She holds her breath, listening for movement on the other side.

Silence.

She nudges the cats to the back wall, away from the door. She'll have to move quickly, before they can escape with her. She presses the button to darken the phone and opens the door just a crack.

All is dark and still beyond.

In a quick movement, she pushes her way through the door and closes it behind her. Good. That's good. The cats are safe.

There's only one way out and that's through the kitchen. Even if she was certain the rickety stairs leading to the direct exit would hold her weight, she doubts she can pry open the diagonal trap door along the exterior foundation. At least, not without making a racket. But all she has to do is make her way up the stairs, into the kitchen, and out the adjacent back door. She can cut across the yard to Odelia's in a matter of seconds and call the police.

As long as Pandora is still safely in her room, everything will be fine until they arrive.

She hesitates, listening, and hears nothing overhead, nothing in the basement. Nothing but the faint sound of her own breathing.

She illuminates the phone screen, lighting her path through the basement. She doesn't even like to be down here with the lights on. There are spiders, and Bella has always hated spiders. She tries not to think about them now, as she covers the distance to the foot of the stairs. She sees the light shining through the crack at the bottom of the door above, and smells the fragrant lamb stew simmering on the stove.

There are footsteps somewhere above. Someone is walking quickly. But not in the kitchen, and maybe not even on the first floor.

She creeps up the stairs, her breath catching in her throat at every faint creak beneath her feet. At last, she reaches the top step. She turns off the phone, slips it into her pocket, and steels her nerves for whatever is on the other side of the door.

She turns the knob, slowly, slowly . . .

She counts to three and then pushes the door open, slowly, slowly . . .

All remains still in the kitchen. When she dares to lean forward and peek, she can see that it's deserted. She sees the cutting board and lime rinds on the counter where Nigel had stood just a short time ago, making a fresh batch of gimlets. There's the back door, just a few feet away. The deadbolt is indeed locked.

Nigel must have done it before joining her and Eudora in the hall.

The footsteps cross overhead again. They're on the second floor, for sure.

She steps out into the kitchen. One step. Two steps.

She hears the rumble of a male voice, and a higher-pitched female reply. Nigel and Eudora. She can't make out what they're saying.

Three steps. Four steps.

She's reached the back door. She turns the lock. Her hand clasps the knob. Slowly, turn it slowly . . .

'I need you to tell me where it is!'

It's Nigel, this time loud and clear, perhaps closer to the top of the stairs.

'And I need *you* to tell me why you want to know!'

Pandora.

She's no longer safely in her room, but at least she's all right. Bella opens the back door. Cold night air rushes in. Freedom.

She puts one foot over the threshold.

Then she hears a scream.

'No!' Pandora shrieks, when the woman who isn't her Auntie Eudora points the gun at Lady Pippa, still cradled in her bony arm.

Unlike Bella's Chance, who sensed the evil in these inter-lopers, the plump little Scottish Fold doesn't seem aware that her life is in peril. She merely looks drowsy.

'Don't hurt her! She's an innocent creature.'

'Aren't we all.' Not-Eudora laughs. 'Don't worry. I won't shoot your little darling. Yet.'

They're in the second-floor hallway now, at the top of the stairs. Nigel has gone to the third floor to search for Isabella.

He reappears, eyes blazing. He, too, is armed with a revolver.

'She can't have got past us,' he says, 'so she must be up here, hiding somewhere.'

'Well, what are we going to do?'

'*She's* going to tell us where to find that Dickens manuscript.' He gestures at Pandora with the revolver. 'Or suffer the consequences.'

'*Dickens manuscript?* I don't even know what you're refer-ring to. You said you wanted the cookbook.'

Nigel and Not-Eudora look at each other.

'Are you playing stupid, or truly stupid?' he asks.

Pandora's thoughts fly to the old recipe book. There was, indeed, a yellowed, long-hand manuscript tucked into its pages – one of Theodora's lackluster literary efforts, she'd assumed.

'Perhaps she really doesn't know, darling.'

Nigel narrows his eyes at Pandora. 'Of course she knows. She's been evading our questions about that cookbook since we arrived. One doesn't have to be a psychic medium to know when someone is lying.'

Pandora heaves a heavy sigh. 'You caught me.'

'Ah, I knew it! It's hidden away in one of those . . . those bootlegger compartments, isn't it?'

'No, I'm afraid the wanker burned it.'

Nigel buckles as if he's been sucker-punched, and Not-Eudora gives a little cry.

'It was a brutal act of vengeance,' Pandora goes on. 'He threw every Marley House heirloom I cherished into a flaming pyre right outside on the shore. I couldn't bear to tell you that our family cookbook was reduced to ashes, Auntie Eudora.'

For a moment, she relishes their horrified expressions.

Then she sees a lethal gleam in Nigel's eye. 'I do wish you hadn't lied, Pandora. You might have spared us all this nuisance. Your dear aunt and I could have enjoyed the rest of our visit and then gone on our way. Instead, you've left me with no choice . . .'

He shakes his head, looking down at the revolver, and she grasps the terrible implication in his pause.

I'm going to have to kill you.

Of course they're not going to move on from this nightmarish episode as if nothing ever happened.

He looks up, meets her gaze, and raises the revolver.

When Bella heard Pandora's scream, she knew she couldn't leave the house. There was only one thing to do, and one way to do it – provided Nigel and Eudora were unaware of the passageway behind a false wall in the powder room beneath the stairs, leading to a cupboard-sized door that opens to the walk-in storage closet in the second-floor hallway.

She doesn't doubt that Nigel looked here during his fruitless search for her. He would have seen only three walls lined with cabinets and shelves that hold cleaning supplies and linens. There would be no reason for him to check it again. But if he does – if she makes the slightest sound to alert him to her presence here – she'll be trapped.

Listening to the hallway conversation, she can tell that Eudora is mere inches from her post, directly against the door. She must have Lady Pippa, and a gun.

So, apparently, does Nigel, and he's about to use it on Pandora.

Bella's hand tightens on the handle of the knife she'd impulsively grabbed from the kitchen cutting board before rushing to the passageway. It's useless, no match for two firearms.

On the other side of the door, Pandora blurts, 'Wait! Spirit has a message for you!'

'A message?' Nigel echoes. 'For whom, and from whom?'

'She's merely stalling, darling,' Eudora says. 'We don't even believe in this nonsense. Let's get on with it.'

'But the message is for you, Auntie Eudora! It's very important, and I'm being told to deliver it while I remain on the earthly plane, or it will be lost. It's – it's very strange, because it's supposedly about . . . your daughter?'

Bella hears Eudora's startled gasp. After a moment, she says, 'But you know that I . . . I don't have a—'

'Now, darling,' Nigel cuts in. 'Let's just hear what Spirit has to say, shall we?'

Pandora goes on, 'Spirit is telling me that you secretly gave birth to a beautiful baby girl, at an Anglican home for unwed mothers in Leeds. You were little more than a lass yourself. Your parents were fiercely religious and they forced you to give her up.'

'No! That's not true at all. It's what I wanted to believe.'

'What?'

'I was raised in a miserable home in Yorkshire by a man who only adopted me because his wife wanted children. She died when I was an infant, and that lout Billy Morton was stuck with me.'

Morton . . .

Bella thinks of the housekeeper who'd disappeared from the *Queen Jane*, and of the long red hair on the duster.

The woman who'd gone overboard hadn't been Tilly Morton . . .

'Darling,' Nigel says, 'you've given yourself away.'

. . . because Tilly Morton is alive and well and on the other side of this door, armed with a gun.

'So what?' she says with a bitter laugh. 'She deserves to hear the truth about her precious aunt, doesn't she?'

'What on earth are you talking about, Auntie Eudora?'

'Let's drop the charade, shall we? We both know I'm not your Auntie Eudora. I'm the daughter she never wanted, and abandoned. All those years, I imagined that I had a loving mother just waiting for me to turn up on her doorstep. And when I did, imagine how I felt when she turned me away, slammed the door in my face?'

'Is that . . . is that what happened?'

'Of course it is. If this darling man hadn't come along in that moment to find me weeping on her doorstep, heaven only knows what would have become of me.'

Nigel laughs heartily. 'And if you hadn't borne such a striking resemblance to that dreary old biddy, I'd still be courting her, and she'd still be . . . well, we won't talk about that, will we?'

'She'd still be . . . alive? Is that it?' Pandora asks. 'But she isn't, is she? You . . . the two of you . . . you—'

'My goodness, luv, why do you look so gutted? I thought you were the all-knowing psychic.' She turns to Nigel. 'I'm growing weary of this. And her. Get on with it.'

'Gladly. Pandora, it's my pleasure to reunite you with your dear Auntie Eudora. Do give her my regards and apologies that it had to end as it—'

Bella jerks the doorknob and shoves the door open. Sure enough, Tilly is directly on the other side. The door slams into her and she's thrown into the opposite wall. She collapses in a heap, losing her grasp on both the cat and her gun.

Pandora dives toward the floor. 'Lady Pippa!'

Nigel whirls on Bella. 'How dare you?'

The knife trembles in her hand, pressed close against her leg. He's just beyond her reach, but if she lunges forward, she might be able to—

'Do drop that knife.'

His preternatural calm sends ice shards through her.

There's no way out of this unless someone – Luther, the police, a pararescue hero, *someone* – swoops in right now to save them.

But no one is coming. She's missed her opportunity to summon help, and nobody even knows what's going on here, and . . .

And if ever there was a woman who didn't need rescuing, it's you.

Nigel is pointing the gun at her. She forces herself not to flinch as she stares into the coldest eyes she's ever seen.

'Drop it. Now.'

She obeys and hears the knife clatter to the floor.

A faint smile curves his mouth. 'Well done. Now then . . .' He takes aim.

'Hubert, wait!'

His eyes widen at her mention of his name.

'I, uh . . . I have a spirit message for you, too.'

'*You?* You're not a medium.'

'Oh, Hubert. Shouldn't you, of all people, know better than to believe everything you're told?' Bella forces a smile. 'The message is from Eudora.'

'Please. Do you expect me to believe that?'

'That's up to you. All I know is that she's been following you and Tilly.'

Tilly – another bit of bait, and she's got him again.

He says nothing, but she can see his thought process: she *must* be a medium – how else would she know their true identities?

'Eudora says she's been watching you snooping through this house, looking for that cookbook.'

'Where is it?' He steadies his grip on the gun. 'Tell me, or I shall—'

'I don't know where it is. Eudora does, but first she wants me to deliver the rest of the message.'

'Then get on with it!'

Bella pauses as she's seen the mediums do, as though she's listening to Spirit.

'She's saying she knows you made up that story about ailurophobia because you realized that Chance sensed that something was off about you two, and you were afraid her behavior might arouse suspicion.'

'That's . . . that's—'

'It's *true*. Drew said cats can sense predators, and you and Tilly panicked, because of course that's exactly what you are.'

He levels the gun. 'This is rubbish.'

'She's saying it was *brilliant*,' she adds quickly. 'The ailuro-phobia ruse. She's . . . she's giving you a bit of applause. She says, "you always were so quick and clever, darling".' Her shaky attempt at a British accent and the compliment seem to appease him for the moment.

'Go on.'

'She's telling me that you eavesdropped on my conversation with Odelia and heard about the pomegranates, so you planted one in the Rose Room to give me a scare. *And* that you made up that story about unsavory characters to throw suspicion away from yourself.'

His startled expression tells her that she's correct, but he recovers quickly. 'I've no idea what you're talking about.'

Hearing a faint movement behind her, she fights the urge to glance around to check on Pandora and Tilly. Hubert seems to have forgotten everything but the message from Eudora.

'Eudora wants you to know she's going to be with you always, Hubert, wherever you go.'

'I sincerely doubt that.'

'She's laughing. She says wait and see. She's going to follow you, and Tilly, too, for the rest of your days.'

He falters, but only for an instant.

'Right, then. I've had quite enough.'

She sees his finger on the trigger, and she knows this is it. The end. The final precious seconds she managed to buy are about to run out.

Oh, no. Oh, Max . . .

She squeezes her eyes closed, and her last thought before the deafening blast is that Sam will be waiting for her, but she isn't ready, she isn't—

She hears a heavy thud as a body drops to the floor with an unearthly howl of pain.

She opens her eyes.

She's still here, still breathing,

There's no Sam.

Only Pandora, holding Tilly's gun in both hands, arms outstretched, trembling violently. And Hubert, writhing on the floor with blood soaking one arm of his tweed suit.

'Pandora! You saved my life!'

She crumples, nods. 'But Lady Pippa . . .'

Bella realizes that she'd had to make a terrible choice: tackle Eudora and grab the gun to protect Bella, or go after her beloved cat.

Turning, she spots the Scottish Fold scuttling along in the shadows at the end of the hall. 'No, she's right there, see? She's fine.'

'Lady Pippa!'

Bella plucks the gun from Pandora's flailing hands as she rushes after the cat, leaping over the unconscious woman in the blue dress. Her gray wig has been knocked askew to reveal a slick of dark red hair. Bella pushes it aside and checks her neck for a pulse.

'Is she alive?' Pandora asks, turning back with her cat in her arms.

'Yes.'

'But she isn't my aunt.'

'No. Her name is Tilly Morton. And his is Hubert Twill.'

'Ah, Spirit told you that, Isabella. You see? Anyone can learn to communicate with the Other Side.'

Bella opens her mouth to correct her, then closes it and shakes her head.

Here in the Dale, believers are going to believe.

And maybe, once in a while, non-believers are, too.

FIFTEEN

April 1st

'Mom, I brought you breakfast in bed!'

Bella opens her eyes to see Max standing in the doorway of the Rose Room holding a tray. He's wearing his favorite Ninja Zombie Warrior pajamas and an impish grin.

'Wow, that's . . .' She sits up to see that the tray is loaded with food. 'Max, did you use the stove without permission?'

'Nope, Miss Feeney permissed me,' he says, setting it on the bedside table. 'By the way, she cooked the food. I just made the coffee. Well, Miss Feeney helped me with that, too.'

'Wow,' Bella says again. Pandora helping Max make breakfast probably shouldn't strike her as the most startling development of all that's unfolded over the last couple of days. But this isn't just any breakfast.

Eggs, sausage, bacon, toast, baked beans, tomatoes, mushrooms . . .

'Dig in, Isabella,' Pandora says, poking her head into the room. 'No better way to start a busy day than with a full English breakfast.'

'And coffee! Drink your coffee, Mom!'

'I will, Max, thank you.'

She reaches for the cup, feigning enthusiasm as Max watches, wriggly with anticipation.

You're going to pay for this, Luther Ragland.

Doing her best not to wince, Bella takes a tiny sip of hot liquid that looks like coffee and tastes like hot water tinted with Gravy Master . . . which, of course, is exactly what it is. She makes a show of sputtering and spitting into a napkin as Max giggles delightedly.

'April Fool's, Mom!'

'You got me!' She laughs and grabs him, pulling him into

a fierce embrace and covering his sweet giggly face with kisses.

'Well played, lad,' Pandora comments, still in the doorway. 'Now, you must go get ready for school. You'll need mittens and boots.'

'OK!'

'Mittens and boots?' Bella looks at the window. Chance and Spidey are curled up on the window seat in a stream of bright morning sunlight. 'But yesterday was beautiful, and it's supposed to be nice today, too.'

'You really must learn to ignore the forecasts, Isabella. A dreadful storm blew in just after sundown.'

'A storm? Wow, I guess I missed it.'

Having spent a sleepless night after the ordeal, and most of yesterday participating in police investigations, Bella had been exhausted. With Pandora here to help Max with homework and dinner, she'd gone to bed early and slept a solid twelve hours.

'Yes, Isabella, we had at least a foot of snow overnight.'

'A foot!'

'Maybe two feet, Mom! March went out like a lion.' Max punctuates that with a loud roar.

Bella's heart sinks. She'd been hoping for a beautiful spring day. Oh, well. It *is* Lily Dale.

'Make sure you dress warmly, Max. And did you finish your story about Chance and Spidey?'

'Yep, and Miss Feeney helped me think of the best title ever!'

'What is it?'

'*A Tale of Two Kitties*.'

Bella grins. 'That is definitely the best title ever. Now go get ready for school.'

Max gallops off down the hall, and she turns to Pandora. 'Thank you for helping him with his homework and for making this amazing breakfast. I won't hold the coffee against you.'

'I can assure you that I had nothing to do with that. I've never been one for silly pranks, particularly amid such difficult times.'

A mere thirty-six hours have passed since Tilly Morton and Hubert Twill departed Valley View on stretchers, tended by medics and heavily guarded by law enforcement. They're hospitalized, Hubert recovering from a gunshot wound to his arm, Tilly from a concussion. They were questioned and confessed to a conspiracy plot hatched when they met in London at Eudora Feeney's doorstep the day she turned away her illegitimate daughter.

Bella has complicated feelings on that matter. It must have been devastating for Tilly to track down her birth mother only to have the door slammed in her face. On the other hand, Luther had heard through the law enforcement grapevine that her motive for finding Eudora might not have been purely emotional.

'She'd spent all her adult life trying to make it as an actress, barely getting by. She needed cash, plain and simple,' he said matter-of-factly. 'She was hoping Eudora had some to spare. Unfortunately, she'd lost her restaurant and come close to financial ruin. The last thing she needed in her life was a long-lost aging daughter asking for a handout.'

Really, the *last* thing she needed in her life was Hubert Twill, a cunning former university archivist who'd escaped prosecution for stealing a trove of antiquarian literature from a library's special collections.

'How did he get away with it?' Bella asked Luther.

'The security measures that make it nearly impossible for outside thieves to get their hands on rare books and manuscripts make inside jobs extraordinarily difficult to uncover and prove. So few people had access to the collection that by the time someone realized treasures had gone missing, the trail was cold and the evidence long gone.'

But not everything about Hubert was a scam or a lie. He was indeed a Dickens scholar, long fascinated by an obscure reference to a short story Dickens penned as a Christmas gift to a neighbor who'd helped tend to his house and children while he and his wife were traveling abroad in America in 1842. Supposedly, it featured a character named Jacob Marley, and was a prequel to what would later become *A Christmas Carol.*

He pinpointed Marley House as the likely neighboring residence and tracked down Eudora Feeney. Reinventing himself as Nigel Spencer-Watson, he manipulated an accidental meeting and embarked on a whirlwind relationship, plotting to get his hands on the priceless literary treasure she'd unwittingly gifted to her niece in America.

When Tilly came along, the two hatched a foolproof scheme to get Eudora out of the way without a murder investigation that might throw suspicion on her enigmatic new suitor. Tilly landed a housekeeping job on the new cruise liner, and Nigel booked a suite on the maiden voyage.

He confessed to murdering Eudora and throwing her body into the sea so that Tilly could assume her identity. As an actress, she was well trained in impersonation, and they correctly guessed that Pandora would likely believe the charade, as she hadn't seen her aunt in many years. They just hadn't counted on Spirit – and Bella – meddling in their masquerade.

Pandora clears her throat. 'Isabella, you've been so gracious, allowing me to stay on as a houseguest until I get things sorted with my living situation . . .'

'It's no problem. You can stay as long as you like.'

'I do appreciate it, luv, but with Luther's generous loan, I'm able to pay the overdue rent, and I expect the utilities to be restored momentarily.'

'That's great, Pandora.' Bella smiles. It had been Odelia's idea for Luther to give Pandora the money he would have spent on their cruise vacation. He'd resisted at first, but Odelia had talked him into it.

'See that? You have that man wrapped around your little finger,' Bella told her.

'Me? He did it for Pandora.'

'He did it for you. He doesn't even like Pandora.'

'Of course he does. She gets on his nerves, just like she gets on mine, but in the end, well . . . you know.'

She'd shrugged, and Bella smiled. She does know.

'Of course I shall pay Luther back, and reimburse Walter and Peter for the meal,' Pandora is saying, 'and compensate you, Isabella, for everything you've done.'

'I'm the one who owes you, Pandora. You saved my life.

But even if you hadn't, remember, that's what friends are for. There will always be a place for you here at Valley View.'

Pandora's eyes glisten, and she bows her head quickly.

Bella looks away, giving her space. She notices a vase on the breakfast tray. It holds a single bloom – a long stem covered with delicate blue blossoms.

'Pandora! Is that . . .?'

She looks up and follows Bella's gaze. 'An English bluebell. Yes, luv. I was at Cotswold Corner early this morning and I spotted it, poking up from the dead leaves and mud. The only living thing in my garden, and far too early in the season. My guides informed me that it was intended for 'Bella blue'. Brilliant, isn't it?'

'Brilliant,' she murmurs, and wipes a tear from her eye.

'Oh, dear. Are you all right, Isabella?'

'Yes, it's just . . . the other day, before . . . everything happened, I started to think, what if Sam is trying to get through to me and he can't?'

'Because you're not open to Spirit?'

'That . . . or . . .' She can't even bring herself to say it aloud.

'Because you've been so caught up in Dr Bailey?'

The agonizing ache in her heart pushes its way into her throat. It takes her a few hard swallows before she manages to say, 'If . . . if dead isn't dead, then doesn't that mean I'm still married?'

'Of course it doesn't! Why, following that logic, every widow and widower who remarries would be a polygamist.'

Bella shrugs, her left thumb toying with the wedding and engagement rings she'd put on for safekeeping and hasn't been able to bring herself to remove.

Pandora sits beside her on the bed. 'Isabella, the love you share with your husband is as eternal as the soul. But marriage, the way we experience it on the earthly plane, doesn't exist on the Other Side. Only love. And that's what Spirit wants us to experience as we continue our earthly journey.'

'Love?'

Pandora nods.

'Your Sam's earthly journey is complete, and he's achieved

another level of existence. You're still here, in this life. You have lessons to learn, things to accomplish.'

'I'm learning and accomplishing, believe me. Most days, I do nothing but learn lessons and accomplish things, morning, noon and night. I'm so . . .' She rakes a hand through her hair. 'It's exhausting. This whole business of *living*. I'm just . . . tired.'

'Aren't we all, luv. Aren't we all,' Pandora says with a sad, weary smile.

'I'm so sorry, Pandora. It's insensitive of me to bring this up when your own loss is so fresh.'

'Oh, I'm accustomed to Orville's absence in my life, although—'

'I meant your Auntie Eudora.'

'Oh . . . yes. Of course. I adored her, and of course I mourn her, and I regret that she met a dastardly demise, but I hadn't seen her in years. This loss, difficult as it is, won't impact my daily life. Losing my husband was a resounding tragedy from which I'm afraid I've never fully recovered.'

'Even now? After all these years?'

'I believe . . .' She pauses, then sighs. 'It seems I've been unable to fully accept it. Acceptance is the only way to heal, but it means letting go – not just of the person you've lost, but a part of yourself, too.'

'I guess . . . maybe I'm not ready to let go of Sam just yet, either. Maybe if I could just talk to him—'

'You can.'

'No, not like that!'

It comes out much harsher than she'd intended, but sometimes she loses patience with Lily Dale magniloquence.

Anyway, death isn't divorce. Sam didn't choose to leave her. They were torn apart by fate.

'I'm sorry, Pandora. It's just . . . I *know* I can talk to him in my head, but I want to know that he hears me. Wait, don't say he can. What I mean is, I want to *hear him*. And I want to see him. I want proof that he's with me, not just all this . . . this . . .' She stares at the bluebell, swallowing the word on the tip of her tongue.

'I understand.'

'Look, I'm trying not to be dismissive of your beliefs. I just want to make sure you're not . . .'

'Dismissive of your skepticism?'

'Yes, and my need for concrete evidence,' Bella says. 'And my inability to accept the idea that I can do what you do if I just try. Because I've *tried*. And failed. And I've never wanted anything so badly in my life.'

'I can assure you that you'll be wistful over your husband's passing for the rest of your mortal life, Isabella. But it will get easier, when you truly accept this loss and resolve to move on. It's something we both need to do, isn't it? Perhaps we can . . .'

Pandora's lip trembles. Bella puts an arm around her bony shoulders.

'I think we can,' she says softly. 'I mean, if we don't take care of each other, who will, right?'

'Yes. Just as long as it doesn't involve a magical miracle elixir.' Pandora wrinkles her nose, and they share a laugh. 'On that note, Isabella, if you wouldn't mind, I'm afraid I require one last favor of you.'

'Anything.'

'Splendid. Dr Bailey rang just now and informed me that Lady Pippa is doing very well.'

'Oh, that's . . . that's great news.'

Concerned about the limp she'd suffered when Tilly dropped her, Pandora had summoned Drew to examine the cat. He'd come right away, and was visibly shaken when he walked into a crime scene crawling with law enforcement.

There was too much commotion for Bella to exchange anything more than a few hurried words with him. He asked if she was sure she was all right, and she told him that she was. He left quickly with Lady Pippa, taking her back to the animal hospital for observation.

'Yes, I'm quite relieved,' Pandora says. 'He said she's ready to be picked up this morning, but I'm afraid I can't do it myself. Would you mind?'

'Pandora, if this is your sneaky way of—'

'It isn't, I assure you.'

'Why can't you do it?'

'Because . . .' She clears her throat, smiling. 'I've a rather urgent appointment. The esteemed member of the Dickens Society with whom I spoke yesterday has caught the first flight out of New York this morning.'

'Pandora, that's wonderful!'

'Yes, it is, isn't it? He examined the photographs I sent of the manuscript, and is most intrigued, and so certain it's authentic that he'll be accompanied by an appraiser. They're due at Cotswold Corner within the hour.'

'And if it's authentic . . .'

'Then I dare say I'll have no trouble reimbursing Luther for his generous loan, or paying Dr Bailey's bill.' Pandora smiles, stands, and heads for the door. 'Do call and let him know what time to expect you, and be sure to extend my gratitude, Isabella.'

'Oh, I will.'

That'll give me at least one thing to say to him that isn't weird and awkward.

She gets out of bed, reaching for her phone on the nightstand and plucking a strip of bacon from the tray. Eyeing the bluebell in the vase, she remembers that Pandora claimed to have found it 'poking up from the dead leaves and mud. The only living thing in my garden, and far too early in the season . . .'

Wait a minute. It would have been poking up from a foot of snow this morning, not leaves and mud. Pandora obviously hadn't discovered it in her garden. Still, her heart was in the right place, wanting Bella to think the bluebell was a mysterious sign from Sam.

Bella shakes her head, biting into the bacon, and dials Drew's number, not expecting him to pick up. Even if he's not busy caring for his patients, she doubts he's interested in hearing from her.

Yet he does pick up, sounding breathless, on the first ring.

'Bella?'

Caught with a mouthful of bacon, she tries to chew and swallow without choking.

'Bella?'

'Yes! It's me! Wait, don't hang up!'

'I'm . . .' He clears his throat. 'I'm not hanging up. How are you?'

'Great. I'm great. I'm . . . Pandora asked me to pick up Lady Pippa for her . . . if that's OK with you?'

A pause. 'Of course that's OK with me. Why wouldn't it be?'

'Because I . . . the other day, when you wanted to come over, I was so . . . and I didn't mean to be so . . . I mean, it wasn't an accident, I guess I did mean it, but I didn't . . .' She hesitates. 'Do you even know what I'm talking about?'

She expects him to say that he doesn't.

'Yeah.'

'Oh. So you figured out that I was trying to . . .'

'Actually, Bella, I'm not sure exactly what you were trying to do. I mean, I'm usually pretty perceptive – when it comes to my patients, anyway. I guess I understand animals a lot better than I do people. Or maybe women. Or just . . .'

'*Me?*' she asks softly. 'Maybe that's because I'm not sure I really understand myself these days.'

'Yeah, well, you've had a lot going on. Way more than I even realized. And I don't want to make anything harder for you, ever.'

'You don't, Drew! You make everything . . .'

Not easier. No, nothing is easy. But then, it never has been.

'*Better*. You make everything better.' She swallows, toying with her wedding and engagement rings. 'And I guess there's a part of me that just didn't realize it until now.'

'Well that's . . . that's good. I'm glad. Because you make everything better for me, too.'

She can hear the relieved smile in his voice.

'Then . . . I guess I'll see you in about an hour?' she asks.

'Yes. And if you can stick around, maybe we can go for a walk in the woods or something. It's beautiful out.'

Beautiful, and snowy. She'll need a parka, gloves, boots.

'I'd like that, Drew. See you soon.'

She hangs up and stands for a long moment, staring down at the phone, considering something.

Yes. It's time.

She goes into her contact settings and quickly changes Dr Drew Bailey to just Drew.

Then she goes over to the bureau and gives the woman in the mirror a firm nod, whispering the words aloud.

'It's time. And it's OK, Bella Blue.'

She hadn't meant to add that last part. It just slipped out, catching her off-guard, almost as if someone else had said it. As if Sam had said it.

She looks again at the bluebell. So what if Pandora bought it from a florist? It's still a sweet gesture to brighten yet another wintery day.

The sun might be shining beyond the window, and the sky a brilliant blue, but the branches are a long way from verdant and lush. Here in the Burned-over District, this difficult season of light and darkness, of hope and despair has a long, long way to go.

Bella notices that Chance and Spidey are awake now, looking out, tails twitching. Stepping closer, she spots a fat robin on a bare bough, above a landscape blanketed in nothing more than dead leaves, patchy grass and mud.

'Pandora!' she shouts. 'Foot of snow my arse!'

'April Fool's, Isabella!' Pandora calls back.

Bella laughs, and turns to the vase.

Maybe Pandora really had found the bluebell growing in her garden.

Maybe the worst of times are behind them at last.

Maybe the best of times are right around the corner.

After all, if March can go out like a lamb in Lily Dale . . .

Nothing is impossible.

ACKNOWLEDGMENTS

With gratitude to Rachel Slatter, Kate Lyall Grant, Natasha Bell, Martin Brown and the team at Severn House; to Laura Blake Peterson, Holly Frederick, James Farrell and the team at Curtis Brown, Ltd.; to Veronica Taglia; to Carol Fitzgerald and company at The Book Report Network; to the real Chance the Cat, Li'l Chap, Sanchez and Lady Pippa; and to all my friends in the real Lily Dale.